CROWLEY

© 2025

Helia James
Sound of Fire Trilogy Book 1
Black Ember

Formatting: Helia James

Cover: Helia James

Publisher: BoD · Books on Demand GmbH, Überseering 33, 22297 Hamburg,

bod@bod.de

Print: Libri Plureos GmbH, Friedensallee 273, 22763 Hamburg

ISBN: 978-3-8192-0835-5

Helia James

BLACK EMBER

BOOK ONE: DRACONIS

I dedicate this story to my Muse, who stood by my side from the very beginning to the very end.

Trigger Warnings for the whole trilogy:

Rape, Abuse, Emotional Manipulation, Genocide, Religious Trauma, Torture, sexually explicit and erotic themes

Spotify Playlist

PROLOGUE

What's the thing dragons fear the most?

It's easy to think that dragons, these mighty and ancient beings, don't have anything to be afraid of. Being an apex predator, that lives for centuries if not millenia undisturbed.

Their scales are impenetrable and their fire strong enough to melt whatever dares to stand in their way.

It doesn't matter if it's fire spewing out of their maws or thunder and lighting bowing to their masters. Dragons are the embodiment of power and royalty. And stilll...

What if even them can get scared?

It's foolish to think, just because dragons are strong that they don't know how it feels to be scared.

Every creature on earth, from the tiniest ant to something as big as a dragon can feel frightened from time to time.

Crowley vowed to himself after he escaped his imprisonment to the Nevermore Island that he would never show fear anymore. He had learned the hard way how it felt to be **terrified.** *And this fear had paralyzed him, unable to do anything. And so he watched his brother die.*

After this day Crowley feared humankind.

The things he had loved as a fledgling now seemed strange and dangerous. His curiousity had endangered him and had killed his brother.

The scars on his skin had stopped hurting. They had become white lines along his black scales. Memories to never forget.

But the scars on his soul never fully healed. He never trusted any of those monsters ever again.

Humans had the power to create, but also to destroy.

A dragon can fight an army, can burn their land, but Crowley had been a child when he got captured. Not bigger than a horse, he hadn't been a threat. He would have died inside of that ship.

The small dragon never felt more isolated and scared than he did in the belly of that hellish ship.

Now that Crowley was an adult, he knew better. He would keep his distance like other Négul did. And he wouldn't let any human get close enough to hurt him again.

He would never be afraid again.

ADAM

Was it worth it?

A few days ago Adam would have answered with an immediate "yes".

The gaze of the young man fell over his shoulder back on the path he had taken up the mountain. With a low sigh he leaned against one of the few trees sparsely growing through the reddish rock and sand.

A few days ago he had reached the foot of the Latu-Trail, a mountain range seperating the two kingdoms of the contintent.

After his first nightfall between rocks and trees, first doubts about his travel had started to form in the back of his mind.

He must have gone crazy.

His journey had started because a pretty girl had batted her eyelashed and asked him to find a dragon. He should be glad it hadn't been a pretty boy or only the old gods knew what he would have agreed upon.

Adams face started to grow hot, the shame about his favored gender still sitting deep within, even after his 20th birthday. Old beasts died the hardest.

The "pretty girl" had been a witch. And she had promised him to return his lost hearing if he managed to find a dragon and get the "dragon's speciality" for her.

There were only two problems:

Firstly, Adam didn't know if dragons were real or not. His uncle used to read him bedtime stories, but those were only stories right?

And secondly, if he managed to find one - what was he supposed to do then? Wouldn't a dragon kill him without a second thought?

Adam had no real fighting experience. With being deaf and all he wasn't allowed in the guard or anywhere near their training grounds. That was especially *why* he had agreed to the witches crazy deal!

All he had were years of sparring with trees and his old childhood friend. Thinking about him still brought hot tears to Adams eyes, which he quickly winked away.

But if he didn't believe that dragons existed, why did he go on this journey? Because he wanted to be part of the guard more than anything.

If there was even one single dragon on all of the continent, Adam would find it. And then he would decide on what to do.

The witch had given him a direction of a cave in the Latu mountains, big enough to host a dragon. This was his first destination.

She had said to go north, almost all the way up to the Frozen Dessert and climb up the mountains. Asliver of uncertainity started to bloom within the blonde man. Maybe he was tricked and the whole deal was an evil joke.

Adam reached into his pocket and pulled out a big golden ring. It was as wide as his palm and sparkled in the sun.

The witch had given him this ring to have some leaverage if the dragon was willing to switch it for whatever this "speciality" was.

The ring was warm in his hand, as he rolled the metal around. Was this thing enough to bribe a dragon?

If this was a trick or prank at least he would be able to trade the gold ring for some food and a ride back home.

Adam slipped the ring back into his pocket and looked up into the sky. Exhaustion started to wear him down and the sun was burning on his tanned skin. Without many trees the harsh sunlight was merciless even for a farmer like himself.

For a moment he thought back to his uncle and their farm. He would return back as soon as possible. It was the end of summer, he would soon be needed on the fields.

Exhaustion made black spots dance on the edge of his vision. One look was enough to see the mountain top clearly against the blue sky.

The stoned path began to grow more and more harsh to walk on and even the last specks of green faded behind the blonde. Up here no vegetation was spared from the harsh cold winds nor from the burning heat.

If Adam continued north he would reach the snow desert in a day. Then he would have to turn around no matter if he found a dragon or not.

The sudden change in temperature after crossing the mountains called for better clothing. Adam looked down at his thin shirt, pants and the small fur cloak around his shoulders. He already started to shiver from the cold winds. The snow desert would be his death.

The blonde rolled his shoulders determined and rubbed cold sweat off his brow. What would he do when he reached the top?

Adam had memorized the map on his way to the mountains. The place where the dragon's lair should be was marked, so what if there was nothing? Maybe he had been tricked. A quiet voice inside him tried to creep up and tell him that he was stupid and naive to follow the words of a woman he barely knew.

A tremor in the ground prevented him from spiraling. Adam lost his footing and fell to his knees with a quiet scream. As quick as the tremor had started, it was over again. The blonde kept kneeling a moment longer, his flat hands pressed to the ground, but there was no other earthquake.

The long silver chain around his neck fell from the collar and dangled between his arms. Exhaustion made his arms tremble, but the blonde still hurried to put the pendant back inside his shirt. The necklace was a remembrance for his mistakes and burned his skin.

Slowly, Adam pushed himself back up. He wouldn't give up, not this close to the top. And if there was no cave up there, he would continue to look for the dragon's speciality. Maybe this was part of his penance and he would take what he was given. This much he owed his lost friend.

Adam's eyes looked up the stonewalls and gently wiggled his toes in his thin shoes. He expected another earthquake and wanted to be prepared. When he fell down he landed on his hands and cut open his palms. The fine debris in his cuts burned, but he had no water left to wash it off.

The last days he only stopped to sleep or eat. Naturally his feet burned and his body was exhausted. Most of his journey he could join a group of merchants. The traveled in carriages across the souhtern parts of the Latu mountains to cross from Altos to Oboros.

Adam accompanied them until they reached the mountain pass, said his goodbyes and went ahead alone. Up the mountain not even a mount like a goat would have helped him.

With his burning hands it hurt when Adam pulled his body up a ledge with a low groan. The sweat under his fur cloak started to cool quicker now that he had reached such an altitude. Adam felt one shiver after the other run down his spine and his teeth started to chatter. His heated breath was visible as small clouds travelling upwards with every exhale. Following his line of sight he noticed an opening just a little upwards behind the next stone ledge - this had to be it!

There was a gap between the ledge and Adam, wide enough that the young man had to jump. Without looking down jumped the blonde over it, hands reaching for the edge of the stone. His full body crashed into the stone wall, but he had made the jump. Adam's muscles ached with the exertion of pulling his weight up. But the gap could have been an abyss and if he had hesitated or slipped he could fall down into nothingness. Pushing his body to the extreme, the blonde finally managed to pull himself up onto the last ledge and crawled tiredly on all fours towards the cave entrance.

Only then did he allow himself to rest and breathe. It was then that he smelled a weird odor coming from the opening in front of him. A warm wind brushed over his face coming from within the cave. It smelled sickly sweet and another cold shiver ran down Adam's spine.

The smell was familiar and the uneasy feeling was growing. But he found a cave where the witch had told him he would find one. So he would march on.

With his last strength Adam pushed himself up on his legs once more an ventured into the darkness in front of him.

He was scared, obviously. Not being able to hear and the mere light coming from the sun in his back weren't the best conditions. He also didn't bring any weapons. Firstly, he still didn't really believe there was a real dragon. And secondly, if there was a dragon what could would a blade do? He would be dead before even pulling a sword out of its sheath.

Adam waited for a long moment with his back pressed against the stone wall until his eyes started to adjust to the darkness around him. The sand beneath his feet was soft, he felt it give way under his thin soles. Suddenly a sharp and biting odor hit his nose, strong enough for him to cover his mouth and nose with his hand. The smell reminded him of burning wood and something sharp like bile.

His blue eyes looked around, but he couldn't make out anything beyond the space lightened by the rays of sunshine coming from the cave entrance.

Without his sense of hearing his gut feeling had become his fifth sense. And right now it screamed at him to start running, that there was something dangerous lurking in the dark. The fine hairs in the back of his neck started to rise, but his feet were frozen in place.

Adam stared into the darkness with bated breath, but nothing happened. Slowly pressed the blonde his body away from the stone wall and took another step deeper into the cave. Had his gut feeling been wrong?

Another step in and something moved along the walls. A shadow? Maybe he had been stupid and this cave was home to an animal like a bear or tiger. Those he could have fought with a sword or at least wound enough for him to escape. But all he had been thinking was that this cave must belong to something bigger. The ceiling was so high he barely could make it out. And he knew how a bear's den smelled. This wasn't it.

The shadow along the wall started to move again and Adam froze. He half-heartedly had hoped not to find anything. Or to find a dead dragon he could bypass, even a sleeping dragon he would have been able to handle. The existence of a real dragon was something the elderly told the young to scare them. Adam was scared alright.

His eyes followed the snakelike movement along the stone walls with his eyes. His heart started to beat twice as fast as normally and his blood pulsed in his ears.

The only thing keeping him from running away in fright was the fact that whatever was lurking in the shadows hadn't attacked him yet. If it was a predator it wouldn't have waited. It would have attacked the moment he had entered the cave and was easy prey. So whatever he was about to encounter wasn't in on killing him quickly.

Adam's throat was dry. But screaming would have been futile, who would have heard him? The birds? Cold sweat started to drip from his brow, but he didn't allow himself to blink it away after it landed in his eye. He was staring at the shadow, watched it move, come closer until a figure formed in the darkness.

Something big stepped into the weak light coming from the entrance. With slow steps a big, black dragon emerged from the darkness. One of its claws the size of Adam's forearm.

Adam watched it move closer. The light danced along the black scales, but what captured his attention were the gold eyes looking down on him. The dragon lowered his head enough for the blonde to see the pupils constricting into thin slits, almost completely swallowed by the molten gold around them.

The exhaustion and the fear finally made Adam's legs give in and he landed hard on his knees. The soft sand eased the impact a little.

This was it. This was the dragon he was supposed to find.

How was it possible that something so big hasn't been spotted? That no one had seen a "real" dragon before? Adam himself hadn't believed the fairtales. Now he did.

All he had to do was to get this dragon to come with him so he could contact the witch and bring her the dragon's speciality. He didn't think about a plan on how to do that exactly since he hadn't believed in dragons up until the last five minutes.

"Come now, Adam. You are smarter than that!", reminded him Silas voice in his head and the blonde's hand found the necklace beneath his shirt. He needed a miracle, but he wasn't dead yet so maybe today was the perfect time for one of them.

Adam tried to calm his nerves with deep breaths. The giant monster in front of him hadn't attacked him yet and was silently watching. He felt goosebumps down his arms.

They were watching each other. Blue human eyes watched gold unreal ones. Time seemed to come to a stop.

Breathe, Adam. Don't blink.

CROWLEY

What's the thing dragons fear the most?

For the dragon Crowley there was only one answer to the question: In all the centuries he had been alive there had been nothing that left any long impression on him. Everything came to an end eventually.

Maybe that was the reason why he hadn't killed the young man who had dared to enter his cave yet.

Taking a human life happened so fast. One swipe with his claw, one bite with his razor-sharp teeth and it would be over. He wouldn't even have time to scream for mercy. It would take a second to sever the blonde head from his shoulders.

But the young man in front of him showed courage to enter a dragon's cave on his own. Even though he hadn't been very stealthy from the start. Crowley hadn't moved quietly himself and still he seemed to have surprised the blonde man to the point where he almost seemed surprised to see a real dragon.

What a weird situation. The black dragon looked wordlessly down onto the human who stared back with huge, blue eyes.

Crowley blinked once, his gaze never leaving the mortal's form, before he moved a little closer.

With a surprised sound the man jumped and fell back on his behind, struggling to stagger back onto his hands and knees. His eyes were still fixed on Crowley's golden irises.

The moment the blonde man raises his hands, the black dragon showed his fangs in warning. But the shaking hands weren't reaching for any form of a weapon. They started to move in odd ways. It took Crowley a moment to understand, that those symbols were forming words.

Crowley was old enough to recognize these form of communication from his past. He understood a few signs, but not enough for a proper conversation.

Dragons just like many other Négul were very curious creatures so during his studies of the human race he had seen them using several different versions of communication. Words, signs, pen and paper and so on.

Négul were known under many different names: Fairytales, myths or simple monsters.

Monsters.

Remembering the things that had been done to a young Crowley, made his whole body tense up and the long line of black scales along his spine started to rattle and raise like the back-fur of a scared cat.

Back then the black dragon had been a naive child, a fledgling, who didn't know about the evils in the world yet. But he had to learn it the hard way. Since then he never trusted another human and they better kept away from him or wouldn't leave his cave alive. It was better to strike first before he got hurt again.

Crowley wasn't a monster, like the humans described him. If there were monsters out there it had to be them!

He would never let a mortal hurt him again.

The young man in front of him still hadn't reached for anythingt that resembled a weapon. If dragon had the facial muscles for it, Crowley would have furrowed his brows.

The signs the human was forming didn't make much sense, why wasn't he just talking?

The continent had several languages and dialects, but whatever language the other spoke, Crowley would have been able to understand more than he did now with the few hand signs.

The black dragon lowered his head slowly to have a better look at the man's hands. The mortal repeated the motions a little slower.

"So you tell me that there is no gold here?"

Gold? Why would he have something so useless here? Maybe he had mistaken the sign for gold? No, you had to point your index finger at your ear lobe and then move your hand away from your ear as you change the handshape into the letter "y." So there was no mistake in the word, but why would a dragon have something like gold?

Dragons were collectors by nature. If you outlived most other things only the inanimate became of worth to you. But gold was hard and useless so Crowley never aquainted any.

After a long moment where he simply stared at the blue eyes of the human still breathing hard in fear he decided on what to do next. There was one way to get answers out of the mortal in front of him. Crowley wasn't sure if he could send his thoughts over into a human's mind like he could do with other dragons, but it was worth a shot if it cleared the situation.

Dragons didn't have any vocal cords like humans did. Flying through the clouds it turned out to be easier to communicate via directly sending your thoughts towards the other and recieve their answer in return.

Crowley would use this opportunity to quell his thirst for wisdom if it was possible to talk to other sentient beings this way. If it turned out to be a lost cause, he could still kill the man.

Why did this mortal walk into his cave, without armor or any way to defend himself? How did he find him?

One way or another, Crowley would get his answers.

FLEDGLING

"Why do we have to leave again?", the Fledgling asked the snowy-white dragon, that loomed over it's small body. It lowered its big head and their snouts touched.

"Because it isn't save here."

Her voice echoed in his head but was as clear as a bell. The strong, white body shimmered in the sun like diamonds.

As young as the Fledgling was he still knew this dragon was special to him. In later memories he would call her "mother".

When it hatched there had been more dragons flying across the lands. Now there wrere only three dragons around him left. Besides the white dragon there was one he barely saw, but he remembered dark scales and cold eyes.

The third one was the same black colour as himself.

That day was the last time the young Fledgling ever saw his mother or the dragon with the icy eyes.

The small dragon grew bigger and started to learn and adapt. It looked up to the other black dragon for guidance and would later call him "brother".

The black dragon's name was Orion and he taught his little brother important things like hunting, but also mundane things like the meaning of a name.

"You don't need a name, but it helps differentiate things, people or other beings. Like you can call me Orion you can choose a name for yourself or let someone you trust give you one. But be careful, names hold power."

The little Fledgling didn't understand what power Orion could have meant at that time.

"The I let you choose. I don't know many words and don't know what a good name would be."

Both dragons were submerged in a river. Orion listened to the sweet and almost naive words and made a sound that could have been a laugh. His little brother wasn't fully grown yet, in body aswell as in mind.

"Then I give you the name Crowley." It had a nice ringing to it. The way Orion said it, maybe he had known someone with that name.

From that day on Crowley started to name all kinds of things. Orion endulged in his little brothers excitement and when it came to important things he took his time explaining the little dragon the real names of things, places or plants.

Orion taught him about the white dragon Crowley barely remembered. That one had indeed been his mother and was called Indina.

Crowley didn't know exactly what a mother was, but Orion only took his time explaining him important things. So a mother had to be very important.

One day the siblings watched from a cliff a group of creatures Crowley never had seen before: humans.

Orion warned him of them and told him to stay away.

What an odd warning. They seemed so small and fragile. If they ever tried to harm him, he would just snap at them and scare them away.

Crowley still needed a few more years to be as tall as his brother, but he still found humans to be small and harmless creatures. But he was an obedient listener.

He kept his distance and only watched humans from afar. How they oddly walked on two legs and treated each other. They were loud and made sounds all the time. Sometimes loud enough for him to hear even from all the way over to his hiding spot.

Their habits were strange but fascinating. Crowley started to inch closer every time Orion was away and left his little brother on his own. He had promised the other dragon to keep away and he would keep his promise. But watching from a little closer up wouldn't do him any harm, right?

Having them a little closer Crowley saw them moving their mouths and making strange sounds. For the first few years those sounds didn't make any sense to him.

Watching those humans was Crowley's little secret. He kept it from Orion so he couldn't really ask him about them.

A few years later Crowley learned the mannerisms of the humans he was watching. He learned about different clans and how their looks differed as much as the colour of a dragon's scales.

The sounds they made turned out to be something called a "language" and also differed from place to place and person to person.

He learned how they interacted, how they showed their happiness and treated the ones dear to them. But he also learned how they showed disdain or even fought each other.

To Crowley they didn't seem that different from the ways Orion had explained him the world. Every living being had something or someone they liked and enough to hate in this world.

One summer the Fledgling watched for the first time how a human man killed a woman. The ruthlessness of the act shocked him to the core, but it didn't really dim his curiousity.

Crowley never showed himself to the humans and even if he would have wanted to, there was no way for him to speak to them. It was a little disappointing that something as fascinating as a human wasn't able to use their voice without moving their mouths the whole time.

Orion explained his little brother that his obsession was misplaced, since there were too many humans in this world for them to be anything special. Crowley didn't care. That only meant that his brother wouldn't scold him for his little secret.

There was never a dull day watching them. Crowley saw humans more than once and tried to remember their faces, but then they left and never returned. Some of them started to visually change, their hair turning grey and one day they just stopped showing up.

Crowley learned that a life-circle of a human was that much shorter than a dragon's. He watched something Orion explained him to be a burial.

A human male with long black hair, slicked back to a tight ponytail was clutching another man that looked almost identical to him.

Humans and animals alike were born, reproduce and die in a for a dragon very short period of time.

Watching the pained expression of that man holdigng the other human even stirred the little dragon's heart. This image burned itself into his core and awoke something he never experience before: compassion.

Humans felt for their kind, they visually suffered after losing someone important to them. A mortal life was very short and it didn't matter if children lost their parents or a mother had to carry her babe to the grave.

If humans and animals were alike, why did it hurt them more to loose one of their kind? Why did a human cry and scream and curse at the stars?

Crowley didn't understand his brother's adversion to the human race, at least not yet. His curiousity made him forget the promise he made his brother decades ago.

He disregarded to be cautious and inched closer and closer.

Orion had taught him to not be scared but wary.

Dragons were the kings and queens of the skies, there was nothing to be afraid of. So with the belief that nothing was stronger than a dragon he became prideful and arrogant.

If he was a mighty dragon what danger could a mere human be to him?

CROWLEY

Maybe the mortal would answer his questions. It depended on how cooperative he would be. By chance Crowley might be able to ask about the world behind the Latu Pass he hadn't seen in centuries. He hadn't left the mountains around his cave for more than a hunt or two.

After everything that had happened in his childhood, Crowley kept as far away from humans as he could. His brother had been right. And now he was dead.

And for the wars and political schemes the people of the kingdoms on the continent got themselves into – Crowley couldn't care less. Humans would use the power of dragons to kill others. *We are no weapons. Don't think you can use us.*

Humans were soft and fascinating things when Crowley had been little. Then he learned how cruel they could be. They would find ways to make use of beings like dragons or other Négul, to fight for them like puppets on a string.

"Of course you won't find any gold here. I am a dragon, why would I have any use for gold or other jewelry? I live here in the mountains so what would I use a single coin for?" A small puff of smoke escaped his nostril.

The mortal in front of him seemed spooked to suddenly hear a voice in his mind. Or maybe Crowleys answer had surprised him.

The black dragon moved slowly. The dark sand under his claws crunched. He lowered his head until he could see the other's form clear. His head was almost as huge as the man before him.

As expected, even up close the human didn't wear any armor, no shield and no sword. Maybe this man was tired of life or he hadn't lied and wasn't here to slay a dragon.

Crowley snorted once and his breath made the blonde locks on the man's head dance.

"Tell me, what's the real reason you are here?"

This time only a quick tremor went through the human upon having a dragon's voice in his head again.

The black dragon lowered his gaze back on the other's hands. Up close it was easier for him to try to read the hand signs.

He knew one or two signs so he quickly lost focus and rather watched the blonde man in front of him a little closer. Short, ashy-blonde hair with soft locks framing a tan face covered in freckles. A clean, but already worn-out shirt and dark slacks.

The fashion on the continent hadn't changed much over the past hundred years.

The only thing he hadn't noticed so far were the icy blue eyes looking up at him. His eyes looked a little glassy and his soft lashes trembled while he still formed words with his hands. Maybe he was holding back tears. Crowley could see his own reflection in those twin pools.

Surprised by his own curiousity the black dragon straight-ened back up. His movement spooked the man who dropped his hands immediately.

"You don't have to form any words anymore, I can hear your thoughts perfectly fine. So I ask you once more: What is the real reason you have sought me out?"

"I have been sent here by a friend."

Even thought Crowley just said he didn't need to form words it seemed like the other was so very used to it that he formed them automatically. Even though, he did *not* form the word for "friend" once.

Adam couldn't lie. Through their telepathic bond whatever he thought Crowley would know.

So why was the mortal in front of him lying then?

The black dragon pulled up one side of his lips and showed a row of razor-sharp teeth.

Was it a ploy? Had someone from the two kingdoms sent a deaf man as a decoy? But Crowley hadn't felt another presence around his cave nor could he smell anything out of the ordinary.

Maybe he was a mere commoner sent here by the crown, but without any defense and all by himself? What odd games were the humans playing?

The dragon's golden eyes were still glued on his visitor. The blue eyes watched him just as intently back.

A growl escaped Crowley's maw, a draconic version of a laugh.

"You really have nice friends, don't you?" Even though they spoke through their minds he could give his words the sarcastic tint they would have had if he spoke them normally.

"Humans send their friends to their deaths, how nice. What if I had bitten off your head the moment you walked in here? Sending friends to look for a dragon without any weapons, ha!" The black dragon opened his maw a little.

"And I would have every right to do so! After everything you humans have done to me and my kin." The words came too quick for Crowley to hold them back. Somehow looking at the human in front of him ripped the walls down he had built around his heart over the years.

This man here wasn't at fault, but humankind was. If he killed this one man not a single dragon would return but one more of those evil creatures would vanish. And still Crowley did not move.

There was something odd about this human in particular. And no it wasn't that he was deaf. There was something unusual that went deeper than the ability to hear.

At first Crowley thought he was dealing with another Négul. They were mostly able to change their visuals to blend into the world and keep undetected. Or maybe he was a wizard or a witch. Something similiar to the black dragon, but still utterly different.

But no. It was simply a human being.

The blonde man didn't smell like magic. Witches had a specific smell to them, coming from their inate magic. Wizards smelled like the ingredients they used for their cantrips and other little tricks.

And some people were given jewelry that gave them powers. Crowley didn't understand most of this type of magic, maybe because it had something to do with those gods some of the humans worshipped.

These people also had no special smell, but those pieces of jewelry made even a big dragon like Crowley shiver. They were unnatural and shouldn't exist.

He also despised wizards and witches, because those were still human. Wizards learned their magic and witches – no one knew where they got their magic from.

It had probably something to do with their blood. Out of all the magic users, witches were the closest to a Négul. Little was known about their magic, about the things they were able to do. And that's exactly what made them so dangerous.

What are you? Crowley still had no answer to this question.

The human's hands stopped trembling, maybe he finally made piece with a dragon's voice in his head.

"You are a weird man, human."

Without the threat of immediate danger the black dragon settled down a little. His tail curled around himself and his wings tucked themselves comfortably in.

After all these years he hadn't stopped being a curious being by nature. But the human better not underestimate their temporary peace. With a low sound he lowered his massive body to the ground.

"Why did you enter my cave without weapons?"

"I did not think I would need them", answered the blonde man and left the dragon speechless once more.

"I didn't really believe in dragons and other fairytales."

Crowley rolled his head to one side which was a weird sight to look at. He seemed like a dog who didn't understand what it's master was saying, but seeing this habit on a dragon was surprising.

"So I am just a story in one of your children's books?", asked the black dragon and a single wisp of smoke rose from his mouth.

The blonde man really had the guts to nod. Crowley bared his teeth in a silent warning.

"Careful, little one. Just because I haven't devoured you yet..." His voice must have been like a thunderclap in the human's mind. Maybe his temper had flared.

The mortal in front of him went down on his hands and clutched his head like he was in pain.

A row of sharp scales along his spine had risen like the fur of an excited kitten. But when he heard the pained whimpering, there was something like compassion welling up in his chest.

Crowley snorted once and tried another question without his full-booming voice: "Why are you only talking with your hands?"

This time the man needed a long moment to respond. It was visible that the man had started to shiver again. But he tried his very best to subdue the tremors in his hands. Once more he began forming words before he remembered that the dragon could hear his thoughts so he lowered his hands again.

"I am deaf. My uncle taught me how to use sign language if I don't have pen and paper around."

Even though he was trembling like a newborn the blue eyes were clear. There was the same curiousity in those eyes that Crowley felt. Both beings wanted to ask their questions.

The dragon didn't think for a single moment to lower his guard, but maybe this man was his only chance to have a proper conversation with a human. No other mortal who had found their way into his cave did hesitate to pull their weapon on a dragon. They only came to plunder, steal and kill. They didn't ask for permission.

Humans saw dragons as monster, but didn't see how monstrous their own race was.

They saw dragons as animals, as things they could hunt and own. Crowley quickly winked away the memories that threatened to come back. He never enjoyed killing humans, but if he had to keep himself save he would set the whole world ablaze.

To distract himself he asked the man: "What's your name, mortal?"

Maybe to make things easier the man formed four letters Crowley understood at the same time as he answered through their bond.

"Adam. And yours?"

No human had ever asked him his name. No that wasn't right, there had been a human boy, but back then Crowley hadn't been able to answer him.

Taken aback the black dragon needed a moment, before he decided to give this unsual man his name. He had given his in return so where was the problem.

"You can call me Crowley."

What use was to have his name? The one who knew it and gave it to him had been dead for a very long time.

The blonde man opened his mouth and a hoarse, raspy voice croaked out: "Crowley."

The black dragon winked once silently. The voice sounded like gravel stuck in the mortal's throat. It sounded very weird.

Crowley still didn't believe the whole "a friend sent me to collect a dargon's gold" story.

Maybe some dragons collected a few coins because they looked pretty but in his whole cave there was not a single coin. Alright, maybe in the pockets of the humans that had died coming here and fighting Crowley in his own home. The blonde could have those if he wanted to.

"So once more, what's the *real* reason you have come here? You can look through the whole cave and you will find a coin or two in the satchels and bags lying around left by the ones before you. Don't try to lie to me, I can read your thoughts."

Talking through a telepathic bond with a being that wasn't a dragon felt unnatural.

"But it's the truth! A friend sent me here. Okay, I agreed to come here, because I didn't believe to see a real dragon in the flesh. I might have declined if I had known..."

"Do you believe dragons exist now?", asked Crowley and slowly unfolded his leathery wings.

"Yes", was Adam's earnest answer, while his eyes followed the movement of the dragon wings.

"So what will you do now? Will you eat me", was the follow up question and the blonde man took an uneasy step backwards.

"No, don't worry. One human isn't even enough to settle my appetite. And it's a rumor that we eat human flesh. At least not if we don't have to", explained the black dragon and crossed his claws over the sandy ground.

"Then tell me, mortal-"

"My name is Adam." Being interrupted like this was a new situation, but for now Crowley corrected himself.

"Then tell me, *Adam*, what do you need the gold of a dragon for? It has to be important if you go the length to find a real dragon."

His cave was almost at the top of the mountain. For a human to end up there "by coincidence" was almost impossible.

"I need the gold to pay off a debt", was the soft answer and the blonde man made sure to avoid looking at the dragon as he answered obediently.

This wasn't the answer Crowley expected.

"Then you better get to work and earn your coin like humans have done for millenia", said Crowley, before he slowly rose from his position.

"No! It has to be the gold of a dragon!"

The human's outburst made the dragon stop. It had to be the gold of a dragon specifically? That sounded like a dare or worse.

"Don't tell me you were dared to find that or made a promise. I have to disappoint you then-" Suddenly there was silence.

Mid-sentence the humans mind had cut their bond and Crowley found himself not able to read into the other's mind again.

This time his dragon instincts kicked in. No normal mortal should be able to cut a connection like this. Maybe he had underestimated the man in front of him. This was no common mortal.

There was still no scent of magic, but what could this man be?

Dragons were able to cut off their telepathic bond, but Crowley would have to loose every single one of his senses to not recognize one of his kin. This man was no dragon.

"What are you?"

For the last time the black dragon tried to build another telepathic bond, but there was no respond, like he was speaking into a well.

Angered and a little uneasy the black dragon rose to his full height and showed his sharp teeth. A low growl eachoed from the walls as he made himself ready to fight whatever he had allowed to enter his cave.

ADAM

Just like this he was back at using his hands. The sudden change in their mood made his skin tingle. Even if he couldn't hear the dragon's growl, seeing the rows and rows of white teeth were enough to freeze him up.

His whole body tensed up and screamed to just run.

At first the voice in his mind surprised him. It was unusal to have a second voice in your head, especially the voice of a dragon. Adam didn't know what he did to stop the second voice in his head.

As much as he had been spooked at first, it was helpful to not have to use his hands for talking all the time.

The dragon had seemed less intimidating with a human voice. It was a soft and melodic sound. For a long time Adam didn't hear voices besides his own in his head. He remembered how his uncle and his best friend had sounded in the past.

Having a humanoid voice took the edge off the dragon, but now looking into those unnatural eyes Adam got reminded that he was facing a monster right now.

Adam thought about Dominique.

She had looked so very thankful after he had agreed to help her. He didn't want to disappoint her. And he still wanted something from him so she would not let him run into his death with her request, right?

Adam's knees buckled as he fell to the ground, never looking away from the golden light the dragon's eyes glowed with. His thin shoes kicked up sand as he tried to move even further away from the monster in front of him.

Without their connection, could they even communicate enough to succeed?

His eyes left the dragon for a quick second to study his surroundings. It was a stony cave with no remarkable features. The light from the entrance illuminated the big creature, but left most of the cave in darkness. Adam imagined the cave being a labyrinth of different tunnels and dead-ends.

His whole attention snapped back to the black figure the moment Crowley started to turn around. The huge creature climbed up a stonewall and dared to vanish deeper into his cave.

No!

Did he fuck up?

He quickly got back up on his feet and hurried after the dragon.

"Come bak!" His own voice cracked as he shouted. He hadn't spoken in a while, so his voice must have sounded raw and unused.

Panicked Adam hurried after Crowley, but as he crawled deeper into the darkness his eyes couldn't keep up anymore. In the end the human didn't see anything.

He put a flat hand against the cave wall. The stone was cold, but it grounded him somehow. Now he was down two of his senses.

One of his hands reached up to his chest and grabbed the pendant around his neck. If he could just get a spark going that would be enough, but the necklace hadn't lit up in the past ten years, not even once.

A single movement in the darkness was enough to get all his attention. He wasn't sure what exactly it had been, but for now what else could lurk in the dark than the dragon?

No other scent was in the air, but the silhouette he was approaching didn't fit the dragon. It was so much smaller. What was going on?

Adam rolled his head to the side and moved a little closer. The figure seemed to be humanoid, maybe there was another human in this cave?

For a second it seemed like the shadowy figure wanted to turn around and run away. Adam rose his free hand and reached for it. No matter what it was, his curiousity won out. Nothing could be more dangerous than a dragon and the one he met hadn't killed him yet.

Slowly the blonde man raised his hand, almost like he tried to calm a spooked animal.

"Stay. Please."

Maybe the figure had understood him. It was no use forming any words with his hands in this darkness.

Even if the silhouette in the dark cave didn't seem big enough to be of a dragon, what else could it really be?

Could dragons change their appearance?

Suddenly a red light started to illuminate the figure. It came like a pulse, like a wave of warm red tinting the walls and everything around them the color of blood.

The shine was strong enough to help the human see what was in front of him. There was no dragon in sight.

It might have looked like a man, but there was nothing human about this. From the posture to the inhuman gaze fixed on Adam.

"Can you do this glowing thing again?", asked the blonde man with shaking hands. He didn't know if the other understood him well enough. Back when he was in his dragon form he had spoken through their minds. Adam had stopped to expect everyone to know the sign language by now, but without pen and paper, what other way way there for him?

Almost immediately after he asked the light intensified and another wave of red washed over him. In the darkness it was almost bright enough to blind him. To Adam it seemed like a pulsing heart.

"You look almost human?", tried Adam again with his hands. Maybe the term human didn't fight exactly. By now he was sure that he was facing the dragon in a human disguise. But it was just that, a form he took on that looked its part, but that was it.

Crowley chose the form of a human male. He was still taller than Adam, but along his neck and chest black scales covered his pale skin. His long, black hair fell in thick strands down his shoulders.

The dragon had chosen a handsome human disguise in Adam's eyes. The blonde man watched how the dragon's lips began to move, but all he could do was furrow his brows. He didn't lie when he had told Crowley that he was deaf.

As sudden as the red light had appeared, as sudden it was gone again.

"Crowley?", asked Adam with his hoarse voice into the darkness again.

With both hands not longer touching a wall, he was again down two senses and a sudden feeling of vertigo started to build in his chest.

Adam slowly sank down onto his knees to put his palms flat to the ground before he started to feel dizzy. When he looked up once more, he almost got blinded by the red light again.

Crowley had walked close enough that Adam had to roll his head back to look into his face. The dragon's eyes were still the same unusal golden colour. His high cheekbones and strong brows gave him a cold and lofty look. Ignoring the black scales Crowley could have looked like an aristocrat like this.

For a moment Adam wondered if the dragon had chosen his human look or if he just mimicked a person he had met or seen and fancied his appearance.

Having him this close the blonde man noticed another thing: After transforming the dragon might have lost most of his scales, but he didn't magically let clothes appear. So with only partly coverage, Adam quickly averted his eyes not to stare directly at the other man's crotch. He felt his cheeks heaten. Did this dragon not feel any shame?

It surprised him when he felt two fingers grabbing him by his chin and forcefully pulling him up to his feet again.

Adam's brows furrowed in confusion. Crowley touched his own lips with his free hand and it took the blonde man a moment before he understood. The dragon was asking him if he could read lips.

With the red light illuminating them both and the fact that Crowley now *had* lips, communicating should be way easier. Adam nodded.

He saw the deep breath Crowley took before his chin was released. The dragon started to speak slowly and carefully formed his words for the other man to read.

"Talking to you seems a real hassle, human. Since you won't let me back into your mind, this should be a temporary solution to answer each other's questions for the time being."

Adam rose a still shaking hand and rubbed his chest.

"Thank you for still trying."

His gaze fell back on the dragon's chest where the red light still pulsed like a heartbeat.

"Is this your heart?" The question was out quicker than Adam could have stopped it. He might be able to read Crowleys lips, but he wasn't sure if this worked the other way around as well. So he continued to use sign language not really knowing if the dragon could even understand him.

Immediately the Crowley's expression turned sour. Yep, it seemed that he understood him perfectly fine.

"No and before we continue I have a warning for you: No human should ever know that we dragon can transform into a human. You have to promise me not to ever tell a living soul what you have seen today. I will know if you broke your promise and I will hunt you down and personally rip your throat out."

Adam watched the other's mouth intently not to miss anything. Like this he noticed the sharp white fangs and he had to swallow hard remembering how big and intimidating those had been in Crowley's original form.

"And now you will answer some questions I have for you", the dragon continued. Adam just nodded, thankful for the possibility to read the dragon's lips since this was the easiest way for him.

It had taken him more than ten years to read them well enough for a proper conversation. But now along with pen and paper it was easy for him to listen into conversations where people believed he couldn't hear them. He just had to concentrate.

For a moment the question reappeared why Crowley had stopped talking to him in his mind, when he suddenly heard the dark, thundering voice in his head again.

"You agreed to a deal with the reward of a dragon's gold, right? Why?"

Adam wasn't sure if the other could hear his thoughts too, so he lowered his hands and answered in his head: "A witch promised me to make me able to hear again. To be allowed into the royal guard this is a basic requirement..." Adam lowered his gaze for a moment.

To others his wish seemed ridiculous, but he had his reasons and he would make it into the guard no matter what.

Upon looking back into Crowley's face it was clear that he had understood him. Well, that made things even easier than the lip reading. But it still left Adam puzzled on how this whole telepathic communication even worked. When was it possible? What could the dragon hear or read? When could they start their conversation and when could they end it?

"The royal guard in Altos?", asked Crowley and Adam nodded, remembering his last conversation with the General. The man had laughed into his face and called him a danger to the whole squad. Just because he couldn't hear?

He was very able to follow orders and even without hearing them, he had studied formations during most of his childhood and knew every handsign regarding war strategy. It was simply not fair.

Adam didn't ask for a lot. All the money he would earn he would give his uncle and the village. He just wanted to finally keep his promise. The necklace under his shirt seemed to pulse along with his heart and he reached up to grab the pendant tightly.

Soon.

Adam wasn't bothered not to hear, but if it was a hindrance to get into the military he had to grab every chance he got.

This time he didn't flinch when the dark voice spoke up again: "And she wanted a dragon's gold for that?"

Adam nodded again. He tried to remember what exactly Dominique had said. Looking down onto his hands he formed the sign she had done.

"Bring me the speciality of a dragon."

Adam looked at his thumb and formed the word again. Oh no. The word for gold and the word for special looked so very similar it was just a shake of the thumb. Had he misunderstood. But wasn't it one and the same anyway? Gold and speciality... What else could it be?

"I thought she meant the gold dragons hoard in their caves. I think I misunderstood..."

It was almost funny that a misunderstanding had let him into a cave he could have very well died in. Maybe he really was a deaf danger.

In the future if he survived this would be a funny anecdote. His uncle might have a heartattack or doubt his nephew's intelligence for a moment, but afterwards they would definitely laugh together.

The words for gold and specialy were similar enough and it was a dumb coincidence. But Dominique even had given him a gold ring to exchange, if the need arose.

In fairytales dragon's liked gold and would probably exchange anything. So what was the specialty of a dragon?

While Adam thought about it, he pulled the gold ring from his pocket.

Parents and the elders of his village often told fairytales to children to teach them a lesson or warn them of dangers. Now the story about dragons hoarding gold had lead Adam straight into the cave of one. It must be pure luck that he was still alive.

"What do you humans think of us dragons?", asked Crowley and crossed his arms in front of his chest, obscuring the beautiful red light. Adam tried not to panic again when the only lightsource faded.

Somehow hearing the other's voice in his head was grounding and helped him remembering that there was still someone or something in front of him in the darkness.

"Where does this nonsense even come from, human?"

"I have name", repeated Adam, before answering the dragon's question: "My uncle told me when I was a child about beings and mysteries in the world. They were fairytales and I didn't believe them when I got older. But then I met you and Dominique and now I think some of them might not be mere stories after all."

"Told? So you were able to hear as a child?"

Coming from anyone else this question for a stranger would have been rude, but Adam remembered he was talking to a dragon. Human social rules did not apply here.

"As a child I got very sick. My ear canals inflamed and treatment started too late. Day after day I lost my hearing until I couldn't hear anything anymore."

This had been now almost 15 years ago it had stopped bothering him. Adam barely remembered how voices had

47

sounded. His hearing had been gone completely a year before Silas-

Adam felt his eyes reddening and he quickly winked the upwelling tears away.

"Let me see the ring myself." Crowley's voice ripped him from his memories before he could succumb to them. Once more he was curious how much the dragon was able to read into his mind.

Judging from the still aloof expression he either didn't care or hadn't read anything.

Adam took the gold ring between his index finger and thumb, when he felt a gentle tug like something was pulling on it. He placed the ring in Crowley's palm.

Studying it Crowley rolled it between his fingers when Adam felt the tug again. Almost like an invisible force his hand reached out like he was about to take the ring back, when it slipped on its own through the dragon's claws.

Like a projectile hit the ring Crowley's chest. It was too small to really do any damage. At least Adam thought so.

The moment the impact happened the gold started to burn its way into the black scales. It looked very painful, but Adam's attention was quickly brought back to his own hand, when it started to feel like it was standing in flames.

A burn scar had started to form around his finger, like an ugly mockery of the golden ring. It felt like his finger was about to burn off. A sharp cry he didn't even know he had in himself escaped him, before he pulled his arm back and pressed his hand against his chest. What had happened?

CROWLEY

Hissing, the dragon tried to grasp the ring and tear it from his chest. The gold had burned into his skin within seconds, now fused directly between his collarbones. Furious, the dark-haired figure reached for Adam, intent on seizing him. This human had brought a cursed ring into his lair. He should have known that a witch wouldn't simply hand over an ordinary piece of gold. Once again, his curiosity had led him straight into danger.

Even with a dragon's reflexes, Crowley hadn't been fast enough to stop the ring from slamming against his scales. It wasn't the impact that hurt. Only when the ring fused with him did Crowley feel the searing pain. Nothing had ever burned him before. A hoarse cry escaped his throat—inhuman despite his current form.

Adam's eyes widened in shock as he instinctively raised his arms in defense, bracing for the clawed hand shooting toward him. But just before Crowley could grab him, he froze mid-motion. This human may have brought the ring into his lair, but he was also the only link to the damned witch who had cursed him in the first place.

Lowering his hand, Crowley focused on the slow ebbing of the pain. The ring, now embedded between his collarbones, was just large enough to fit around a human thumb. Beneath his scales, a red light pulsed wildly, like a caged bird thrashing against its prison.

"Crowley?" Adam's voice was laced with confusion as he pressed a hand against his chest, as if trying to dull the lingering burn.

"What just happened?" Adam's question carried pain, though perhaps it only seemed that way because of his agonized expression. Even in the nasal sound of his voice the hurt was audible.

Crowley placed his own hand over his chest. The ring was unnaturally hot. Foul witchcraft.

There was no metallic scent, apart from the smell of molten gold, and gold was certainly not one of the five elements of elemental mages.

Adam must have allied himself with a powerful witch.

For a fleeting moment, Crowley considered that he might have walked straight into a trap. But the bloodshot eyes of the blonde and his labored breathing were too genuine. Adam looked just as surprised by what had happened as Crowley was. He wanted nothing more than to rip the cursed piece of metal from his chest.

Witches were dangerous creatures. It was unnatural for humans to wield such power. Elemental mages received their abilities from the gods. Sorcerers learned their tricks through books, rituals, and alchemy. Every kind of magic had an origin, an explanation, and a limit. But witches? They could simply wield magic.

As long as they kept to themselves, Crowley didn't care how they lived.

"Are you okay?" Adam's voice in his head dragged Crowley from his thoughts.

Damn them all—this wretched witch, this mortal, and, above all, his own cursed curiosity.

His chest rose and fell with labored breaths, the pain flaring with each inhale. He should have known better. The ring must be a safeguard for the witch, and he had been foolish enough to take it. Now he was paying the price.

Maybe the stories about greedy dragons held some truth after all. The thought sent an unpleasant shiver down Crowley's spine, raising the ridge of dark scales that ran along it, even in his human form.

Dragons did not like being backed into a corner. They demanded open confrontation—something they could win. Now, stripped of his advantage, Crowley felt exposed. And the rhythmic pulse of the ring felt like mocking laughter.

He focused, willing the pain in his chest to dull enough to think clearly.

No witch had approached his lair. That meant the curse had been placed on the ring beforehand, and Adam had unknowingly carried it to him. He had been nothing more than the messenger in this whole scheme.

But why would a witch go through the trouble of deceiving an ordinary boy just to curse a dragon?

Had he angered a witch in the past? Could this be some kind of revenge?

"I need you to listen carefully, Adam," Crowley finally said.

He waited until Adam gave him a nod, indicating he was paying attention.

"Whatever you did earlier to push me out of your thoughts—don't do it again. If we have to work together, don't make our communication any harder than it already is. Understood?"

For a moment, Adam looked as if he wanted to argue, but then he simply nodded again. Good. At least that was settled.

"This ring—it's your witch's curse," Crowley explained.

Adam's confusion was evident, so he elaborated.

"She cursed it. And only the one who cast the curse can break it."

That much, Crowley knew about witches.

Unfortunately, he had no longer any way to contact his kin after fleeing north. His brother, Orion, would have known more.

The thought of Orion sent a sharp pang through his chest, a pain more profound than even the burning of the ring.

Adam must have seen the displeasure written across Crowley's face, but he, too, was clearly struggling with the situation.

Crowley saw Adam's face flush with what he guessed was shame. Clicking his tongue, he turned away.

"If I want to get rid of this ring, I suppose I have no choice but to accompany you back to your witch."

A low growl rumbled in Crowley's throat.

When he was younger, he had been warned about witches. He didn't know what power this one held over him now, but not knowing was just as dangerous as knowing.

He had to find her and break the curse as soon as possible.

The thought of willingly seeking her out made the scales along his spine rise once more.

"She's not my witch," Adam retorted, sounding almost offended. "Her name is Dominique."

Crowley watched the man stubbornly cross his arms in front of his chest and sighed. It was a little bit relatable, finding out that you had been used as an errand boy at most. But Crowley wasn't any happier about the situation.

With a raised hand, he signaled for Adam to wait.

Apparently, he was leaving his lair for the first time in ages—and in an unfamiliar form, no less.

He needed clothes. He surely had something left from a past visitor. If they were to travel unnoticed, he needed to blend in.

"Wait here. I need to find something to wear. Looks like I'll be stuck in this form for a while," Crowley muttered before vanishing into the shadows, leaving Adam in the dark.

Without the glow of the ring, the cave was once again swallowed in blackness.

As he searched for a shirt, pants, and shoes, Crowley kept an eye on Adam.

For someone who couldn't hear, he moved slowly but steadily through the cave. Crowley gave a small nod of approval after getting dressed and followed him toward the entrance.

This time, it was Crowley who blinked against the bright afternoon sun.

Adam hadn't heard him approach, and Crowley's curiosity got the better of him.

He observed the blonde in silence.

A broad nose, tanned skin, sand-colored hair. Had his hair been darker, he could have passed as someone from the desert cities of Oboros.

Adam shifted impatiently, tapping his foot.

Satisfied, Crowley finally stepped forward into the light.

He felt Adam's gaze sweep over him, scrutinizing his form.

Crowley wiggled his toes inside his shoes. Two legs felt vastly different from four.

The adjustment was quick, but he still felt the ghostly presence of his missing limbs—especially his tail.

That, too, was gone.

But his mission remained clear. Break the curse. And return home.

Before he had put on his clothes, his gaze had fallen on the dark scales covering his body. They had made him feel less human, which had comforted him. But if he wanted to return home as quickly as possible without drawing attention, he would have to look just like a real human. He had shed his scales unwillingly, but the ridge of scales along his spine had remained.

In a relaxed state, the black scales lay flat against his back and were well hidden by the shirt he wore. As Crowley rolled up his sleeves, he studied his forearms and hands. He hated this form. As long as he was forced to travel as one of them, he would avoid his own reflection.

He would get used to this different body. And as soon as he got rid of the ring, he would immediately shed this monster's skin and fly home. He had only himself to blame for things having come this far.

After giving Adam enough time to study him and rolling up his sleeves, he turned his thoughts back to the blond man.

"As long as you don't throw me out of your thoughts again, we can communicate this way. It works like any other conversation. I'll tune you out when I'm not speaking to you, so maybe it will feel less unpleasant. And I expect the same from you."

Adam nodded immediately. Good, at least they agreed on that.

"So, what's the plan?" Crowley asked, already beginning the descent.

"Well, I hadn't expected that," Adam admitted honestly, pointing at Crowley's chest before following him. The top buttons of Crowley's shirt had been torn off. Adam's gaze was fixed on the ring, and under the intense scrutiny, Crowley grew restless. As they walked, he fastened the top button of his shirt and pulled the frayed band at his waist, what had once probably been a belt, out of the loops, using it to tie his hair into a high ponytail.

The form he chose resembled the human twins he had watched centuries ago during one of the burials, but the length of his hair threw him off for a moment.

"I didn't expect it either. That makes two of us," Crowley replied. He made no secret of the fact that he was unhappy with their forced situation.

"We should head back to Dominique first. She lives in Vitris. I met her at the market there," Adam suggested, jumping down from a rock ledge. Crowley followed suit.

Speaking through telepathy had turned out to be a good decision. Their journey would have been unnecessarily delayed if they had to stop every time they needed to communicate—just because the young man needed his hands to talk.

"Vitris? What a coincidence that this witch happens to be from Altos' capital," Crowley remarked. "How long did it take you to get here?"

"A few weeks. I traveled the first part of the way with some merchants, so it was faster than going on foot. I could have borrowed a horse, but I would've had to leave it behind before reaching the mountains. I didn't know exactly where to find your cave, so I spent the last two weeks in the mountains, traveling north along the border," Adam explained.

Crowley snorted. The human had really gone to great lengths to find him. The Latu Mountains stretched from north to south, splitting the whole continent in half.

"It wouldn't have helped us anyway. Animals are usually afraid of dragons," Crowley said with a shrug. So, they would travel on foot.

As a dragon, it would have been easy for him to take to the skies, but with a human in tow—especially on the journey to Altos' capital—it would be complicated. The risk of being discovered was too great.

For a moment, Crowley furrowed his brow. Had he seriously just considered flying a human all the way to Vitris? Maybe the ring was already playing tricks on him, messing with his mind.

They would take the path through the forest and fields—it was the most direct route to the capital. They would only stop when it was necessary for the mortal.

Crowley sighed and rolled his shoulders.

"Let's go. The sooner we get there, the sooner I can be rid of you and this cursed ring and return home." His words were cold; even now, it took great effort to travel in a human's company. He was probably one of the few dragons who actually feared humans. He had been captured as a child, and that memory had burned itself into his mind even deeper than the golden ring in his chest.

They made their first stop at the foot of the mountains long after the sun had set. Neither man slept much, but after the difficult descent, a short rest was welcome. As a dragon, Crowley didn't need many breaks, and Adam didn't dare close his eyes longer than necessary.

The dragon sighed, wondering how he could make the other man understand that, for now, he posed no threat to him. They both wanted the same thing at the moment, and to achieve it, Adam needed to sleep.

How long could a human last without sleep? Two days? A week?

He had to figure something out.

Thanks to Crowley, wild animals gave them a wide berth. Adam had rolled onto his side and closed his eyes. Crowley wasn't sure if he was actually asleep or just pretending. Maybe the stubborn human had finally realized that he needed rest.

Slowly, exhaustion crept into Crowley as well. It had to be this human body.

His gaze fell to his hands. He studied his long fingers, the backs of his hands, and the soft pads of his palms. He closed his eyes briefly before looking up at the sky. The stars were so clear. Compared to them, even a mighty dragon like Crowley felt small and insignificant.

He lifted his hand, pretending to hold a star between his thumb and forefinger. Forming a circle around a bright star, he peered through the gap. When he clenched his hand into a fist, he could see the muscles shifting under his skin. It was fascinating—and equally unsettling.

This wasn't his body, and yet it obeyed his will completely.

A pulsing sensation throbbed in his head, forcing him to close his eyes to fight the nausea.

This body felt like a cage.

His own personal cage of flesh and blood.

A cage?

That was his last thought before his eyes slipped shut.

FLEDGLING

The first thing Crowley noticed was the scent of saltwater and iron. It was dark and freezing cold. His young body was wedged between the iron bars of a cage—one built to hold a rabid dog or perhaps a wolf, but not a dragon.

Even for a young dragon like Crowley, the cage was far too small. His wings were bound tightly to his body, and a rough rope muzzled his mouth shut. Chains pressed against his delicate limbs, squeezing and digging into him, while the oppressive darkness around him filled him with fear and suffocation.

The coarse material had chafed the skin around his muzzle, leaving it raw and burning with pain.

Where was Orion? Where had they taken his brother?

A sheet had been thrown over the cage, preventing Crowley from seeing where they had brought him. They had captured him, just as they had captured Orion. And all because he had been curious about those ships.

His shimmering black scales were scratched and dirtied, his breath trembled with fear, and his heart pounded wildly in his chest—like a frightened bird trapped in a cage.

"Why is this happening?" he wondered, but the only sound he could make past the gag was a faint whimper.

"I didn't mean any harm... I just wanted to fly, to get a closer look at the ships. I was just curious." A pained noise escaped his throat, making the cold around him feel even more unbearable.

"Orion always warned me not to fly alone, to be cautious of humans. But I was so curious, so foolish. And now I'm here, alone... Where is my brother?"

Weakly, he reached out with his mind, searching for his brother, but in the icy darkness, he heard and felt nothing. The chains clinked softly as he shifted, a cruel echo in the silence.

"I'm so scared."

Crowley didn't dare close his eyes as tears rolled down his face, leaving hot trails along his black scales.

"What will they do to me? I've heard what they say about dragons, how they fear and hate us. But I'm just a child!"

He thought of the vast, open sky, of the sun's warmth on his wings.

"Will I ever feel that again? Will I ever be free again? Or is this the end?"

His mind tormented him with visions of hunters — hard-faced men, iron, and fire.

"Maybe they'll kill me... or worse. Maybe they'll keep me in this cage, put me on display like an animal, mock and hurt me."

His thoughts spiraled, and nausea rose within him. His small, black body trembled from both the cold and sheer terror.

"I can't bear this. I don't want to end up like this. I want my freedom back! I want to go home to my brother, to the warmth and safety of his wings."

A sob escaped him as he dug his claws into the cage floor. He had never felt smaller or more vulnerable.

"Please, if anyone is out there, please help me. Don't leave me alone in this cold, in this fear. I don't want to die—not like this."

A single wisp of smoke drifted from his nostrils, swallowed by the merciless darkness around him. And in the silence, all he could do was cry, his tears unheard, lost in the void.

Crowley had not yet been a fully grown dragon. Besides his older brother, he had no one. Their parents had left Crowley in Orion's care and slowly disappeared after the All-King had died. The kingdom had shattered, and ever since, war had raged along the border between the humans of the continent.

Humans.

The very same humans who had captured him, thrown him into this tiny, suffocating cage, and left him in the dark.

The thick ropes around his snout dug into his scales as he tried to open his mouth, hoping to reach the sheet covering his cage. A quiet whimper escaped him as the cage suddenly lurched forward, shifting violently.

There were voices all around him—too many to distinguish.

No chance.

With a racing heart, Crowley pressed his black-scaled head against the iron bars.

A sharp pain in his left wing reminded him of the searing agony that had shot through him when the humans had struck him from the sky with a harpoon. They had removed it but had left the wound untreated.

"He'll survive," one of the men had said before they had bound him.

Crowley was terrified. Overwhelmingly so. His brother's words echoed in his mind:

A dragon does not fear. Fear what? We are the strongest, most powerful beings in this world. Even the gods do not stand above us. Pull yourself together, Crowley!

But the fear was too deep. His young dragon body shivered uncontrollably, no longer obeying him.

With a dull thud, the cage was roughly set down, making Crowley's teeth clack together from the impact.

Then the sheet was ripped away.

Instinctively, Crowley pressed himself against the iron bars at the back of the cage, like a frightened animal.

His pupils narrowed into thin slits as the firelight from four torches flared up in front of him.

Leave me alone!

His golden eyes darted around, searching desperately for a way out. They were in a cave—one he did not recognize.

His breath came in quick, panicked bursts, forming small, white clouds in the cold air. His body trembled—not just from the chill.

None of the human faces around him were familiar. In their eyes, he saw nothing but greed and cruel amusement.

At that moment, he did not yet understand that this would become the longest, most agonizing period of his life.

That realization only struck him when one of the men stepped forward with a pair of large iron tongs—and ripped the first scale from his leg.

A strangled scream tore from his throat, but the ropes around his mouth held firm.

Another scale was ripped away, and the world around him blurred.

He had never harmed these humans.

He had only wanted to return to Orion.

Back then, he had not yet known that he would never see his brother again.

CROWLEY

Crowley's eyes flew open, needing a moment to orient themselves. It felt as if he had surfaced from icy water. He could feel how fast his heart was pounding, how quickly his breath came.

The sun had risen just a few minutes ago. He was no longer in that cage. His head throbbed painfully, and his hands trembled as he looked down at them. Human hands.

Bile rose in his throat, and he turned to the side to vomit, but apart from a mouthful of saliva, there was nothing to spit into the grass.

A quick sidelong glance at the blond man beside him helped pull his mind back to the present. Slowly, the dream faded, and the events of the past day returned.

The witch's curse and her ring.

With a deep breath the black-haired man focused back on reality. He was no longer in that cage. It had just been a nightmare.

Crowley's gaze dropped back to his hands, which had finally stopped shaking. He hated looking like one of those monsters. But if he wanted to end this ordeal as quickly as possible, it was a sacrifice he had to make.

Had this human body triggered the memories of that time?

Crowley forced himself to suppress the renewed trembling that overtook his entire body.

But the darkness of the forest around him felt suffocating, almost like an invisible shroud tightening around his chest. His heart hammered wildly, so loud it pounded in his ears—too loud. Too fast.

He could feel every vibration within his body, as if he were on the verge of shattering. The dream—his nightmare—was fading, yet suddenly, distorted and terrible images flashed through his mind again.

Fear surged through his veins.

It felt too real, as if he were back in that cage.

His breath grew shallow and rapid, as though no matter how deeply he inhaled, his lungs couldn't take in enough air. His fingers dug into the damp earth of the forest floor, but it suddenly felt rough and dry, like coarse paper beneath his fingertips.

His chest tightened—tighter and tighter—like an invisible hand crushing his heart, stripping him of any control.

He tried to focus, but the forest and the remnants of the burned-out campfire blurred before his eyes. His entire body began to tremble, the cold spreading from his nape down to his fingertips.

He wanted to move, to stand up, to run—to do something.

But his legs felt as heavy as lead.

He was trapped, here, in this moment, between what was and what is. The nightmare clung to him like a shadow that refused to fade.

A strangled sound escaped him as he desperately tried to suppress the panic clawing its way up from his core.

His hands pressed against his chest as if he could push the tightness away, but it only grew worse.

His stomach twisted, a dull pain spreading inside him.

Everything felt wrong.

The world spun, his body refused to obey him—until his gaze landed once more on the sleeping blond man beside him.

He had to pull himself out of the past.

Back to the here and now.

Adam.

The young man had appeared in his cave. Because of the ring embedded in Crowley's chest, he was now forced to travel alongside him in this human body.

This was the western forest beyond the Latu Mountains—not the belly of a ship.

His gaze drifted upward to the star-speckled sky.

Up there, he could feel the wind beneath his wings. No chains biting into his flesh.

Slowly, Crowley parted his lips as if to scream.

No gag to silence him.

He—was—here!

His eyes closed gradually, and he focused on his breathing—slow and steady.

He waited until his heartbeat returned to normal before nudging the human's foot lightly with his own, waking him.

With a mask of ice, he gave no hint of what had dragged his entire being into darkness just moments ago.

In silence, they continued their journey.

ADAM

Adam lived with his uncle on a farm, a good day's ride from the village where he had grown up.

Vitris, the capital, lay almost at the center of the kingdom of Altos, surrounded by several village communities and their respective fields. Adam's birthplace was one of these communities east of the capital.

He had spent the first years of his life there. Several families from closely neighboring villages had formed a clan, and under the leadership of a clan chief, they handled most matters independently.

Adam's uncle Theodore was their clan leader, responsible for seven families and their lands. Theodore was not truly Adam's uncle but more like a foster father. However, as soon as Adam had been old enough to form the sign for "uncle" with his hands, he had insisted on calling Theodore that.

When Adam grew older, his uncle told him that his parents had been killed in a bandit attack on their village.

Since then, he had lived with Theodore. On the way to Vitris, they would have no choice but to travel through the lands where his uncle and the other clan members tended their fields.

It was the fastest and most direct route to the capital. Adam hoped his uncle wouldn't ask him any questions. At over twenty years old, Adam was no longer under constant supervision.

Still, because of his impairment, his uncle was often overly cautious when it came to making decisions. Adam sighed and looked up at the sky. Crowley's cave lay so far north that it would take only another day's march on foot to reach the frozen wasteland along the northern coast.

As the largest desert on the continent, it stretched from the Western Sea across the entire northern coastline to the port city of Corre in Oboros on the eastern shore. After resting at the foot of the Latu Mountains, they would soon reach the first forests surrounding the entire mountain range. The trees effectively kept out the cold, ranging from sparse conifers to the dense deciduous forests in the west.

Without Dominique's description, he would never have found Crowley's cave. The moment they had set off again, Crowley had naturally taken the lead, as if he knew exactly where he was going. Adam was perfectly fine with that. It gave him more time to think—and to stare at the broad back before him, barely concealed by a sun-bleached shirt.

Crowley's human form was beautiful.

Adam knew that he was more drawn to male bodies than female ones. He had often observed men's physiques before—stealing a glance or two wasn't a crime, was it?

Being gay wasn't a punishable offense in Altos, but neither was attacking someone for it. The royal soldiers didn't even bother to hide how repulsed they were by people like him. Adam didn't know how the people in the big cities felt about homosexuality, but in the countryside, it was a different matter altogether.

He kept his secret carefully because one wrong word and the entire clan would know.

He and Silas had often watched men and women training at the garrison in their village community. The jokes that had been made then made it very clear what the men thought of others like him.

Looking back, Adam could only roll his eyes. Just because he was attracted to men didn't mean he was any less capable of serving in the royal guard. But his personal handicap was already enough of an obstacle—he had no desire to add another reason for rejection.

Being gay wasn't the problem, but between that and being deaf, chasing his dream had never been easy.

As a teenager, he had always stuck close to Silas at village festivals. Without his friend, he never would have met so many other young people from the village.

For some reason, other children seemed to find it unsettling to befriend a deaf boy, as if his condition were contagious.

Lost in thought, Adam's gaze remained fixed on the muscular back in front of him. The strong muscles beneath Crowley's shirt moved smoothly with every step he took.

Crowley lifted a hand and ran it through his ponytail, pulling it over his shoulder and exposing his neck.

In the sunlight, Adam could make out dark scales there. So, Crowley still had scales on some parts of his human body. Why hadn't he hidden them like the rest?

Maybe those particular scales were special, or perhaps he simply couldn't make them disappear.

A single drop of sweat caught Adam's attention as it rolled down behind Crowley's slightly pointed ear. He was walking close enough behind him to track its descent with his eyes.

Crowley was a dragon, even if he currently had a human form.

Adam shook his head and quickened his pace, moving up to walk beside the taller man rather than behind him. He needed to think about something else before Crowley caught on to how closely he had been analyzing him.

Back in the cave, Crowley had told him that this telepathy thing worked like a normal conversation. That meant he should have been able to hear Adam's thoughts.

But Crowley hadn't reacted and kept walking in silence over rocks and tangled undergrowth.

Fine, then. Adam would test the limits of this telepathy thing. Focusing intently, Adam thought about a steaming bowl of cabbage soup—and his stomach immediately grumbled.

In his mind, he heard Crowley sigh.

"I already told you—I don't care what you think about, as long as it's not directly about me. But for your own sake, maybe think a little less. Your thoughts buzz like a beehive, even when I try to block them out," Crowley remarked, glancing at Adam from the corner of his eye.

So, theoretically, Crowley could hear everything Adam thought if he wanted to.

That was... unsettling, to say the least.

Adam turned his focus to Crowley's face. By that logic, he should also be able to hear the dragon's thoughts. But after Crowley's explanation, there was nothing.

Frustrated, Adam furrowed his brows.

A faint smirk tugged at Crowley's lips before he pulled a branch aside, allowing both of them to duck under it.

"I'm used to speaking this way," Crowley explained matter-of-factly. "You, on the other hand, have never communicated with someone like this before. I know how to think quietly and how to direct a thought at you."

That made sense—but it still felt unfair.

Fine. He would think less. That was easier said than done. How did someone think less?

As Adam continued pondering how to "think quietly," they reached the first rows of fir and pine trees. His gaze wandered back to Crowley, observing the muscles in his arm as he bent down to lift a fallen log out of the way.

The sheer strength behind the movement almost concealed the slight unsteadiness that followed.

But Adam was watching too closely to miss it.

It seemed Crowley still had trouble with balance. Not surprising—dragons typically had four legs, and Crowley was now walking upright on two.

The dark-haired man wiped sweat from his forehead and grimaced in disgust.

"Are you alright?" Adam asked directly.

"Human bodies are disgusting," Crowley shot back.

Adam barely managed to stifle a grin as he watched Crowley sniff his hand—the same hand he had just used to wipe away sweat.

"Don't tell me dragons don't sweat," Adam asked, curious.

Crowley shook his head.

"Unusual," Adam mused. "Doesn't every living being sweat when it gets hot?"

"I'm a fire dragon. We don't get hot," Crowley stated flatly. "So, we don't sweat. But this body is struggling to handle my elevated body temperature."

He wiped his hand on his pants with a disgusted look.

Curious, Adam reached out and touched Crowley's arm. His skin was scorching hot, and Adam immediately pulled his hand back.

"You could just take off your shirt until your temperature adjusts?" he suggested.

Crowley lifted a hand to his neck, covering the black scales there.

"Better not," came the simple reply before the dark-haired man turned away and continued walking.

Adam had the feeling that Crowley had misunderstood his suggestion. Heat rushed to his face, and he quickly inhaled the forest's fresh scent to calm himself.

To calm himself, he took a deep breath, inhaling the pleasant scent of the forest. It was only then that he realized he had followed Crowley without thinking. He didn't know this part of the woods, and unease crept into his stomach.

Normally, he chose well-lit paths or ones clearly used by multiple people as a safety measure to ensure nothing would happen to him. Over the years of living without hearing, he had come up with ways to navigate life on his own.

Crowley had led him down the mountain without him stumbling even once. Despite his new form, the dark-haired man moved gracefully from ledge to ledge. However, Adam's trained eyes noticed every time the dragon hesitated before jumping.

He allowed Crowley to show him which stones could support his weight and which ones were best avoided. Perhaps he was reading too much into Crowley's actions. Adam shook his head. He had promised himself he wouldn't overthink things.

Curious, the blond man raised a hand and pressed it against the cool trunk of a fir tree. Adam liked the forest. It was cool, and he enjoyed the scent of moss and wood.

He followed Crowley deeper into the woods, already able to feel the difference between loose gravel and forest soil through the thin soles of his shoes. Deep in his heart, he believed he could hear the birds if he closed his eyes. Without thinking, his eyelids had fallen shut—only to walk straight into Crowley with a dull thud as the man had stopped in front of him.

Reflexively, Crowley grabbed Adam's upper arm before he could fall. Even through the fabric of his shirt, the dragon's hand was warm, and his grip was strong enough that he could break Adam's bones if he wanted to. A small, heated shiver ran down Adam's spine, and he quickly took a step back, freeing his arm from Crowley's grasp.

"What is it?" Adam asked, puzzled.

"You are truly peculiar, human," Crowley noted, raising a brow. "You cannot hear, and yet you close your eyes without hesitation. You willingly take away two of the most important senses your kind relies on."

Adam bit his tongue, fighting the urge to blush again. He must look like an idiot in Crowley's eyes. Yet the dragon's face remained largely unreadable, giving away nothing.

Adam could only guess what the other man was thinking. He had hoped that telepathy would make things easier, but unlike a true dragon, Adam couldn't filter Crowley's thoughts any more than necessary. And Crowley's blank expression wasn't much help.

"I've been in this forest before. And I have a name," Adam replied stubbornly, crossing his arms over his chest. Not needing his hands to communicate at the moment was a novelty, and he planned to use his gestures to their fullest extent.

"I'm not afraid that anything will happen to me, in case that's what you're worried about," he quickly added.

"I'm not really worried about you," Crowley responded with a shrug before they continued walking.

If something happened to Adam, Crowley would simply seek out Dominique on his own. Finding a witch wouldn't be difficult for a dragon, especially now that he knew she was in Vitris. Adam was merely the ring-bearer in this story — the proof that he carried something special from a dragon.

And yet, Adam couldn't shake the feeling that Crowley was looking out for him. That he was deliberately choosing paths with fewer obstacles, ensuring Adam didn't trip or face unnecessary dangers.

His gaze fell on Crowley's chest as the ring caught the light of the sun, now high in the sky. But when Adam glanced back at Crowley's face, a shiver ran down his arms. The dragon's dark pupils had narrowed into slits.

The only feature that still made Crowley look slightly inhuman was the subtle point of his ears. Maybe they could find a headband somewhere to cover them. Otherwise, perhaps his long black hair was enough to hide them.

They continued their way through the forest in silence. Adam stared straight ahead, determined. Crowley had never been thrilled about wandering through the woods with a human to find a witch. That much had been clear from the start.

Sure, he made sure Adam didn't fall and break his neck, but in the long run, looking after the blond man was purely self-serving. With Adam's help, Crowley would find Dominique much faster than if he searched for her alone.

Under Adam's gaze, Crowley's eyes had turned cold. The dragon pulled the wide collar of his shirt up slightly, as if to shield the ring from view. As if Adam's staring was an intrusion. But this whole thing with the ring had been an accident. And it was partially Crowley's fault, too—he had asked to see the ring out of curiosity.

"If you hadn't asked me about the ring, we wouldn't even be here," Adam blurted out, making the dark-haired man halt in his tracks.

He hadn't meant to say it aloud. But once the thought had formed, he couldn't stop it. And the moment the words left his mind, he wished he knew how to block his thoughts from a dragon.

He knew he had just triggered something.

The next thing he felt was a hard impact—his back slammed against the rough bark of a tree, knocking the air from his lungs.

Panic shot through him as he realized what had happened. Crowley had grabbed him by the upper arm and shoved him against the tree. The same hand that had caught him earlier was now gripping him with a strength that left no room for escape.

A strangled sound escaped Adam's throat, and tears stung his eyes from the sheer force of Crowley's grip. The dragon's nails—sharp like claws—dug into his flesh. Reflexively, Adam's free hand shot up, grasping Crowley's wrist.

Frantic, he pulled at the dragon's arm, but Crowley's grip didn't loosen. Fear spread through Adam's body, locking his limbs in place.

Since leaving Crowley's cave, Adam had not felt fear in the dragon's presence. He had even slept for a few hours the previous night, pushing aside the reality that he was traveling with a dragon. The human-like appearance had lulled him into a false sense of security.

But now, the illusion was gone.

Since entering the forest, Crowley's eyes had looked more human—darker, almost like a deep brown. But now, his true nature was on full display. His eyes glowed with a venomous yellow, and his bared teeth were razor-sharp, like those of a predator.

If it came down to a fight—man against dragon—Adam would lose. His only hope was to persuade Crowley that he needed him to find Dominique.

Just as he was about to struggle again, Crowley's head twitched to the side, and his pupils suddenly dilated. His grip on Adam's arm loosened slightly, allowing the blond to duck under his arm and put some distance between them.

With a quiet groan, Adam clutched his arm. A moment longer, and the bone might have snapped under the pressure.

Blinking away his tears before they could fall, he quickly wiped his eyes with the heel of his palm. When he looked back at Crowley, he noticed the dragon's pointed ears twitching slightly.

Was he hearing something?

CROWLEY

He hadn't wanted to hear the truth, but his body had reacted to Adam's statement before he could stop it. Damn it, Adam was right. His curiosity had led him to pick up the ring, and now it was firmly fused into his chest.

He was just about to justify himself when a faint sound made him stop. He took a step back, and his pupils dilated so much that they almost completely engulfed the golden ring of his iris. His instincts had alerted him. There was the sound again—the neighing of a horse, followed by the dull thud of hooves on the forest's earthy ground.

"If we don't want to be discovered, we should get out of here," Crowley warned without looking at Adam. Still staring into the forest, the black-haired man let out a low growl. Of course, Adam couldn't hear the approaching hooves, and when he stepped around the tree, he was suddenly confronted by the tip of a sword pointed directly at him.

Crowley ducked back into the shadows and crouched low. From his position, he could watch as the riders emerged from the thicket one by one, surrounding Adam.

He had been so focused on arguing about the damn ring that he had heard the riders far too late. Annoyed, the black-haired man clenched his teeth.

He should have noticed the three riders much earlier; then they wouldn't have gotten themselves into this situation. Now, he had no choice but to wait.

Adam wanted to be a knight—perhaps he even knew these men. Crowley quickly dismissed the idea when he saw another man draw his sword and aim it at the blonde man.

Crowley was about to rise but held himself back at the last moment. How would the blond man handle the situation without him? Adam had pressed his back against the tree Crowley had shoved him against earlier. The horses pranced nervously in place, their nostrils flaring, but the knights seemed oblivious to their unease.

Adam's eyes widened as he followed the blade that one of the riders pressed against his throat. The knights wore dark blue uniforms with silver armor on their arms and legs. Those were the colors of the neighboring kingdom of Oboros. Crowley spotted what appeared to be a crest on the saddle of one of the men—a silver dove on a dark blue background.

"Well, what do we have here?" asked the knight whose sword rested against Adam's neck. Crowley could see Adam trying to read his lips. But with the knight sitting high on his horse, his face was too far away for Adam to make out the words. Crowley watched as the knight grew impatient, receiving no answer. A muscle in the dragon's neck twitched, but he waited to see what Adam would do next.

"Are you deaf? I asked who you are," the knight scoffed, lifting his sword slightly to tilt Adam's chin up with the tip. The knight had struck gold (haha) with that.

When Adam tried to retreat, his back only pressed harder against the unyielding bark of the tree. Like a fish, he opened his mouth, but no words came out—only a faint noise. Crowley frowned. Adam was completely unarmed—that much was clear now.

He wouldn't stand a chance against three armed knights on horseback. Crowley's body tensed as he prepared to pounce. A human's body was different from a dragon's. If he still had a tail, it would be lashing in agitation.

For a moment, Crowley focused on Adam, who sent a single, unmistakable thought his way: "Bastard!"

Crowley grinned and pushed off the ground with both his hands and feet.

"You called?" he answered in Adam's mind before turning to the three knights. Even in a human body, Crowley was fast.

With all his strength, he propelled himself forward, shooting toward the first knight like an arrow. The man had no chance to lift his sword in time. Crowley crashed into him with such force that both knight and horse were sent tumbling.

The horse let out a pain-stricken whinny, but as soon as it realized what had struck it, it scrambled to its feet and bolted through the trees. Crowley could feel Adam's gaze on his back as he slowly rose from the motionless knight.

"What the hell was that? Who are you?" the second knight shouted, drawing his sword. Crowley's ears twitched briefly.

Since his traveling companion was deaf and their conversations took place in their minds, the man's loud voice rang unpleasantly in Crowley's ears.

Crowley growled in response, which was enough to frighten one of the remaining horses into throwing its rider and galloping away in the opposite direction. The third horse, held tightly by its rider, trembled, its flanks quivering and nostrils flared.

Nervously, it pranced on the spot while Crowley fixed it with his gaze. The animal knew exactly what it was facing—the largest and most dangerous predator in the land. Crowley's current form might look human, but nothing about his movements was.

With a trembling hand, the last knight drew his sword. Crowley's eyes widened when he saw the mark engraved just above the hilt.

He would recognize that symbol anywhere. Like a trident, three serpents coiled around an eye.

Cold dread spread through Crowley's veins. It was the same symbol burned into the outside of his left thigh, the size of a clenched fist. For a fleeting moment, he thought he could smell charred flesh.

"I'll ask you one last time—what are you?" the knight demanded, snapping Crowley out of his frozen state by lifting his sword and preparing to strike.

For an instant, the steel sword blurred before Crowley's eyes, turning into a glowing brand. His body locked in place.

Images from his nightmare the night before flickered through his mind, so vivid that his thigh burned as if the wound had reopened. His pupils shrank into slits, and a deep snarl rumbled from his throat. Blinking, he forced himself back under control, and the brand dissolved into the depths of his subconscious.

He wouldn't allow his past to paralyze him in front of a single, pathetic human.

Out of the corner of his eye, he saw Adam push away from the tree and start toward him.

"What—", Crowley began, but he never finished. The blond man had thrown himself against the dragon's side.

His branded leg buckled beneath him, and Adam's full weight actually managed to knock him off balance, sending him sprawling to the ground.

Crowley landed hard on the forest floor, growling as he grabbed Adam by the collar of his shirt.

"What the he—" He stopped mid-sentence, eyes locking onto the blade that had barely missed him, slicing through the air just above Adam's shoulder.

While Crowley had arrogantly smirked at the last knight, the second one—the one thrown off his horse—had gotten back up and drawn his own sword.

Adam had protected him.

This time, Crowley saw the knight raise his blade again. In a swift motion, he rolled Adam off him and grabbed the sword by its blade before it could strike.

A gush of dark blood spilled from the deep cut, soaking Crowley's outstretched arm. Pain lanced through his limb. Without his scales to protect him, the crude slash cut deep.

Only the knight's shock at Crowley's inhuman resilience allowed him to yank him off his feet.

The knight cursed, trying to wrest his sword free from Crowley's iron grip. As if in silent agreement, Adam leaped forward, smashing his elbow into the knight's outstretched arm.

The sickening crunch of bone snapping echoed through the trees, followed by the man's piercing scream.

Crowley's ears twitched again at the sudden loud noise, but a satisfied smile spread across his face.

The air was thick with the scent of blood and fear.

The knight, his arm broken, dropped his sword and stumbled to his feet. Crowley saw Adam eyeing the abandoned weapon but making no move to pick it up.

They had taken down three knights, but if an entire army lay in wait beyond the trees, they were in trouble.

Impatiently, Crowley grabbed the fallen sword and shoved it into Adam's hands, smearing his own blood over the hilt and Adam's fingers.

"You have to kill him! We can't let him escape. If he raises the alarm, we'll have more than just these three on our backs," Crowley growled, giving Adam a push toward the injured man.

Crowley didn't watch to see if Adam would go through with it. Instead, he focused on the knight with the marked sword.

His fear would not win. Apparently, the man facing him had realized that he was not fighting another human, because for the briefest moment, pure fear flickered in his eyes.

"Monster," the knight breathed, raising his sword in front of his face.

Crowley's human body had a different center of gravity than his massive dragon form. As he lunged toward the man, he stumbled and fell to the ground.

Startled, the horse that had just thrown off its rider reared up, flared its nostrils, and bolted away. It seemed that this man was the leader of the group, because instead of fleeing, he swung his heavy iron sword.

Crowley tried to dodge the strikes but had clearly overestimated himself. In his true form, he would have effortlessly knocked the human down and torn his head from his shoulders.

With an upward slash, the knight cut off a long, black strand of Crowley's hair.

The blade came dangerously close—he could see his own reflection in the polished steel. His pupils were dilated, and he recognized the panic on his own face.

A malicious grin crept onto the knight's lips. He must have noticed the fear in Crowley's gaze.

Damn gods.

Just as the knight raised his sword for another strike, he suddenly froze mid-motion and collapsed sideways to the ground.

Behind him, Adam appeared, panting heavily, clutching a large stone in both hands. The edge of the stone was soaked in a dark liquid.

Adam let the stone fall and sank to his knees himself.

Crowley looked from the blond man to the motionless knight on the ground.

Adam had just saved his life.

FLEDGLING

The chains tugged at his wings, cutting deep into his scaly skin, and every small twitch sent waves of pain coursing through his body. The stench of burnt flesh hung in the air—his own flesh.

Sparks danced around him as the iron, heated to a glowing red, struck his scales once more. The dull hiss of metal against his skin echoed in his ears, his muscles convulsing, but he suppressed the scream.

How long had he been trapped here? Judging by the movements around him, he guessed he must be in the belly of a ship. No daylight reached Crowley's cage, leaving him with no sense of time—no difference between day and night.

They had begun tearing out his scales, one by one. At some point, his mind had stopped sending him pain signals, replaced by a white noise that drowned out the loud voices and laughter surrounding him. Just before he lost consciousness, the scent of hot coal had filled his nostrils.

Again and again, they had dragged him back into the present, pressing burning iron into the soft skin between his scales. They would not let him slip away into unconsciousness. They wanted him to suffer.

He was a dragon. An ancient, powerful creature—more than flesh, more than blood. And yet, he felt fragile. Every breath seemed to drive the pain deeper into his bones. His flanks trembled as he fought against the agony.

Why were they doing this? What did they hope to gain?

Once, a man had appeared, dressed in expensive garments. It was early in Crowley's captivity, and he had questioned his hunters as if he were bidding on a prize at a market.

The man kept returning. Sometimes, he would stand silently by the cage; other times, he would not even glance at Crowley. He was tall, with brown hair that caught a reddish hue in the dim lantern light.

A full beard obscured his sharp features, but his green eyes gleamed with hunger whenever they settled on Crowley's cage. This man knew how to break a dragon.

They had broken one of his wings. If only he could stretch it out, it would heal without issue. But the cage wasn't even large enough for him to turn around.

He squeezed his eyes shut, trying to recall the wind rushing beneath his wings, the warmth of the sun on his scales. But the memories were like distant dreams, fading beneath the screams of his body.

The iron was pressed into his side again, and this time, a growl escaped him. A sound deep from his chest, raw and uncontrollable. His breathing was labored, and he opened one eye.

The world around him was wrapped in a haze, everything moving sluggishly. The man approached him at an agonizingly slow pace, as if time itself had stalled. He stopped right in front of the bars. If Crowley had been able to move, he would have snapped at his fine vest or lunged for the human's head as he looked down on him.

The dragon's golden eyes locked onto the silver pin on the cruel man's chest. If he ever escaped, he would remember that pin.

He would hunt this man down and make him feel the same humiliation, the same pain he had suffered. His breath came in short, ragged gasps, and he felt the burning cold sinking deep into his core. They wanted to break him, and perhaps they already had.

The fire that had once raged inside him was now just a spark. A tiny, trembling flame, flickering as it slowly faded into smoldering embers.

He thought of Orion. His brother would get him out of here. He would come to save him. And then he would scold him for being so naïve. And Orion would be right.

Crowley had never feared humans; they had fascinated him. But now, his body trembled with fear of what these monsters might still have planned for him. He felt the cold creeping into his heart. The chains wrapped around his body were his prison, turning him into nothing more than a shadow of himself.

ADAM

He could no longer feel his legs. Every breath burned in his lungs, and his thoughts raced. The roaring in his ears was so loud that Adam imagined his thoughts must sound like a beehive.

He had killed someone for the first time. And not just anyone—two knights. His vision blurred as tears welled at the edges of his lashes.

As a knight, death was inevitable. Adam knew that much—he wasn't a child anymore. And these deaths had been necessary, an act of self-defense for himself and Crowley. And yet, his entire body trembled, and he felt bile rise in his throat.

As soon as his breathing had steadied, he rolled to the side and vomited beside the corpse of the knight, whose head wound was still bleeding.

"You're hurt." That was the first thought he could grasp amid the chaos in his mind.

Slowly, Adam lifted his gaze and made out Crowley's blurred figure before him. The black-haired man had crouched beside him, whether intentionally or not, blocking his view of the dead knight.

"Am I?" Adam weakly countered. He raised both hands to examine them, but aside from a few small scratches, he was unharmed. Instead, he noticed Crowley's hand, completely covered in blood.

"Easy for you to say—your hand! Let me see it!" Carefully, he took Crowley's hand and inspected the wound. Dragons seemed to have remarkable healing abilities.

The cut had already almost completely closed, and the blood could be washed away. Adam let out a relieved breath and quickly released the hand that had, just moments ago, pinned him against a tree.

"You protected me," Crowley noted in surprise, and Adam looked up at him. Even before the fight, Crowley's eyes had returned to their old golden hue, but now they were once again the warm brown of his human disguise.

Adam liked both colors, though the brown made Crowley—he thought for a moment—seem more vulnerable. Or perhaps it was just the way the dragon was looking at him.

Adam's gaze drifted to the first knight Crowley had thrown to the ground. His legs shook slightly as he stood and walked over. Something wasn't right.

For years, he and Silas had observed knights from both Altos and Oboros. When they passed through the village barracks to rest or train, the two boys would watch eagerly.

They had even snuck onto the barracks roof, watching the men and women practice from above. But the way these three had fought didn't match what Adam had learned as a child.

"These three men were definitely not knights," Adam shared his thoughts with Crowley. He crouched beside the body. Without the blood, the man almost looked as if he were merely sleeping.

That made it easier for Adam to overcome his revulsion as he reached for the dead man's shirt.

The crest of Oboros was emblazoned on his chest, but a real knight's uniform would have the insignia intricately embroidered with fine thread. These uniforms were fakes. That explained why they had attacked without question.

"So we took out three impostors? Then we've actually done the Crown a favor without meaning to," Crowley said, before standing and dusting off his pants.

Adam made a quiet sound of agreement and stood as well. His gaze fell to one of the swords on the ground. If bandits ever got their hands on it again, it wouldn't hurt to be armed. He bent down and picked up one of the swords, fastening it to his belt.

For a moment, he thought Crowley might object, noticing the dragon's look, but instead, Crowley simply turned away and stepped over the knights' bodies without a second glance.

For a brief moment, Adam considered burying the men. Then he reminded himself that they were frauds who had trampled on the honor of true knights. Frowning, he hurried to follow the dragon.

As the unlikely pair moved on, Adam found himself noticing a similarity between Crowley and his childhood friend.

When Adam had been younger, there was only one boy who hadn't cared that he was slowly losing his hearing. That boy had been so stubborn that he had insisted on befriending the strange, quiet blond boy next door. And so, Adam had gained his first—and best—friend, Silas.

After their first year of friendship, his condition had worsened rapidly, and within a year, all the sounds he knew had disappeared from his world. But some things had remained as fragments: the warm voice of his uncle, the excited chatter of Silas, and the melody of an old song often played at village festivals.

Silas had been reckless and braver than anyone. If he were here now, he would have been impressed by Crowley.

The memory of Silas pulled at Adam's heart, and he couldn't shake the emotions that always overwhelmed him when he thought of his friend.

"Are you okay? Why are you crying all of a sudden?" Crowley's voice pulled him from his thoughts.

Quickly, Adam wiped his eyes with his sleeve. The memory of Silas still ached, even after all these years. The silver pendant around his neck felt heavier than ever.

He didn't want to think about his old friend anymore, but he also couldn't lie to Crowley, not when their connection ran this deep. Adam's gaze flickered to the sword at his hip.

"It's just… the first time I've killed someone," he admitted. It wasn't entirely a lie, but it wasn't the full truth either. The deaths of those three men weighed on him, whether they had been bandits or not.

Crowley looked at the sword with a mix of disgust and wariness.

Adam was about to ask what was wrong when Crowley's injured hand caught his attention again. The blood had mostly dried, but he wanted to be sure the wound had fully healed.

"Let me see your hand again."

Irritated, maybe even hesitant, Crowley extended his hand, allowing Adam to inspect it. With both thumbs, Adam tried to wipe away the dried blood.

Restlessly, the black-haired man attempted to pull away, but Adam doubted he was actually hurting him.

"Hold still," Adam thought, tightening his grip.

Crowley had elegant hands, with long fingers. Adam ran his thumb over his palm, tracing the lines of his fingers. Crowley let out a quiet growl but ultimately held still, allowing Adam to examine him.

Adam deliberately avoided looking up. He could feel Crowley's gaze on him. The dragon's body temperature was still unnaturally high, but he seemed to be adjusting to his human form—his skin was no longer damp with sweat.

"You don't have to make such a fuss over a scratch," Crowley muttered. It was probably taking all his self-control not to pull his hand away.

"A scratch? You stopped a sword with your bare hand," Adam countered.

"You seem to forget—I'm not human," Crowley stated matter-of-factly.

Adam's eyes widened in realization. He had forgotten. For a moment, he had treated Crowley like any other person. For him, this must have been child's play.

As the memories of the fight returned, Adam let go of Crowley's hand. For a brief moment, the dragon's fingers hovered in the air before he slowly lowered them.

"You're pretty good with a sword. Are you sure you can't become a knight?" Crowley resumed their mental conversation as they set off again.

"The Grandmaster won't let me into the academy as long as I can't hear. Without you, that last strike would have killed me. I didn't hear it coming. Maybe the old man was right—I'd be a danger to myself and others on a real battlefield."

Like a dog, Crowley tilted his head, one pointed ear twitching. Adam suppressed a quiet laugh. The gesture would have looked strange on anyone else, but somehow, it suited Crowley—he was still getting used to pretending to be human.

"I don't understand your obsession with becoming a knight. But if you want it that badly, your deafness won't stop you. You even walked into a dragon's den for it", Crowley noted with a shrug.

Was that… a compliment?

Their conversation ended there as Crowley lifted his gaze to the sky. The sun was setting.

"Let's keep moving a bit longer and set up camp. We'll still have a full day's journey through this forest tomorrow," he said, nodding toward a sloping hillside.

Adam glanced up as well. The sky was clear. No rain. Another night under the open sky. Maybe they would find a cave or something to hide in.

The closer they came to the outskirts of the capital, the more people they might encounter. This time it had been a group of imposters, but who knew what came next.

Since the attack, Adam kept his gaze on the trees to see if there wasn't another ambush. He was travelling with a dragon, he almost forgot. Soon he relaxed and for now he trusted in Crowley to warn him if there was anything strange around them.

It had been him as well who detected the bandits first. For now this was enough to trust the dragon until they reached the forest's edge.

From there on Adam knew the way by heart and it was way harder to sneak up on them on open land.

CROWLEY

Suddenly, the black-haired man heard something rustling in the underbrush, and his pointed ears twitched in the direction of the sound. No animal had dared to come this close before. Adam furrowed his brows in question and reached for Crowley's forearm.

At first, Crowley wanted to pull his arm away from the grip, but the human's fingers around his wrist prevented him from doing so.

The dragon's eyes wandered through the dark trees until a slight smile crept onto his lips. Adam didn't understand what Crowley had seen in the darkness. The black-haired man raised a finger to his lips, signaling the other to stay silent.

"You humans don't only have stories about us dragons, do you?" Crowley asked without moving a muscle.

"My uncle used to read me many things when I was younger. Back then, I could still hear him, but it got worse and worse until I eventually lost my hearing completely. I already told you-," the blonde replied, leaning forward curiously.

His eyes widened slightly as he, too, faintly made out something silvery between the trees.

"What is that?" he asked the older man, just about to move closer, when Crowley raised his hand to stop him.

"These creatures are very shy and do not show themselves to humans. They protect the forest and the animals within it. Stay behind me and imitate what I do as best you can," the black-haired man ordered before straightening up to his full height, his body once again becoming covered in black scales.

Adam gasped in surprise, but his attention was drawn to the creature that turned its head toward them curiously and slowly approached. The blonde man's eyes widened, and a feeling of reverence swelled in his chest. He couldn't believe his eyes—he was already traveling with a dragon, so how crazy was it to now be standing before a living, breathing unicorn?

Slowly, Crowley bent one knee and lowered his head. Adam could only stare at him. He had never expected that such a proud creature as a dragon would bow before such a delicate being as a unicorn. Too late, he remembered Crowley's words, and the unicorn turned away with a quiet whinny.

"No, wait!" Adam thought desperately and clumsily dropped to his knees. His eyes were wide, and his cheeks burned with heat.

With trembling fingers, he reached for his face, wiping away the silent tears that had fallen onto his cheeks.

Slowly, the unicorn also inclined its head, as if bowing in return, and walked past the two kneeling figures before disappearing back into the underbrush.

Adam stared for a moment at the spot where, just moments ago, a real unicorn had stood. He wiped both hands over his face before looking up at Crowley, who had already risen to his feet beside him.

"What just happened?" the blonde asked in confusion.

"Unicorns are among the purest beings. I'm surprised one dared come so close to a human. Its presence must have moved you to tears," Crowley explained with a shrug. For a dragon, a unicorn probably wasn't anything special.

The black scales on Crowley's body withdrew back into his skin, leaving the blonde with more questions than answers. But before he could question Crowley about it, the dragon had already disappeared among the first trees.

Adam got to his feet with slightly unsteady legs and brushed the dust from his knees.

There were dragons and unicorns—that much he had learned on his short journey so far. He had met a real witch too.

How blindly did humans walk through the world when it was filled with such beautiful things?

Adam watched as Crowley pulled the scales back into his skin. In an instant, a dragon could look completely human.

Maybe other creatures also had different forms and lived hidden among humans without them ever noticing. With newfound determination, Adam followed the black-haired man into the increasingly dense undergrowth.

After sunset, their progress slowed. They had taken a few breaks to eat from Adam's rations and rest. Crowley didn't need to eat often—he could go days without food.

Once the matter of the ring was settled, he would catch something large and devour it with pleasure. Just the thought made his mouth water.

When they reached a larger clearing, the black-haired man came to a halt and surveyed the area.

"Let's set up camp here before you trip over something in the dark," he decided, already looking for a comfortable place to sleep.

Crowley wasn't truly worried that Adam would fall. Even without hearing, the young man managed well on his own—that, Crowley could admit. But after their encounter with those knights, he didn't want to risk any unnecessary delays. As much as he disliked the thought, he needed Adam.

Out of the corner of his eye, he watched Adam navigate the darkness, stepping carefully over a large root. He could imagine worse travel companions, as strange as that thought was. Despite being human, Crowley could tolerate the blonde—at least until they reached the capital.

"I can't even see my own feet in the dark," Adam admitted tiredly, collapsing onto the large root he had just climbed over.

The black-haired man looked at Adam's face, marked by exhaustion.

Crowley wasn't sure how much strain a normal human body could endure. He had been moving quickly, expecting the other to keep up.

The sooner they reached that witch, the better. She would remove the ring from his chest, and Crowley wouldn't spare either of them a second glance.

And yet, he studied the tired features of the blond man. Maybe he was imagining it, but there was a vulnerability in Adam's gaze that didn't quite fit the brave, if reckless, human.

"So, you really can't hear anything?" Crowley asked directly.

Surprised, Adam lifted his head, and their eyes met.

"Why would I lie to a dragon about that?" came the immediate response. Despite his exhaustion, the young man was quick-witted—Crowley had to give him that.

"I was just curious. You manage surprisingly well, even without a sense of hearing," Crowley admitted honestly and stood up again to search for firewood.

Around their campsite, he gathered small, dry twigs and moss to start a fire.

Entering a pact with a witch for whatever reason was foolish. Adam had blindly followed her orders to get his wish granted, a wish Crowley still couldn't understand. What was so great about the royal guard that you willingly looked for your own death?

Witchcraft was mysterious. No one knew exactly where it came from. It was passed down to the eldest daughter, but even Crowley knew little beyond that.

Further away, the dragon collected larger logs and carried them back to their campsite. He watched as Adam built himself a makeshift bedding of moss and twigs, so he wouldn't have to sleep on the hard ground.

Crowley felt Adam's curious gaze on him as he stacked the wood and, with a deep breath, ignited it with his inner fire. For a brief moment, the core in his chest glowed as the flames gathered there.

Adam scooted a bit farther from the fire and busied himself adjusting his bedding, breaking off a few small branches.

Crowley noticed Adam's intrigued look at his core and instinctively turned his upper body away, focusing on keeping the fire going. He tugged at the collar of his shirt, but the top button was missing already, so he could only pull the thin linen fabric up slightly—though it didn't completely obscure the golden ring and his core.

"I keep forgetting that you're not actually human," Adam admitted, looking up. Crowley studied the blue eyes for a moment.

"It would be dangerous to underestimate me. I may look like your kind, but I am still a dragon," the black-haired man warned.

"Believe me, I know that," Adam replied simply, his gaze dropping to the ground beside his feet.

The events of the afternoon still lingered in both their thoughts. Crowley glanced down at his hand, the same one that had caught the blade, before looking back at the fire. The flames flickered in Adam's blue eyes like sunlight on ocean waves.

He hadn't been to the sea in a long time.

"You should sleep. I don't mind staying awake. As long as I'm here, even the creatures of the forest will leave us alone. I'll wake you if anything happens," Crowley suggested, having noticed how Adam's eyes kept drooping shut.

The dragon clicked his tongue once and threw another piece of wood into the fire, causing a small burst of sparks. He saw Adam scoot a little farther away. Had the sudden sparks startled him?

"I can see your eyes are barely staying open. Lie down and get some rest. Otherwise, we won't make any progress tomorrow if you're exhausted," Crowley growled, making it clear that he wouldn't tolerate any protests.

He needed Adam awake and alert. Once they left the forest, the blond would have to take the lead and guide them to Vitris as quickly as possible. Crowley only knew the route from the sky. On foot, the best he could do was keep heading west through the trees.

His words seemed to make sense to the young man, and, albeit reluctantly, Adam curled up on his makeshift mattress. Within two minutes, he was fast asleep. Crowley watched as the tension gradually left the young man's stiff body.

Crowley doubted that anything in this forest would be foolish enough to attack them. Most creatures weren't concerned with appearances; they could sense what he was. The three horses had known what he was even before their foolish riders had seen him coming. This would be a peaceful night.

Or so Crowley thought.

Just before sunrise, Crowley was pulled from his resting position when Adam curled in on himself beside him, almost as if he were in pain.

"Adam? Are you awake?"

At first, Crowley tried to reach him with his thoughts, but subconscious minds weren't affected by telepathy. Not even dragons could connect while sleeping.

His parents had been mates, and when Crowley was still a young dragon, it had often seemed like his father knew what his mother was thinking before she even spoke. That had been so long ago now. The memory was faint and full of holes, but Crowley was sure his parents had loved each other.

After they had left him and Orion behind, he had spent years searching for them. But dragons weren't creatures that lived in family groups. Orion would have left him too, once Crowley had reached adulthood. But that had never come to pass.

The memory of his brother sent a sharp ache through Crowley's chest. He placed a hand over his heart, feeling its strong, steady beat beneath his palm.

Adam kicked in his sleep, his foot connecting with Crowley's hip. Shaking off the remnants of his memories, the dragon refocused on the human beside him.

Was he having a nightmare?

Crowley turned his gaze away from the curled-up figure and instead stared into the fire, which had burned down to mostly embers.

Maybe the human was cold? Crowley knew that the closer they got to the capital, the warmer it would become. He himself never felt the chill—his inner fire burned too hot for that. Taking a deep breath, he reignited the flames.

A few moments passed, but the pained sounds beside him only grew louder. The warmth hadn't helped; Adam's entire body was still trembling like a leaf in the wind.

Had he been injured during their fight? No, Crowley hadn't smelled any blood on him after they'd left the three knights behind. So it had to be a nightmare.

Under Crowley's golden gaze, the blond man tossed and turned. When he rolled to face the fire, Crowley noticed the sweat beading on his forehead. He sighed before making another attempt to wake him through their telepathic link.

"Adam?"

The young man's body twisted as if fighting off invisible hands. His fingers dug into the earth and scattered leaves as if searching for something to hold onto.

Crowley hesitated, unsure if he should touch him.

What did it matter to him if the other had bad dreams?

Adam's head suddenly jerked to the side as if someone had struck him, and a faint, choked whimper slipped from his lips.

Carefully, the dragon reached out and brushed a single blond curl away from the mortal's damp forehead with his nail.

Crowley frowned as he observed him. It was remarkable how a man who supposedly couldn't hear still slept so deeply. Every breath, every shudder of his body revealed how deeply Adam was trapped in this nightmare.

The flickering light of their small campfire cast unnatural shadows across Adam's pale features. Another twitch. Another fear-laced whimper.

Crowley had no idea what was haunting him.

Annoyed, and perhaps a little sympathetic, the dark-haired man reached for the blond's shoulder.

A strangled cry tore from Adam's throat, and his eyes snapped open. Reflexively, he lashed out at the hand that had grabbed him and scrambled away from the fire in panic.

Adam gave him the same look a frightened rabbit would give a fox. Right now he was the hunter that had frightened his prey.

Crowley hadn't meant to scare him so badly, but at least he was awake now. Slowly, he raised his hand to show that he was no longer touching him.

"You were having a nightmare," Crowley explained.

Adam was awake, but his unfocused, glassy stare told Crowley that he wasn't entirely present yet. Maybe he still thought he was dreaming.

Like a frightened animal, the blond crouched beside his moss-covered bedding. His blue eyes were veiled, as if he were lost in his thoughts, somewhere far away.

Did he not recognize who was in front of him?

Cautiously, Crowley lifted both hands, palms facing outward, in a gesture meant to reassure him.

"I just wanted to wake you. The sun will rise soon," the dark-haired man said calmly.

Slowly, the tension in Adam's body eased, and the vacant look in his eyes faded.

Had he truly been so terrified of Crowley that he saw him as a threat the moment he woke up?

Crowley exhaled sharply and then stomped out the last embers of their fire. He stood, not wanting Adam to see the unease and uncertainty swirling inside him.

He was not a monster.

ADAM

It had taken a while for Crowley's voice to reach him. Only then did the veil of the dream slowly fade.

Adam had dreamed of the knights. Of their fight in the afternoon and of Crowley.

In his dream, the dragon had been in his true form and had made short work of the impostors. Adam's subconscious had drawn from the images in the dragon's cave and had made him appear far more monstrous than he really was. The bloody images still lingered heavily in the blonde's thoughts.

Silently, they continued their journey after sunrise. Adam's gaze wandered up to the leaves of the trees swaying in the wind. What must that sound like?

He hadn't been deaf from birth. But many of his sound-filled memories had faded over time. Sometimes, he saw something and wished he could hear it. Over the years, he had learned to live with it. That didn't change his longing, though.

As he watched the leaves, his gaze fell on the profile of his traveling companion. Crowley's human form was handsome. The long black hair and sharp features made him look like a southerner from Oboros. Many of them traveled along the trade route from Korintha over the mountains to Vitris.

"You're staring," he heard the dragon's voice in his head.

"I haven't had the time to look at you properly until now," Adam answered honestly.

"Don't get too used to it. As soon as we find your witch and I get rid of this ring, we'll never see each other again," Crowley snorted, quickening his pace. What was with him? Maybe the dragon hadn't slept well.

On foot, their path led them through the forest, past small hills and caves. Adam no longer recognized this part of the woods.

He had entered Crowley's cave from another direction and slowed his steps. The black-haired man stopped beside him and raised an eyebrow.

"Why are we stopping? Is something wrong?"

Adam didn't know how the dragon would react, but he had to be honest. What good would lying do now?

"I didn't come through this part of the forest. I need a moment to see if something seems familiar."

"So, we're lost," the dragon concluded, unenthusiastic.

Adam ignored the remark and started looking around the clearing where they had stopped. The trees were so large that their branches still stretched over the entire clearing, allowing only patches of sunlight to reach the ground.

That was when Adam noticed indentations carved into the reddish sandstone around them. Curious, he stepped closer and examined the stone. The rock seemed natural, but the indentations had been deliberately chiseled. Had they stumbled upon a memorial site?

In some of these alcoves, small and large stone blocks had been placed. A few bore stone plaques inscribed with markings. Intrigued, the blonde approached to inspect one of the plaques more closely, but the symbols were unfamiliar to him.

He sensed someone stepping up behind him just before Crowley appeared at his side. They hadn't been traveling together for long, but the prickling sensation of danger at the nape of Adam's neck hadn't quite faded. He still couldn't read the dragon.

"That's Compassé, an old version of the script you humans use today. These plaques must have been placed here hundreds of years ago," the dragon remarked, running his fingers over the smoothly polished stone. Surprised, Adam looked up and met the black-haired man's gaze.

"Can you read it?" Adam asked before turning his attention back to the stone.

"No, I never learned to read your script. I only recognize the symbols."

"How old are you?" The words slipped from Adam's mouth before he could stop himself.

He clapped a hand over his lips as if to take them back. Was it weird to as a Négul their age? Did they even age? Adam was at a loss.

But Crowley didn't react at all; instead, he turned away from the stone tablet.

Adam glanced around again and now noticed smaller figures beside the stone plaques. These must have been altars. Perhaps merchants had prayed for good fortune here, or hunters before setting off into the forest.

To his left, a figure had been carved from the stone, hands raised in a gesture of blessing. Its face was hidden beneath a hood, but a faint smile was visible. At its feet, serpents coiled, their bodies sculpted so finely that they seemed to glisten in the dim light.

To the right stood a smaller statue on one of the stone blocks that served as altars—a warrior, holding a massive shield and a sword pointed toward the sky. His eyes were empty, but his expression was resolute, as if guarding the pass and its travelers from unseen foes. His stone-carved cloak appeared to billow in the wind, though no breeze was present.

Further ahead stood a third figure, the one that drew the most attention. A woman of overwhelming beauty, her arms spread wide as if embracing the entire world.

Her stone eyes gazed into the distance, and at her feet, tiny plants sprouted from the cracks, as if life itself was flowing from her.

Time had worn down the figures and plaques, making them blend with the surrounding rocks and debris, but the old gods still seemed to reign here.

Adam stopped, his gaze fixed on the goddess as he felt a strange energy fill the clearing. The silence was heavy, but it was as if the forest itself was whispering—as if the gods, immortalized in stone, were still watching over their domain.

He stepped closer to the goddess, reaching out to touch the cool surface of the stone.

For a moment, he closed his eyes and imagined he could feel a faint vibration running through the statue. Almost as if the goddess's heart was still beating, hidden deep within the stone.

The scent of damp rock and ancient roots filled his nose, and for an instant, he thought he could hear the breath of long-gone worshippers. But then, he lowered his hand, took a step back, and turned away.

It was eerie, even for someone like Adam, who had spent his whole life believing in the old gods. Yet he had never felt so close to them as he did now.

He allowed himself a sideways glance at Crowley, but the dragon either didn't sense the energy or simply didn't care. He had climbed onto a small rise and was now looking down at Adam.

"You coming?"

With quick steps, Adam hurried to leave the altars and statues behind.

CROWLEY

The next few days of their journey were also spent mostly in silence. At least the wild animals left them alone thanks to Crowley's presence. The dragon noticed that Adam's thoughts were never still.

They always hummed quietly, like waves, or buzzed like a beehive. What had initially been annoying had turned into an everyday occurrence. Adam hadn't had another nightmare either.

One evening, they stopped by a small river, and Adam seemed to think it was time to talk about that night.

"Crowley, I haven't properly thanked you yet for what you did with those impostors."

Impostors? Weren't the three men knights from Oboros? To Crowley, all humans under the blue flag belonged to Oboros, and those under the red flag to Altos. Whether frauds or not, they had defended themselves—there was nothing to thank him for. Shrugging, he replied, "You don't need to thank me. We fought together, and they attacked us."

"But I want to thank you," the blond interrupted, poking at the campfire with a stick. "The fight scared me a little," he admitted hesitantly, and Crowley took notice.

Had he scared Adam?

"I've never killed a person before."

Ah.

"And that frightened you?" Crowley asked, confused. He had seen humans kill each other countless times. He had assumed it was nothing unusual. But Adam nodded.

"I know that dreaming of becoming a knight sounds ridiculous if a single death unsettles me this much. But I saw the look in those men's eyes. They would have killed me without hesitation, without remorse, without a second thought."

That made sense to Crowley. Those men wouldn't have hesitated to kill two complete strangers.

He was just about to say something when Adam continued: "But you protected me. I know you're only keeping me alive because you need me to bring you to Dominique.

But I still wanted to thank you. That night afterward was unpleasant, and I had to process it first, but I think between you and those impostors, I'm glad to be on your side, even if only temporarily."

It took a moment for Crowley to fully grasp Adam's words. He had assumed that Adam had been trapped in his nightmare out of fear of him.

Maybe he had simply been startled upon waking up. For a brief moment, Crowley felt something close to guilt stirring in his chest and sighed. Adam had taken a step toward him—he could do the same.

"With or without hearing, I'm glad to have you on my side too. You fought far better than those three wannabe knights ever could." Shrugging, Crowley was about to rekindle the fire when he noticed a faint glow between the trees. Adam raised an eyebrow.

"What's wrong?"

"Will-o'-the-wisps," Crowley replied, starting to scatter dirt over their fire.

"Will-o'-the-wisps?" Adam repeated, confused, watching Crowley uneasily as he buried their only light source. The dark-haired man took pity on him and gestured toward the trees.

"See those lights? Those are will-o'-the-wisps heading toward the mountains. You wouldn't have encountered them on your journey to me—they only appear at night. They're cautious and often hide in the mist. It seems they feel safe enough to travel tonight."

Crowley smiled as he watched the colorful lights drifting like small blossoms through the trees.

"What exactly are will-o'-the-wisps? And why did you have to put out the fire?" the blond asked, remaining completely still.

"You can relax, just don't make any sudden movements— you might startle them. Will-o'-the-wisps are Négul, just like me and the unicorn."

It wasn't unusual to encounter Négul; they were living beings, just like animals and humans. But many of them were skittish, and it was impressive to see that two had already approached Crowley despite the presence of a human.

From the corner of his eye, Crowley noticed Adam's figure relax as he watched the dazzling display with wide-eyed wonder.

"Will-o'-the-wisps fear fire, that's why I put out our campfire. Once they've passed, I can relight it."

At the mention of their fear of fire, Adam flinched. Did the blonde also fear fire? Over the past few days, Adam had always kept a safe distance from it. Crowley had taken care of lighting and extinguishing it.

As soon as the tiny lights disappeared, the dragon breathed life back into the embers. The flames cast large shadows around them.

One might have thought they had only imagined the will-o'-the-wisps' passing.

"You must be something special," Crowley began as Adam lay back down on the ground. Confused, the blonde sat up again.

"What do you mean?"

"Négul are wary of humans, and yet you've already encountered four of us."

Was it just his imagination, or had Adam turned red at his words?

"And now sleep—we still have a long journey ahead of us," Crowley snorted and closed his eyes. He wouldn't sleep deeply, but he could afford to rest. If even will-o'-the-wisps weren't afraid to approach him and Adam, then he could trust himself to close his eyes for a moment.

In the end, he fell asleep leaning against a tree. And he dreamed—of home. The Latu Mountains had become his home after he lost Orion.

Alone and uncertain, he had fled into the mountains, traveling further and further south until he found a tunnel system. Over the years, he had turned the abandoned tunnels and caves into a nest he could always return to.

In his dream, the sun shone over the mountain peaks like a golden caress. A new morning had dawned. Crowley had just awakened. His scaly body gleamed in deep black, like wet obsidian.

As he did every day, he stretched his wings wide and soared into the sky. His shoulder cracked slightly—an old wound that would follow him for the rest of his life—but his flight through the clouds was still a majestic sight. The trees and houses below looked like tiny specks in the landscape.

Even after all these decades, he could still hear Orion's voice warning him not to fly too low. Humans didn't care whether they shot a bird or a dragon from the sky.

After a while, he landed softly in a forest clearing to hunt for food. His sharp eyes scanned the terrain. He could have searched for prey from the air, but he didn't want to risk being seen.

Effortlessly, he caught a deer and carried it back to his cave.

To many, the life of a dragon might seem dull, but Crowley cherished his solitude. He had become more cautious since his captivity.

His escape had only succeeded by sheer luck, and thanks to his brother, he had survived.

Once, he had indulged his curiosity, observing humans at will. Now, he only allowed himself careful glances from a safe distance. He would never be that naive again.

Satisfied, he allowed himself another flight and landed by a small brook to quench his thirst. The sounds and scents around him were so familiar that he felt no need to worry about danger.

This was his home.

With a sudden jolt, Crowley's eyes snapped open, but the forest was still shrouded in darkness. The fire had gone out—how long had he slept? Had he really dozed off?

He glanced at Adam, but the human was sleeping soundly, and the forest around them was deathly silent.

Surprised, Crowley touched his cheek and felt warm liquid.

Tears? Frustrated, he wiped his eyes and looked up at the sky. He would return home soon. This human body was a curse, a prison, and the dark-haired dragon had sworn never to be caged again.

With his home in his heart, Crowley waited for the sunrise before gently waking Adam.

ADAM

By the time they reached the forest's edge, the two had spoken more than they had before their encounter with the will-o'-the-wisps. That quiet moment of trust had melted a big layer of ice between them.

Even if they were only traveling together until Vitris, it was still easier with someone one didn't outright despise.

As the trees grew sparser, the forest's border finally came into view. But the closer they got, the slower and quieter the dragon became.

The landscape around them had changed, just as the weather was beginning to shift. While the eastern part of the forest had been dominated by conifers, the western edge was lined with deciduous trees, shrubs, climbing plants, and the lush green of moss.

The temperature began to rise noticeably.

Having started his journey from his uncle's farm further south, Adam had made good progress thanks to traveling merchants and reached the forest's border within a few days. He had rested with them before their paths diverged. He would have liked to continue with them.

Apparently, their destination was the great market city of Korintha, west of the Latu Mountains in Oboros. Adam knew from his uncle that merchants from across the continent gathered there, but he had never been to that market himself.

The blond-haired man took the first step out of the dense treeline into the dim light of the setting sun. Out of the corner of his eye, he noticed Crowley hesitating briefly before stepping onto the dusty path as well.

Adam wondered if Crowley had ever traveled this far from his cave before.

Shaking his head, he reminded himself that a dragon could surely travel farther than a few forests if he wanted to. Crowley had probably been all over the continent—a fact Adam found himself somewhat envious of.

"What's wrong?" the blond asked curiously, coming to a stop.

"Nothing. I've avoided humans for years. Now I have to walk among them, wearing the skin of one of them. I can think of more pleasant things to do," Crowley replied with distaste. Adam could see the tension in the taller man's shoulders.

The remark made Adam grin, though he tried to hide it behind his hand. Luckily, only he could hear Crowley's thoughts. That brought up another idea, and he turned his attention back to the dragon.

He was sure now that his thoughts were reaching the other man. This kind of mind-reading was strange—completely foreign to someone like Adam.

"Can others hear the thoughts we share?" he asked Crowley. Earlier, during their encounter with the false knights, he hadn't paid much attention to it.

The dark-haired man halted, furrowing his brows before answering.

"I don't think so. But you're also the first human I've ever spoken to this way. Honestly, I don't want to hear any more human thoughts. Yours are chaotic enough."

Had Adam imagined it, or had Crowley's voice sounded unusually soft in his head just now?

After the strange dream, the blond had worried things might become awkward between him and the dragon.

He had told Crowley that he needed time to process everything—after all, it had been his first time killing someone. And he had seen a real dragon fight, even if it was in human form. He couldn't put it into words, but the sight of Crowley snarling and attacking had been enough to haunt him for an entire night.

Soon, they would reach the first farmlands. Adam had hoped to avoid the lands belonging to his village, but he couldn't think of a good excuse to justify the detour to Crowley.

Together, they pushed through the tall grasses toward the first marked properties. Adam recognized the boundary markers, and his palms began to sweat. He had left home without telling his uncle. A queasy feeling settled in his stomach as he thought about how his uncle might react to him bringing home a real dragon.

Crowley hesitated at the boundary marker, just as he had at the last row of trees.

Adam was about to reach for his hand when the dark-haired man made up his mind and stepped forward. He adjusted his pace to match the human's, allowing Adam to take the lead.

The mountain and the forest had been Crowley's territory—these fields belonged to humans. They were the same fields where Adam had played as a child with the other farm kids until the sun had set.

He led them along the wooden fences, careful not to startle the smaller animals, like goats and lambs. But avoiding them proved more difficult than expected, especially with a dragon in tow. Adam could feel Crowley watching him curiously, observing how he wove through the fields.

Even without hearing, the dragon somehow knew how to avoid unwanted eyes—whether human or animal.

He was used to navigating through overgrown landscapes. Crowley stayed two steps behind Adam at all times, as if waiting for him to show the way, just as the dragon had guided him down the mountain.

Adam focused entirely on keeping the larger animals away. Naturally, they approached to protect their young, and his plan to completely avoid the livestock didn't seem to be working. But as soon as the sheep and goats caught sight of Crowley, they scattered.

"Why do they recognize what you are? You look human right now. The knights yesterday didn't recognize you as a dragon, but the horses nearly went mad," Adam asked, puzzled.

"Because animals are sometimes smarter than humans," Crowley replied with a shrug.

"They have a sixth sense for danger. They don't rely on appearances—they trust their instincts, which tell them what I really am. Dangerous," the dark-haired man explained. That made sense to Adam.

By now, he had been traveling with Crowley for some time. Occasionally, he caught himself studying the dragon's "disguise."

The only features that might give him away—if one knew what to look for—were his slightly pointed ears and the golden glow of his eyes when he was excited or had spotted something interesting.

Surprised at how well he could read Crowley's body language, Adam lowered his gaze, feeling his face grow warm.

Instead, he focused on one of the rams in the pasture, which had spotted them and declared them enemies. Adam stopped, and Crowley came to a halt right behind him.

He could feel how close the taller man had stepped. If he wanted to, he could lean back and would feel the other's chest against his back. Instinctively, Adam tensed.

Crowley stepped past him without hesitation, staring at the ram. From Adam's position, he could only see the glow in Crowley's golden eyes before the ram bolted in a panic. Adam chuckled quietly and walked past Crowley to continue their journey. At least the animals wouldn't be a problem. The humans, however, were another story.

Once they had passed the first pastures, Adam's stomach growled. They decided to take a short break under a large oak tree. Adam gathered whatever edible plants he could find growing freely in the area, only to return to the tree without Crowley.

"Crowley?" Adam asked in his mind. Without seeing the other, he wasn't sure if his thoughts would reach him. How far apart could they be and still hear each other? Maybe he'd ask Crowley that someday—if the opportunity ever arose.

He suddenly felt a faint pull on his scarred hand, as if someone were trying to take it and lead him forward. His left hand lifted slightly on its own.

Startled, Adam yanked it back and pressed it to his chest. What was going on?

As if sensing his unease, the dragon's deep voice resonated in his mind. "Don't worry, I just went to find something to eat myself. I'm not satisfied with a few berries and roots."

Though he had only recently started hearing Crowley's voice in his head, the initial fear had almost disappeared. It felt less like hearing a voice in his mind and more like Crowley was standing right behind him, speaking to him.

After their respective meals—and after Adam's disgusted request that Crowley wash the pig's blood off his hands—they resumed their journey.

Adam had initially wanted to scold him for stealing a pig from a farmer, but Crowley had simply hunted for food. He couldn't have known that the animals in the fields belonged to nearby villagers.

So, he let it slide this once. But once they left the farmlands behind, he would make sure Crowley followed human dining customs until their agreement ended.

Adam grimaced at the thought of that conversation. That was going to be fun.

CROWLEY

The dark-haired man wrinkled his nose as the scent of cows filled his nostrils. Adam didn't react at all. For a brief moment, Crowley wondered if Adam might be one of those farmers himself.

His gaze traveled over the other man's frame. He wasn't thin, so he wasn't someone who had to beg for his food. Even though the blonde had been wearing the same clothes for days, they were too neat for a slave and too simple for a servant.

Maybe Crowley's first instinct had been right—perhaps Adam was a farmer or a craftsman from a nearby village.

Crowley followed a few steps behind him, giving himself the opportunity to observe undisturbed. Adam was slightly shorter than Crowley's human form. His blond hair curled over his ears, and his skin had a light bronze hue.

He must work outside a lot.

Broad shoulders tapered into a slim waist, and the dirty shirt Adam had been wearing since their first meeting clung loosely to his torso. He was strong and well-built, not someone who shied away from working with his hands—or from grabbing a sword if necessary.

Crowley's gaze wandered back up Adam's back, just as the blond turned his head over his shoulder to look at him. Their eyes met, and Adam gave a small smile.

"What?" he asked.

Crowley just shook his head.

"Nothing, I was just thinking," he admitted.

His eyes drifted back to Adam's neck and shoulders. Every muscle, every contour radiated strength. But it wasn't just physical beauty that held Crowley's gaze—it was the way he moved. Confident, whether he could hear or not, as if the world couldn't touch him.

Crowley forced himself to look elsewhere. Why had he been staring at Adam for so long?

He gestured vaguely toward the fields, but without words, the movement felt awkward. Luckily, they were alone on the dusty road.

"If you're asking whether I'm a farmer—yes, my uncle owns a farm," Adam answered before casting Crowley a sideways glance. His brows drew together as he studied Crowley's face, and the dark-haired man hesitantly lifted a hand to his cheek.

"Do I have something on my face?" he asked, puzzled.

Adam shook his head. "Your ears probably don't stand out too much, but just to be safe, I'd get you a headband."

Crowley didn't really understand, but if Adam thought it would stop people from staring at him, then fine—he'd wear one. This one time.

His presence made the animals in the fields restless, making it almost impossible to sneak past the farms unnoticed.

Still, they crept as close as they could to one of the farmhouses. Crowley watched in surprise as Adam grabbed a piece of fabric from a clothesline and took off running.

For a moment, the dark-haired man stood frozen before chasing after him. With his speed, he caught up effortlessly within a few meters.

"What was that for?" Crowley asked, ducking beneath another clothesline.

"I couldn't think of anything better. Until we can get proper clothes in the city, we'll have to make do with whatever's available," Adam replied, slightly out of breath as he presented his spoils.

He had snatched two linen tunics, a pair of simple trousers, and a cloth belt that dangled from his fingers—probably meant to serve as the headband he'd mentioned.

"You've got quick hands," Crowley teased with a grin. "Have you always been in the habit of taking things without asking?"

Adam hesitated. "No, that was the first time."

Maybe Crowley imagined it, but for the briefest moment, a smile flickered across Adam's lips.

A little rebel.

He wouldn't have expected that from him after their short time together.

Crowley had assumed knights were celibate, devout men serving the Crown, dedicated to upholding law and order. Apparently, not only were humans full of prejudices about the Négul, but Crowley had his own misconceptions too.

Only when they reached one of the narrow dirt paths winding between the fields did Adam slow his pace. Crowley adjusted his steps to match. Unlike Adam, his breathing was barely affected. The blond was still catching his breath, but soon, his heavy panting turned into laughter.

Crowley's eyes widened in surprise.

Adam's laughter lacked the usual ups and downs in pitch—it didn't sound like laughter normally did. To Crowley's ears, the sound was foreign. If he hadn't seen Adam's shoulders shaking, he wouldn't have recognized it for what it was.

The blonde threw his head back, and the laughter grew louder. Crowley's ears twitched at the sudden noise, but soon, he felt his own mouth start to twitch.

Adam's laughter was infectious, and before long, both of them stood there, laughing until their sides ached.

Slowly, their mirth subsided, and Adam looked up at him with eyes shining.

"Let's take a detour to the river," he suggested. "We can wash up and change there. By midday, no one's usually around—most people draw their water at sunrise for the whole day. We should have some peace and quiet."

He ran a hand through his hair, but a damp strand clung to his temple.

Crowley nodded and followed him, watching as Adam expertly maneuvered through the underbrush along the path.

By now, the sun hung high in the sky, casting a golden halo over Adam's curls. His hair was a mess from their escape, and his face was slightly flushed.

Crowley furrowed his brows in confusion and let himself fall a step behind. He placed a hand on his chest, feeling the wild thumping inside. This time, it wasn't the ring.

For the past few days, the dragon had repeatedly tried to contact the witch through the ring, but he'd received no response. The ring had been fused to his chest to ensure he would obediently follow along. Crowley clicked his tongue.

If it wasn't the ring pulsing, then what was it?

"Can I ask you something, Crowley?"

Adam's voice pulled the dragon from his thoughts.

For the first time, Crowley was grateful that he was skilled at speaking telepathically—it made it easier to hide his thoughts from Adam than the other way around.

To Crowley, Adam's mind sounded like a buzzing wasp's nest. He usually ignored it unless the blond directed a thought at him.

The taller man caught up so they could walk side by side again. Adam glanced up at him over his shoulder, and Crowley nodded in response.

"Are there other dragons besides you?"

Adam was clearly uncomfortable asking the question, but his curiosity had won out. Crowley watched as he nervously rubbed at the scar around his finger.

At first, Crowley wanted to ignore the question.

He didn't want to trust humans anymore. Adam wasn't like the people from the ship of his childhood. But the uneasiness still clung to his bones and it was only because of the damned gold ring that he even accompanied the blonde man next to him.

It wasn't dragons who were the monsters—it was greedy men who took pleasure in flaunting their power.

His old scars began to itch, and his steps unconsciously quickened.

"You don't have to tell me if you don't want to. I was just curious," Adam said, his voice warm in Crowley's thoughts. "But it seems like my question upset you. I'm sorry."

Crowley turned to him in surprise.

The worry that had been in Adam's voice was written plainly on his face.

If Adam could speak properly, Crowley thought his voice would sound just like it did in their shared thoughts.

The dark-haired man shook his head and gave a small smile.

"I lost my brother to hunters, and I can't say where my parents are. Dragons are solitary creatures, but we'll always exist—that much is certain."

Over Adam's shoulder, Crowley could already see the river he had mentioned. The faint murmur of the water reached his ears.

For a brief moment, his pupils narrowed into slits before widening again.

When Adam had said "river," Crowley had expected a stream. But this water was wide enough that if they reached the middle, it would likely come up to their waists.

As they approached the water's edge, Crowley watched Adam pull off his shoes with a relieved sigh and step into the shallows.

"Would you turn around?" Adam asked, lifting his hands to the top button of his linen shirt.

Crowley tilted his head.

"There's no need to make a fuss. Just take your dirty clothes off," he said simply.

But the moment Adam started undoing the buttons, that strange pounding feeling returned in Crowley's chest.

He tore his gaze away, focusing instead on the flowing water beside him.

Kneeling next to the stream he put his hands into the cool water and sighed softly. Maybe he could really use the time and wash himself a little.

Crowley never learned to swim properly. Being on a ship and almost drowned at sea hadn't helped.

The river wasn't too deep and if he kept to the shallow edge he would be fine.

With his wet fingers he combed through his long black strands and watched his reflection in the water. The face looking back at him was so strange and unfamiliar that he started to growl at it. Annoyed, he punched the surface until the face distorted and wasn't recognizable anymore.

ADAM

At first, Adam had thought that Crowley would be watching him. His neck had become quite warm at the thought. Fortunately, it didn't take long before the water caught the attention of the dark-haired man.

Adam quickly stripped off his clothes and waded step by step into the water.

It was midday, so the cool water felt good on his overheated body. He went to the middle of the river and sank to his knees in the water, allowing it to cover him up to his chin.

As if by instinct, his eyes found their way back to the dragon. It was sitting by the water, staring at its reflection. When Crowley suddenly punched the water and stood up, Adam flinched in surprise. He didn't really understand the other, but that wasn't surprising. They were two completely different beings.

The water felt good, and the blonde took a deep breath so he could dip his head under. When he resurfaced, he pushed the wet hair out of his face. That's when his gaze met Crowley's.

The dark-haired man was watching him. Adam remained with his upper body under the water, but it felt as if the dark-haired man's gaze could pierce through his skin.

Quickly, Adam lowered his gaze and watched the gentle ripples in the water around him. The river wasn't cold enough to make him lose his bodily functions, and Crowley's human form was very attractive. Adam bit his inner cheek.

As the only gay man in his village, Adam had enough practice keeping his feelings concealed. Even his uncle didn't know about his sexuality.

At 25, Adam was the oldest bachelor in his village, but due to his deafness, no one dared to ask him about it.

Only Silas had known.

The memory of his best friend made Adam's chest tighten.

"You're caught in old memories again, aren't you? I can read it on your face what you're thinking, even if I can't hear your thoughts," Crowley's voice suddenly appeared in the swirl of his thoughts.

Surprised, Adam lifted his head and saw Crowley standing before him in all his glory. He should have closed his eyes or at least focused on the other's face. Instead, his gaze wandered down the strong neck of the dark-haired man, down over his well-defined chest.

In Crowley's cave, it had been too dark to observe the other's human form. Besides, he had been terrified.

After the brief time together, the dark-haired man had given him no reason to be afraid.

He was a monster who had taken the form of a human for their journey. But since they had left Crowley's cave, other humans had been far more cruel than the dragon. Crowley had protected him and was ready to accompany him to Dominique.

It took all of Adam's self-control not to let his eyes wander further south. This wasn't fair; didn't Crowley know how good he looked?

Adam took a deep breath and tried to calm his thoughts. It would be better for both of them if the dark-haired man didn't know what his appearance was doing to the blonde. With all his might, the young man lifted his gaze to meet the dragon's eyes.

"Is there a reason you look like this as a human?" Adam tried to change the subject.

Crowley didn't seem to mind standing there naked, but he kept a certain distance from the water. Were dragons afraid of it? That couldn't be, could it?

"I once saw a human couple who looked exactly alike. One buried the other. That image has stayed with me. I think I subconsciously chose to look like this," Crowley replied.

It seemed like a secret Crowley was sharing with him. Adam knew nothing about dragons, and it still felt surreal to be traveling with a real one.

But what Crowley was willing to share, Adam would take. Since leaving the dragon's cave, there had been an unspoken understanding between them that they were both pursuing the same goal and needed each other to achieve it.

To ease the tension between them, Adam teased lightly, "Are you planning to put down roots here, or are you coming into the water?"

Crowley's reaction surprised him. The dragon looked like he... hesitated? Slowly, Adam stood up, the water now only reaching his navel.

"You can stand here," the blonde tried to reassure the other.

Still skeptical, Crowley looked at him, and Adam lifted his hand from the water, extending it to the taller man.

"Come, nothing will happen to you." He hoped his smile would calm the other.

Somehow, it made the dragon seem less monstrous—that he was afraid of the water made him feel more human to Adam.

Slowly, Crowley moved closer. His steps lost their confidence once the water lapped at his bare ankles. Adam waded closer to the taller man, making sure his torso remained submerged.

He didn't trust his body, as he could clearly feel a warmth building in his gut. The last thing he wanted was to explain to Crowley why he had suddenly gotten aroused.

The dark-haired man hesitated to take the extended hand, but Adam didn't pull him in too quickly. Together, they made it back to the middle of the river.

"See, that wasn't so bad," the blonde tried to reassure the dragon. Crowley just rolled his eyes, but his tense posture had loosened slightly.

Adam released Crowley's hand, but contrary to his expectations, the dark-haired man stayed close to him, not making any move to create distance between them.

Well, then it would be Adam who would retreat. They were much too close, and he could even see the many small scars scattered across Crowley's chest.

They seemed old, as Adam hadn't noticed them until he allowed himself to examine the dragon's chest more closely. Adam cursed himself for staring at the taller man.

In a panic, he tried to divert his eyes elsewhere. But as soon as they moved lower, he was reminded again of the size difference between their bodies. Where the water reached Adam's navel, the larger man's hip bones jutted prominently from the water, inviting the blonde to follow the line of his muscle strands down from his side abs.

Adam felt his breath become heavier and squeezed his eyes shut. His body was frozen, and he had to pull himself together and fight the rising arousal. All these years, he had been able to keep his secret, and now he had to desire a dragon, simply because he looked so incredibly good.

"What's the deal with that pendant?" Crowley asked, breaking the spell that had begun to cloud Adam's thoughts.

Adam's eyes snapped open and met the warm brown eyes of the dragon. Crowley had leaned forward, and his fingers were about to touch the red pendant at his chest.

Reflexively, Adam shot his hand up, pushing the larger hand aside to grab the pendant and hide it in his fist.

Adam was about to start a story, but Crowley would know he was lying about their connection. The dragon was close enough that Adam could have counted the golden flecks in his brown eyes.

"It belonged to an old friend. I'm just holding on to it for him."

It wasn't a lie. He didn't have to mention that this was the last thing he had from that friend.

Adam took another step back, as though he could retreat from the memory attached to the piece of jewelry. Now, he could breathe a little easier.

Crowley looked at the blonde man silently from his brown eyes. Whenever he stared too long at the pendant or felt the hard metal under his hands, his heart would start to race, and his throat would tighten.

He couldn't panic now.

How could he explain his behavior to the dragon? But if he left the water now, he'd have to explain his half-erection, which, despite the tightness in his chest, hadn't quite gone away.

Sometimes, Adam cursed his body.

Desperately, Adam squeezed his eyes shut again, wishing for a hole to open up beneath him. Instead, he felt a warm hand on his cheek.

Surprised, the blonde opened his eyes and stared at the man before him.

Crowley's hand was warm on his cheek. Strangely, Adam felt as though his face was already on fire, yet the dark-haired man's hand was even warmer.

Crowley's thumb began to move slowly. Adam felt the larger man brushing a wet strand of hair from his cheekbone where it had stuck. The blonde's heart was pounding in his throat, and he was sure the dragon could hear the loud thumping.

"It's a beautiful piece of jewelry," the dark-haired man said simply, not removing his hand from the young man's cheek.

Adam inhaled sharply.

The other's words stung a little, but the shadows that had threatened to overtake him began to recede.

Slowly, Adam let go of the pendant and stared into the other's eyes. The color of them had slowly shifted from an ordinary brown to a warm gold.

They were so close again. A fresh wave of goosebumps ran down Adam's arms at the way Crowley was looking at him.

There was something in the dragon's gaze, something in the shine of his golden iris. To get some space between them, the blonde cleared his throat and turned his head to the side.

"Do all dragons fear water?" Adam asked, a slight smile creeping onto his lips. His distraction worked, as Crowley straightened to his full height and removed his hand from Adam's cheek.

"Keep your cheekiness to yourself, little human," Crowley grumbled, but the slight grin on his face revealed the amusement behind his words. With a dramatic gesture, he splashed water at the blonde.

Panting, Adam fell back and gasped for air as a wave of cold water splashed into his face.

"Just wait, you giant lizard!" Laughing, Adam grabbed both of his arms so he could splash the other just as much. Crowley shook his head like a wet dog and reached into his hair to pull out the piece of cloth that had served as a hairband.

The thin band had loosened enough that most of his hair had already fallen over his broad back. With one hand, the dark-haired man tossed the band aside and ran his long hair back. Adam stared at him with slightly parted lips.

"What?" The dragon asked, raising an eyebrow with a mischievous grin. Adam wasn't about to ask any more foolish requests with his thoughts.

Instead, he closed his eyes and submerged himself fully. The cool water helped him calm down, and he could breathe easier once he surfaced.

Crowley turned slightly to the side and cupped water in both hands, pouring it over his head. Apparently, there was some kind of fear of water, as he couldn't just dive in. Without asking, Adam began running his fingers through the long black strands.

He hadn't expected Crowley to grab his wrist. But just as quickly as the dragon had reached for him, he loosened his grip. He didn't let go of Adam entirely, though; his fingers remained loosely wrapped around his wrist. It was impressive to see someone with so much strength also be so gentle.

"What am I thinking?" Adam wondered to himself, but he didn't pull his arm back. Instead, he took a step closer to the other. Now, he had to tilt his head back slightly to look into Crowley's eyes.

Adam's gaze fell to the other's lips.

How must they feel?

Crowley had touched him first, hadn't growled or pushed him away, so surely he could stare just a moment longer? Adam allowed himself to rise onto his toes so they were on the same eye level.

He just wanted to give in to this longing. As a teenager, he'd tried a lot of things, but as an adult, he couldn't afford to do so much. In the countryside, it was difficult if you were interested in your own gender.

Maybe it was easier for people like Adam in the city, but here in the community, everyone knew everyone, and secrets never stayed secret for long. It was a miracle no one knew about Adam's preferences yet.

But Crowley wasn't from the village. He was a dragon. The blonde had to remind himself of that again and again as he studied the distinct face of the dark-haired man.

"I don't know what's louder, your thoughts or your heart," the dark-haired man interrupted. A small smile crept onto his beautifully curved lips. Adam felt his face flush and sank back onto his heels.

"Then don't listen," the blonde retorted, but the smile on the taller man's face only made his heart race faster. It was really unfair.

"I like the sound of your heart," the dark-haired one said, and it took a moment for Adam's mind to process the words.

How could this dragon say things like that without batting an eye? It was driving him crazy.

Adam used his voice to hiss a loud "Shh" and tried to push the other away by his shoulders.

He had forgotten that his opponent had the strength of a full-grown dragon and didn't budge an inch. Instead, Crowley even pressed back against Adam's hands, wearing a pleasant grin.

Was he making fun of the blonde? Adam pressed harder, and soon, the two men were wrestling with each other in waist-deep water. Laughing, Crowley stepped aside, causing Adam to fall into the water. Adam surfaced, gasping for air, and grabbed the other's arm, pulling him down. Had Crowley not lost his balance on the slippery stones, he could have easily shaken off the grip.

Adam groaned as the larger man fell on him, Crowley's knee digging into his side. The pained noise quickly turned into a soft chuckle, which grew into full-blown laughter. It felt good to tussle with the larger man. Adam was proud he had brought the dragon down.

It took a moment for him to realize the position they had ended up in.

Crowley knelt over him, one hand on each side of Adam's blonde locks, supporting himself. The dark-haired man's chest rose and fell with the effort of their wrestling, and his black hair tumbled over his broad shoulders, falling forward. One of the long strands tickled Adam's neck.

Their little fight had brought them closer to the riverbed. The blonde could feel every stone in his back, but his attention was captured by the beautiful man above him.

Since Silas, no man had captivated him like this. What had left a large hole in his chest might now be able to be filled, even if just a little.

Maybe his body moved on its own, or maybe it was because Crowley didn't pull back, but whatever had happened, Adam pushed himself up on his elbows and placed his lips on the other's.

CROWLEY

The human kissed him. The concept of a kiss wasn't foreign to Crowley, but he didn't know what to do. Should he end it? After all, he was kissing a human.

His human body was new, and its reactions to certain things confused him. There was a heat that had gathered in his belly. It felt like his core just before it spewed fire.

Like a piece of lava slowly dripping down. As if a simple kiss had rekindled the embers within him, threatening to burn him.

His lips grew warm, where they rubbed against the human's. It felt good, so Crowley leaned in a little closer to him. He could feel Adam's hand grab his shoulder.

The dark-haired man smiled into the kiss, mirroring the younger one. Adam had far more experience handling a human body. Crowley would imitate him as long as that warm feeling behind his navel didn't stop.

He kissed the blonde like in a trance. When Adam ran his tongue over Crowley's lips, the latter opened his mouth on its own to receive him. His body knew how to react. Crowley could only hear the rapid heartbeat of the man beneath him and feel the heat in his belly moving south.

He knew what arousal felt like, but this heat in this body was so completely new that Crowley didn't know what to do. His first instinct was to push Adam away, but the quiet first groan of the man beneath him threatened to turn the embers in his core into a raging, unstoppable inferno.

Breathing heavily, the two of them parted. Crowley could see his own reflection in the glassy eyes of the human. The man's pupils were so large that only a small rim of his sky-blue irises was visible.

Crowley felt a heat inside him that was so foreign, it began to scare him. This wasn't just arousal, it was a hunger that threatened to control him.

He pushed himself away from Adam and sat back in the shallow water. It was then that he noticed his own erection, hard and hot between his thighs.

The blonde followed him and sat up as well. In Crowley's ears, Adam's heartbeat still pounded, drowning out all other thoughts. He wanted more of it, but he didn't know what would happen. This body and these feelings weren't his, were they?

Crowley lowered his gaze and saw that Adam too had an erection, one not too different from his own. Did the blonde feel the same way?

Unsure, the younger man clasped his legs together. He had probably stared too obviously. Crowley lifted his hand to place it on Adam's knee. He wanted to examine it more closely, but midway through the movement, he stopped. As a dragon, he could rely on his instincts.

But as a human, he had to relearn that confidence. Until now, he had been imitating Adam, adjusting his actions to the human. If Adam withdrew now, that was probably the right approach, so the dragon followed suit.

The heat in his loins began to grow uncomfortable, but he let his hand drop and simply stared at the blonde. Adam looked at him with blue eyes, his pupils having returned to their original size. An unusual silence hung between them.

Since they had set off together, they had always had something to say, or Adam's thoughts had been like a loud swarm of insects flying around. Now, the dark-haired man only heard his own rapid heartbeat.

The blonde took a deep breath, and a small smile crept onto his lips. Through the heavy fog in their minds, Adam spoke first: "That was unexpected," the young man admitted nervously, but he held the dragon's intense gaze.

"Was it wrong of me to go along with it?" Crowley asked, confused. Adam merely shook his head.

"Your body reacted as naturally as mine did; there's nothing wrong with that. I just didn't expect that..." Adam began to explain, before a warm raindrop landed on his nose. When he tilted his head back, another drop hit his forehead.

Crowley too looked up at the sky just as thunder rumbled.

"A summer storm is rolling in," the dark-haired man observed and pushed himself off the ground to stand.

"There's a cave further down the river, we can take shelter there," Adam suggested as he stood up and pulled his new tunic over himself. The dark-haired man followed his lead, slipping the garment on.

Adam's version was more fitted and clung to his body. Crowley felt the pull in his loins again. It was a mix of pain and restlessness. Normally, arousal in his usual form passed after a few moments, so why was it so much harder to control his human body?

The collar of Adam's tunic was high and embroidered with small designs. The sleeves were long and wide, gathered at the wrist with fine ribbons.

The hem of the tunic reached just above Adam's knees, adorned with a jagged border, also embroidered with small symbols. Crowley knew by the roughness of the stitching that it had been made by an amateur. Yet the garment looked truly good on Adam's muscular frame.

His own tunic was less fitted, and unlike Adam's white one, it was midnight blue. The blue band intended for a headband might have been the belt for Crowley's robe, but he liked how the soft fabric lightly brushed against his body.

They reached the cave just in time before a torrential downpour began, accompanied by a roaring thunderstorm.

"If we'd waited a moment, we could have spared ourselves the bath," Crowley grinned as he watched the rain intensify. Just like the thunder, the heat in his body still pulsed. It had felt good to kiss Adam. Something like euphoria fluttered behind his navel, demanding attention.

"Was it so bad that you would have preferred standing in the rain and washing yourself?" Adam asked.

The dark-haired man turned to look at him. Adam had taken their old clothes and was folding them to store them in his bag.

Crowley wasn't sure whether Adam was referring to the bath in the river or their kiss. Slowly, he approached the younger man and sat down beside him on the rocky ground. The sound of the rain had grown so loud that Crowley winced and twitched his ears.

He froze when he felt Adam's hands over his ears, holding them to block out the loud noise. Adam had crouched in front of him and was gently covering his ears with a slight grin.

"Not being able to hear anything can sometimes be a blessing. With this much rain, it must be deafening out there. Are your ears hurting?"

Crowley stared incredulously into Adam's blue eyes. He saw the small smile, but there was the slight arch of Adam's eyebrows and the expression in his eyes. The blonde was nervous. Crowley could feel his hands trembling over his ears. His hands were warm, so it couldn't have been from the cold.

Slowly, Crowley shook his head.

"I'm afraid," he admitted quietly. He didn't know why he had shared this thought so openly with Adam. But it was the truth. This whole situation, the reactions of a body foreign to him, it all scared him.

He didn't want to appear weak in front of a human, but his connection with Adam laid him bare, as if he were ripping open his chest and exposing his core. Crowley swallowed hard, but Adam's hands remained where they were.

"That's okay, I'm scared sometimes too," the blonde confessed. "I have nightmares often. You've shown me that dragons aren't just fairy tales. That means you can be afraid too. What are you so afraid of?"

Crowley's body acted on its own when he laid his forehead against Adam's. A gesture dragons often made when offering comfort to one another. Quickly, the taller man pulled back again.

Being so close to each other was unusual and far too personal. Crowley lowered his gaze and slowly confessed, "This body doesn't feel natural to me. Humans have hurt and tormented me, and now my only option to return to my old life is to accompany you, in human form, to Vitris."

He hated being so vulnerable. Above all, he hated this human body!

No, that wasn't right. He hated that this body allowed him to feel things he didn't understand.

Adam sighed softly. "If this body wasn't a part of you, you wouldn't have been able to transform, right? I don't know much, but you're still the same dragon I met in the mountain cave, right?" he tried to explain.

Slowly, the blonde removed one of his hands from Crowley's ear and placed it instead on his chest. Directly beneath his palm sat the golden ring, fused with his skin. The rain had lessened in intensity and was now just a soft patter in the background.

"I saw your chest glow after we kissed. And your eyes briefly changed from brown to gold. You're still just as much a dragon, whether in human skin or not. Is this your first time as a human?" Adam's thoughts felt like a warm cloak wrapping around Crowley, shielding him from the cold of his fear. The young man continued to surprise the dragon again and again.

The dark-haired man nodded.

"I once saw my brother in his human form. He hated it just as deeply as I do. But there are enough dragons who have permanently shed their natural form." Just like that, one of the greatest secrets of the dragons slipped from his lips.

Crowley briefly bit his tongue before continuing: "Since I was once captured, I haven't given any thought to human forms." He could only hope that Adam wouldn't use this knowledge against him.

But the young man, after all the time they had spent together, didn't seem like someone who would hunt dragons in human form based on that knowledge.

Adam looked him in the eye and took a deep breath, as though trying to encourage Crowley to do the same. The air smelled of fresh rain, and the nausea inside Crowley seemed to ease.

"My body feels things differently, it moves differently, it feels like I have no control over myself," Crowley began, almost hesitantly explaining his feelings. Admitting this was probably the biggest hurdle, and for a moment, the dark-haired man wished he could take his words back.

"You just have to get used to it. I think it would be way harder for me to adjust to a dragon's body than the other way around. You're not stumbling through the world like a baby; that's a good start. And I can help you when you hit your limits," Adam suggested, his ears slowly turning red. Crowley only noticed because they were so close, and his eyes had adjusted to the faint light in the stone cave.

"Do dragons kiss?" Adam asked curiously.

"If not, then that's something you learned on your own. You can take some pride in that, you lizard," Adam teased, removing his hands from Crowley's body. However, the dark-haired man just smiled and wrapped one of his hands around Adam's that was resting on his chest, holding it there.

"I've learned from you," Crowley replied, watching as the redness in Adam's cheeks deepened.

"You're awful, you know that?" the blonde responded, embarrassed, but his attempts to free his hand were half-hearted. Adam sighed and looked Crowley in the face.

"Do you want an encore?" the blonde asked bluntly, rolling his eyes. Crowley knew the question was a joke. But his body reacted on its own, leaning in and kissing the corner of Adam's mouth.

The heat inside his body hadn't truly dissipated and was now reignited.

They were so close that Crowley could smell Adam's scent for the first time. His fragrance tingled on the dragon's tongue. He had never experienced this feeling with anyone else.

Was Adam truly mortal?

Had his senses not been so clouded, he would have asked that question. Instead, his mouth opened as if on its own, as if he wanted to devour the young man.

Where did this hunger come from? And why did he want this human with all his being?

ADAM

The surprise was written all over Adam's face. When Crowley bit his lip, he could only groan in pain. But as soon as the initial pain subsided, warmth began to spread in his stomach again. He should have pushed Crowley away, should have ended this.

The dragon's entire demeanor had changed. His eyes glowed golden even in the darkness of the earth cave, and Crowley's breath hit Adam's lips, hot and heavy.

Adam felt fear, as if he needed to run from the other, yet he remained where he was, studying the beautiful face of the creature beneath him. Not human, he had to remind himself again and again. He could feel Crowley's heartbeat under his palm.

Should he kiss the dragon again? His rational side urged him against it; it was ridiculous.

"Crowley?"

Adam tried to reach the other, but all he felt under his palm was a growl, causing goosebumps to rise on his arms.

"Hunger... touch me..." the broken words came through their connection, as if Adam were allowed to glimpse a deeper, more primitive side of the dragon.

He shouldn't exploit Crowley to release years of sexual frustration. Besides, the dark-haired man was a dragon. But just the feeling of being wanted like this was worth being consumed.

Adam was frustrated, and Crowley was perhaps only following an instinct. The blonde didn't know how this would end. Maybe Crowley would kill him.

Yet, Adam shifted a little closer. Leaning forward like this was uncomfortable, so he simply climbed onto the dragon's lap and sat on his thighs.

In doing so, Crowley finally let go of him. Adam felt a heat beneath him that stole his breath away. Crowley lowered his now free hand and dug his claws into the ground beneath them, leaving gouges in the dirt.

"You can touch me if you want," Adam said, masking his nervousness by leaning further forward and brushing his lips across the other's.

Immediately, a hand was on his hip, clutching the fabric there. Was he imagining it, or were Crowley's nails sharper and pointier than before?

Adam looked into the other's face. It was still the same face he knew, even with the golden eyes. But behind those golden eyes was something else, something more dangerous, something he had noticed back at the river.

"Is everything alright?" Adam wanted to ask, but by then, Crowley had already claimed his mouth, clearly showing how quickly dragons could learn things.

Years of frustration had built up in Adam, and Crowley's kisses burned like a forbidden temptation after just a few minutes. He soon knew how to use his tongue to make Adam moan softly into their kisses.

Maybe it was just the blonde's imagination, but the dragon's tongue seemed longer and quicker than an ordinary tongue. His own tongue also brushed over a sharp fang from time to time.

Adam's hands had tangled into Crowley's dark hair. It took all his self-control not to press his whole body against the taller man. Crowley's hand had not left his hip, but eventually, his fingers began to twitch restlessly.

Adam bit Crowley's lower lip to get his attention. He probably shouldn't have done that.

With a single move, the dragon rolled them over, so now Adam was the one lying on his back on the hard earth, looking up at the dark-haired man. The long, black hair hung like a veil, blocking out reality.

The blonde could only see the golden eyes and once again felt a wave of fear. This mixed with his arousal into a completely new feeling, one he couldn't escape.

When their eyes met, Crowley's eyes glowed like two golden rings, and his heavy breath hit Adam's face. Without thinking, Adam's gaze wandered briefly to the dragon's chest.

Dominique's ring rested beneath the blue tunic.

As Adam lowered his gaze further, he noticed a distinct bulge beneath the dark blue fabric. A warm shiver ran down Adam's back.

They should stop before this escalated further. But on the ground, he felt almost defenseless, at Crowley's mercy.

CROWLEY

„Crowley."

The dragon felt the human reach for him through their telepathic bond, but he ignored it. A feeling way stronger than that started to fill his body. Something he never had felt before.

His body seemed to be on fire. An amusing thought regarding the fact that he was a fire dragon. With the need to hunt his whole body yearned for that heat.

Mine.

Crowley knew he would harm the mortal if he gave in and burried his teeth into his tender flesh. He hadn't hungered for human meat before.

Wait. This wasn't the hunger he knew. This was a feeling way stronger. And he didn't want to eat his companion, he needed to *devour* him.

The dragon's body moved on its own. Again they pressed their lips together and only Adam's hands pressing against his chest forced him to back off a little.

He watched the human gulping down lungs of air almost choking on them, before he dove back in to kiss him hard on the mouth once more.

The metallic taste of blood started to spread on his elongated dragon tongue. Only then did he break the kiss by himself.

The hands on his chest were trembling, but Adam did not push him away again.

Crowley's golden eyes locked on to the glistening lips and the pink tongue swiping over the bloody marks his fangs had left in them.

His body started to loose focus. If he transformed back into his usual state he could kill the man beneath him.

So in a last resort, the black-haired man pushed himself away and leaned back on his elbow. Eyes fixed on the stone cave ceiling he watched his heated breath leave his human nose.

„Crowley?"

His name reached him through the fog in his mind.

The dragon lowered his head almost hesitating and instantly regretted his choice.

Adam had pushed himself up on one arm and looked at him with his golden locks in disarray and his lips plush and red.

His clothing had come loose around his shoulder and the young man looked so confused. Crowley wished he could explain himself. But this was nothing that could have come up naturally between two males after knowing each other for barely a month.

Even from a distance could Crowley smell the scent of arousal and see the wide pupils of the other's eyes.

"Adam... I am sorry", he tried, but for what exactly was he apologizing? The bite? He didn't regret it. The kisses he almost choked the hua´man man with? He didn't regret those either.

"You didn't really hurt me, it's okay. I was just surprised. Is everything alright?"

Adam's question was so very sweet and Crowley couldn't even explain him what was going on. He wanted to nod, but also shake his head at the same time.

The blonde man reached out for the other and before the dragon could even think about it, his body had reacted for him. He leaned into the touch and pressed his nose against the warm palm of the human's hand.

"I don't want to hurt you."

Crowley thought and said these words at the same time, forgetting for the moment that the other couldn't hear him.

His lips brushed the rough skin on the young man's hand before he used his fangs again to lovebite Adam's wrist. As soon as he noticed what he was doing, he immediately let go again.

The heat came in waves. And it seemed like nothing was enough to feed *this* type of hunger.

Adam lowered his gaze and another hue of red freckled his tanned cheeks.

"May I?"

Crowley needed a moment to understand what he was referring to, before he simply nodded.

Everything, anything just to make the heat bareble and without him ripping the delicious flesh from the human's bones.

This had never happened before. Not once had his arousal been this harsh and delirious. It was as delicious as it was vicious.

The blonde man took his hand away to brush the blue fabric aside and free the dragon's dick. Crowley growled and another cloud of smoke left his nostrils.

Normally he never had a problem to control his arousal, but when his companion wrapped a curious hand around his member his brain evolved back to that of a mere stupid lizard.

Crowley's pupils turned to slits which made the human jump surprised as he pulled his hand away.

Greedily, the dragon snatched the other's wrist and pulled him back to wrap both their hands around his member.

Adam didn't resist but his face had turned the color of cherries. The black-haired man smiled and used his free hand to grab the young man by his chin. Surprised, Adam's eyes snapped up into the other's face. The human's mind sounded like a hornet's nest.

"Everything alright?" Odd that he asked this while burning up himself, but he didn't want to make things even more awkward.

Right now the blonde man could snatch his hand back and walk away. Crowley would fight the urge down no matter what, but tonight it seemed like he didn't have to.

Adam smiled, showing the small gap between his front teeth before he took the lead again and tightened his grip around the dragon's member.

Crowley lowered his own hand and instead burried his elongated nails in the earthy ground of the cave. It felt too good.

While he focused on the feeling, both men felt goosebumps down their arms. The need to thrust up into the damp palm of the human man started to become overwhelming.

From the corner of his eye, he noticed Adam moving closer. One hand of his shot up and grabbed the front of the human's clothes.

"Wait... Stay back. I don't want to loose myself."

Crowley forcefully loosened his grip and instead put his hand at the other's hip to have something to hold on to. His nails pricked the fabric and maybe even the soft skin underneath.

"It's okay to loose control sometimes."

Adam's words reached him like the first rays of sunshine after a long and harsh winter.

"It's probably not good... I haven't- I can show you, if you let me..." The young man's rambling combined with the red splotches across his cheeks and neck were almost endearing.

Crowley hesitated. This was a line they shouldn't cross. Afterwards things would never be the same.

With a shallow breath, he closed his eyes and focused on the scents around him and the still lingering taste of Adam's blood on his tongue.

The hand felt good around his dick, but not good enough so he nodded.

More.

Tha dragon rolled his hips and fucked once up into the mortal's fist. Fuck, yes.

The scales along his spines vibrated in excitement.

Crowley watched out of narrowed eyes how the blonde moved his hand up and down over his shaft. When it felt good he moved into the touch as if to reward Adam for doing good.

He heard his own breath coming short and laboured. He wanted to come.

With his free hand, Adam grabbed his own tunic and pulled it upwards to bite down on the hem. Like this it wouldn't get dirty. Afterwards he pushed Crowley's own tunic even further up.

The dragon's abs worked hard while he tried to stay still, but all he wanted, all he *needed*, was to grab the soft meat of the blonde human and make him submit.

In his hazy mind it took him a while before he noticed how Adam was moving against him. How the young man was rubbing against him. And only then did he feel the mortal's own hot cock stirring against his thigh.

With one of his hands, the black haired man reached between them and touched the blonde just as he was touching him. But he was very careful with his nails.

A hoarse moan escaped the human's mouth.

The dick in Crowley's hand was hot and velvety. He mirrored Adam just like he did before when they were kissing.

The dragon kissed the man on the mouth to dampen his voice as the broken moans started to echo from the cave walls.

Adam's hand lost it's rhythm.

With hazy eyes, the blonde moved his hips into the dragon's hand and almost forgot to move his own.

Not knowing how to help more, he let go of Adam's cock and instead reached for his rear. The skin of his cheeks was soft and plump as it gave into the tight grip of Crowley's hand.

With his grip, he pulled the human closer and felt something twitch against his leg. Something sticky dripped down his thigh. The scent of sex intensified.

He wasn't stupid. He knes the other had just orgasmed against his leg. Slowly, Adam started to move his hand again but his soft and pliant body against Crowley's torso was enough to make him cum too.

With a hoarse growl the dragon came in waves between their sweatty bodies.

With heavy breaths Crowley made sure to keep the other close, with one arm around his still trembling body.

The first wave of hunger had subsided, but he wasn't satisfied yet.

Only out of the corner of his eyes did he notice Adam whincing and quickly wiping his hands with a piece of their clothing. Maybe his cum had burned him. Since it directly came out of his body it must have been unnaturally hot to the touch for a human.

Adam spoke reassuringly to the dark-haired man while his trembling hands stroked the taller one's sides up and down.

"Okay?" That was all he said. But he shook his head with a grin, as if he couldn't believe what had just happened.

Crowley's head felt clouded, like it was wrapped in cotton. So he only nodded and waited until the pleasant sensation in his body settled into a gentle simmer. Only then did he loosen his grip on the other.

In the meantime, the rain had eased. In the silence that had now returned to the cave, Adam avoided Crowley's gaze.

"I need to get some fresh air for a moment." And with that, the blond disappeared from the cave, leaving behind a confused dragon.

His heartbeat had returned to normal, but something still pricked at his chest as he watched Adam. That ring had to be removed from his body as soon as possible.

Some fresh air wouldn't hurt him either. This cave was a good hiding place, so Crowley left his tunic there before stepping outside and shifting back into his true form.

Instantly, he felt like himself again, and with a powerful beat of his wings, he was airborne.

ADAM

After both of them had enough time to process the situation, they returned one after the other. Adam was the first to reach the earthen cave, and for the second time, he feared that Crowley had left him.

After what had happened, not only panic but also shame rose within him. He had hoped that, for once in his life, he would be allowed to feel desired and to embrace his own sexuality. Now, he had been abandoned.

Before the panic could fully take hold, a massive shadow fell over him.

Startled, Adam turned around, ready to defend himself. But at the sight of the large black dragon before him, his knees went weak—just as they had the first time.

"Crowley, is that you?" Adam asked uncertainly.

"How many black dragons do you know?" came the smug reply, and with a lowered neck, the massive dragon stepped into the cave.

Adam remained motionless until the enormous body curled around him.

"Don't tell me I actually scare you?" Crowley asked, his large golden eyes glowing. Adam had to admit, in his dragon form, Crowley was far more intimidating. But he was also stunning.

And was the dragon just joking right now?

Their tryst last night seemed to have loosened the tension in not only one way, it seemed.

At last, Adam could take his time to really look at the dark creature before him — as long as Crowley allowed it. Slowly, Adam's gaze wandered over the dragon's body while Crowley observed him in silence with his golden eyes.

"What?" Adam asked, caught in the act.

"You're a strange human." Adam had heard that sentence from Crowley before.

"Is that a good or a bad thing?" the blond asked as he cautiously sat down again.

The large dragon didn't respond.

Instead, he simply closed his eyes. Somehow, it gave Adam a warm feeling in his chest, knowing that Crowley felt safe enough to do so.

Curiously, Adam let his gaze wander over the massive dragon's body. Now that he was this close, he could make out the individual black scales, as well as spots where some were missing. On the dragon's dark skin, there were white lines and curves — clearly old scars.

Adam's heart clenched. What had happened to Crowley? Were there battles between dragons that left such marks?

"You're staring," the blond heard the dragon's deep voice in his mind.

Caught, Adam lowered his head. Slowly, the great golden eye opened halfway, fixing its gaze on him.

"I just noticed all the scars. And you're missing some scales on your sides and back," Adam remarked.

As if the mist curling from Crowley's nostrils had seeped into his own body, the dragon's eyes grew hazy.

For a second it seemed that he would uncurl his body and move away. His entire black form vibrated with tension before it gave way to something close to lethargy.

"Old wounds," came the simple, tired explanation.

Adam knew there was more to it, but he wasn't sure if he was in a position to pry.

"Your dragon form is beautiful, you know that?"

At those words, the dragon's eye opened fully, and his slit-shaped pupil widened slightly.

"The black scales look like gemstones," Adam added in explanation.

Crowley's chest rose and fell steadily with his breath, but he said nothing.

"I don't know a single human crazy enough to call a dragon beautiful."

"I thought you didn't know any humans," Adam smiled, and almost absentmindedly, he lifted his hand and placed it against Crowley's neck.

Both of them froze at the sudden, instinctive movement.

The dragon's pupil expanded further, swallowing more of the golden iris, but he didn't move away from the touch.

Surprisingly, the scales weren't as hard as Adam had expected. They felt more like the scales of a snake.

"I didn't mean to startle you," the blond reassured the dragon before him.

Crowley exhaled again, but he didn't pull away from the cool hand on his neck. Adam carefully traced his fingers over the scales, deliberately avoiding the spots where half or even whole scales were missing.

Slowly, the great golden eye closed once more. Adam's hand moved along the dragon's neck until his fingertips reached the large bone where his wings began.

They were folded against his massive body, but the thin membrane shimmered faintly in the weak moonlight filtering through the cave entrance.

Upon closer inspection, Adam noticed that one of the wings sat at a slightly different angle than the other.

Perhaps Crowley had once been caught in a battle, and his wing had never fully healed?

But during their fight against the false knights, the dragon's wounds had healed instantly.

Whatever had happened to Crowley, it had left marks—marks that were clearly visible if one took the time to look.

And if Crowley allowed someone to get close enough to see them.

As Adam studied his hand, his gaze fell on the burn scar around his finger. He didn't know if he would ever be able to get rid of it.

The ring had physically embedded itself into Crowley's chest, and the scar had appeared on Adam's finger. As soon as they reached the capital and found Dominique, he would demand answers.

Adam had only been to the capital, Vitris, twice before. The first time, he had been just a child, but the stairs leading up to the market had seemed so grand and imposing to him that he could still remember them years later.

The second time, his uncle had taken him up those very stairs to the marketplace. That was when he had met Dominique. That meeting had set everything into motion.

That day, his ears had burned with excitement. His uncle, Theodore, had only smiled at him and said, "When I first came to the great marketplace in Vitris with my father, I looked just like you do now."

His uncle, his uncle's friend Cain, and, once upon a time, Silas were among the few people who had learned to speak with their hands for Adam's sake.

Theodore was a middle-aged man with light brown hair and blue eyes. His hands, hardened from years of laboring in the fields, were a bit stiff, so the words he signed came slowly.

Adam was used to his uncle's pace, but the excitement that buzzed through his body that day made him shift restlessly on the carriage bench.

The blond had spent his whole life in and around his clan. A trip to the largest city in the kingdom of Altos was thrilling and entirely new to him.

Throughout the journey in Theodore's horse-drawn wagon, his uncle was bombarded with Adam's endless questions. The answers came slowly, as Theodore had to hold the reins with one hand and often had to think about which signs to form.

Although he had learned sign language, he mostly wrote things down for Adam, so many of his responses consisted of simple "yes" and "no" answers.

Along the way, they stopped at waystations, where travelers could rest for the night and horses were cared for. Even there, Adam's curiosity was unstoppable.

More than once, he asked his uncle to question the people at the neighboring tables during dinner on his behalf.

Theodore knew his nephew well and was a naturally sociable man. Striking up conversations and gathering information from merchants or fellow travelers was easy for him, and he would relay everything to Adam on a piece of paper.

On the third day of their journey, the gates of the capital came into view, towering before them like a great rock formation. The pale brown stone of the walls gleamed in the light of the rising sun, resembling warm sand.

As soon as Theodore brought the horse-drawn wagon to a halt, Adam frowned and stared at the closed gates in front of them.

"Are we too late, Uncle?" Adam asked, uncertain.

But his uncle patted his shoulder reassuringly before slowly forming the words with one hand.

"Don't worry, the gates of Vitris are open from sunrise to sunset. Even if we had left earlier, it wouldn't have made much of a difference."

As if his words had triggered something, the massive wooden gates began to open slowly.

Amazed, Adam watched as life gradually stirred within the city, where moments ago everything had seemed silent and abandoned behind the closed gates.

Some residents were leaving the city, while others—like Theodore and his nephew—waited for permission to enter.

"Why are the gates closed overnight?" Adam asked, noticing the two guards stationed on either side of the entrance. "And the guards—are they knights?" he signed quickly in his excitement.

Theodore laughed at his nephew's boundless energy.

"Slow down, Adam," the old farmer signed, still chuckling.

With a wistful look, Theodore gazed up along the towering city walls.

For lengthy explanations and conversations, he didn't rely on the words he could form with his hands.

Instead, he handed Adam the horse's reins, retrieved a piece of paper and a quill from a small sack, and began writing out his response while the two knights at the entrance gates started inspecting the incoming goods.

"Many years ago, the continent was divided into two kingdoms between the two sons of the All-King, Alduin. The western lands were given to Brondor, who named his kingdom Altos. He declared Vitris its capital and set out to expand it, turning it into the most glorious city on the entire continent."

Adam's eyes followed his uncle's elegant handwriting. With no formal education, he only knew what he had picked up in the village about his own country's history. His uncle and Cain had taught him how to read and write when he was young.

Short descriptions and signs weren't difficult for him, but reading entire books was a struggle—there were simply too many words he didn't recognize.

His uncle and the other farmers often spoke poorly of the royal family, saying that no king after Alduin's bloodline had been worthy of the devotion that people gave the All-King.

The first time Adam had visited Vitris, he had noticed the many statues of the king. His uncle had explained that people in the larger cities worshipped the All-King as if he were a god.

But the scraps of information Adam knew about Alduin didn't make him seem divine at all.

He had been the first king of the continent when the land was still free and uninhabited. Arriving from across the sea, he had displaced the old gods of these lands and established his own empire.

However, the farmers in Adam's village still worshipped the old gods. Sometimes, this had led to conflicts with passing knights. Once, it had even escalated into a brawl.

Adam no longer cared who worshipped the gods or the All-King. He lifted his hand and placed it over the necklace hidden beneath his tunic.

While he was lost in thought, Theodore had already written several more lines.

*"After Brondor turned the capital into what you see before you today, his brother Barnabas grew jealous of Altos' splendor. He launched repeated attacks on Vitris.

Brondor grew weary of the constant assaults on his city, so he ordered the gates to be sealed overnight, making it unreachable to enemies on foot. During the day, everyone was welcome, but at night, he wanted to offer his subjects a place of safety."*

Theodore set the written page aside and took back the reins as the city guards waved them through the gate. They passed under the archway, and as if stepping through a veil, life around them suddenly burst into motion.

Hundreds, if not thousands, of people filled the streets in the bustling early morning activity.

Their horse-drawn cart moved forward slowly, and when they reached the grand marble steps leading up to the raised marketplace, they had to leave the cart behind and carry their goods on foot.

With practiced ease, Adam jumped down from the cart and began dividing their merchandise into two baskets, which he slung over his back. The grains and fruits weren't particularly heavy.

This year's wheat harvest had been good, and they had an abundance of meat, milk, eggs, and wool. Their cart was packed with various goods from their village.

Each time, a different clan representative would travel to Vitris with all the products the village had produced. This time, they had so much that Adam would likely have to make two or three trips up and down the market steps.

Theodore couldn't carry as much as his nephew, but Adam was happy to help his uncle however he could.

His uncle had warned him to stay close for the entire walk. They both had their hands full—literally—so there was no way for them to communicate.

Obediently, Adam adjusted his excited pace to match his uncle's slower steps. Theodore wasn't young anymore, and the climb was making even Adam break a sweat.

Once they reached the top, they found an open space, and while Theodore expertly laid out their goods, Adam's eyes wandered over the marketplace.

If he could hear, the place would have been overwhelming, but for Adam, it was the most beautiful sight he had ever seen.

The marketplace of Vitris was a whirlwind of color, filled with merchants from all walks of life. Thousands of scents mingled in the air—enough to overwhelm anyone experiencing them for the first time.

Adam's heart pounded so hard it felt like it might burst from his chest. He was so lost in thought, so caught up in staring, that he didn't notice the young woman standing beside him.

Just as he turned toward the vegetable basket one last time, he nearly collided with her—hard enough that she might have fallen.

On instinct, his hand shot out, grabbing her arm. Almost automatically, his other hand moved to his chest, tracing a circle with his fist before he stopped.

His uncle had learned sign language for his sake, but he couldn't assume that everyone he met would understand it.

He was about to open his mouth to mumble a verbal apology when, to his surprise, the woman raised her hand, signaling that she was okay.

"You understood that?" he signed, astonished.

Even if his voice couldn't carry his surprise, his face surely could.

"I like learning new things," she responded simply, her words accompanied by a warm, open smile.

For a brief moment, Adam thought he saw a flicker of surprise in her gaze as well. Most people he met were either caught off guard or confused when he spoke with his hands.

"My name is Dominique, but you can call me Domi. Is this your first time in Vitris?"

"Dominique? That's a long name", Adam laughed and struggled to form each letter quickly.

They both laughed, and for a fleeting second, Adam wished he could hear her laughter. He imagined it was beautiful.

Dominique was a small woman, barely reaching Adam's chest, but her gaze was steady and confident. She didn't seem the least bit bothered by the fact that everyone around her was taller. Her face was framed by white-blond ringlets, and the fringe over her forehead made it impossible to guess her age.

Her skin was pale—much paler than his. She had to come from wealth; she didn't look like someone who worked under the sun, unlike him and his uncle. Her skin had the same translucent quality as her hair. Adam had never seen a woman so fair before.

"My name is Adam," he signed.

With his thumb, he gestured over his shoulder toward Theodore.

"My uncle brought me along today because he needed help," he explained openly.

"Your uncle? You don't look alike."

"I hear that a lot. He always says I take after my mother. After my parents died, my uncle took me in and raised me." Adam only shrugged.

"Do you have a stall here too?" he asked curiously.

Dominique shook her head.

"I live in Vitris."

For a moment, she studied his face, as if he looked familiar.

The blonde woman shook her head slightly before forming her next words, a peculiar expression crossing her features—one Adam couldn't quite interpret.

"What do you think about magic, Adam?"

The question took him by surprise, and for a moment, he wondered if he had misunderstood her.

As if on cue, he felt the phantom warmth of the necklace against his skin. It had been broken for ten years now, yet sometimes,

Adam could still feel the heat, as if the fire from back then was still trapped inside the piece of jewelry. He resisted the urge to touch it.

"Magic is dangerous," he admitted cautiously. "It took my best friend from me."

Out of the corner of his eye, he saw Theodore watching them. Adam hated talking about Silas in front of his uncle or the villagers.

"My uncle only really needs me to carry things. I'm free for the rest of the morning. Would you show me around the city?"

He quickly informed Theodore that he would be stepping away for a while.

He skillfully ignored the knowing smile on his uncle's face. When would the old man stop trying to pair him up with every girl he met?

Dominique was enchanting, but he couldn't picture himself with a woman. He had kissed girls in his youth—that had been enough experience.

Dominique led him through the bustling streets, far enough from his uncle's stall that Adam felt like he could breathe more easily.

She seemed to notice that something weighed on him but didn't press. Instead, once they had left the thickest part of the crowd behind, she simply repeated her question.

Then, she began signing again.

"Would you look at me differently if I told you I'm a witch and that I sell medicine?"

Her pale eyes locked onto his, peering at him through her fringe.

A witch?

Supposedly, they were the fourth form of magic in the world.

When Adam was a child, his uncle and his uncle's close friend, Cain, used to read to him and Silas—stories of kings and knights, but also of monsters and other beings: the Négul.

These creatures had their own kind of magic and were meant to be left alone by humans. Back then, Adam had thought of them as nothing more than fantasy, so he had never taken their "magic" seriously.

The second form of magic belonged to the gods. They could share their power with mortals by gifting them enchanted jewelry, infused with elemental magic.

Silas had received such a necklace—and had become an elemental mage.

The third form of magic was the weakest among the known types and could be learned by most people. It consisted of small spells that required little magical ability. People could train as wizards at the Academy in Oboros. Some of them were so talented that they were almost on par with witches in the eyes of the common people.

Witches possessed the most powerful magic. It was said that they never died and were capable of anything.

And now, Adam was supposed to have just met one?

Dominique crossed her arms over her chest, looking at him with an offended expression, as if accusing him of thinking, "What, you don't believe me?"

It was simply too far-fetched, and Dominique didn't look anything like how he imagined a witch would. Slowly, the blonde woman lowered her arms again and let out a quiet sigh.

"Then let me make you a proposition," she began again, before taking Adam's hand and pulling him from the marketplace into one of the narrow side streets.

Confused, he let himself be led.

The young woman brought Adam to a fountain embedded into the stone wall that surrounded Vitris.

The marketplace held all the city's bustle, but here, apart from them, there was only another couple by the fountain.

Adam studied the stone figures adorning the fountain's edge, raising an eyebrow at all the romantic motifs.

Why had Dominique brought him here?

Just as he was about to ask, she began signing again.

"How about a little test? You complete a small task for me, and I'll show you my magic. How does that sound?"

Admittedly, the blonde was curious—just how powerful could a witch's magic be?

Could she make him a knight for Silas' sake?

There was only one way to find out, so he nodded firmly.

Dominique immediately beamed at his willingness. Her smile was so infectious that Adam felt his own lips curve upward in response.

She rummaged in a hidden pocket sewn into the skirt of her dress and pulled out a small golden ring, holding it out to him on her open palm.

"I want you to go and bring me something special from a dragon. You can take this ring and trade it if necessary."

Adam stared at her for a moment.

He must have misheard.

Had she just said dragon?

Slowly, he raised a hand and mimed breathing fire, questioning if she meant a real dragon.

The blonde woman nodded and pressed the ring into his hand.

"Don't worry, I'll cast a protection spell. Nothing can happen to you until you return. I've heard of a dragon in the border mountains."

When she named the place, something flickered in her eyes—something Adam couldn't quite decipher.

"How do I know you're not just lying to me? How do I know you're really a witch—"

His cocky remark was cut short when he suddenly had to grip the fountain's edge with both hands.

Black dots danced in his vision until, suddenly, everything went completely dark.

Panicked, Adam's hands shot to his face, feeling his eyelids.

He was unharmed—yet he couldn't see a thing. Nothing but darkness.

Deprived of two of his senses now, fear surged through him. His breathing quickened, teetering on the edge of hyperventilation.

His body refused to obey him.

Then, he felt a gentle pull on his arm, and all at once, light and colors rushed back to him.

Blinking in confusion, Adam shook off the last lingering black spots. His vision had returned, completely restored.

"What the—" he started, but before he could finish, Dominique's pale hands closed around his.

With an almost innocent smile, she squeezed his hands once, before letting go again to continue signing: "You wanted proof that I'm a witch. There you go. So, can I count on your help?"

Was he imagining things, or did Dominique sway slightly after signing those words?

Adam's heart was still pounding.

He could still feel something strange—like static tingling on his tongue, as if a lightning bolt had struck inside his mouth. Sometimes, after a bad storm, he tasted something similar.

The young woman before him had simply taken away his sight. And then, just as easily, she had given it back.

This demonstration of her power hadn't been meant to harm him—he had foolishly challenged her, and she had proven, without a doubt, that she possessed magic.

"And if I complete my task, what then?" the blonde asked, still skeptical.

The sparkle in the witch's light eyes grew even stronger, and Adam's heart started beating faster all on its own.

A gust of wind rushed through Dominique's long, white-blond hair, tossing her curls into a wild mess, yet her gaze remained locked onto him with unwavering intensity.

Under her piercing stare, Adam felt goosebumps rise on his arms.

"Then you can wish for anything you want."

Her lips curved slightly.

"Anything. Absolutely anything."

CROWLEY

The following days, Adam hadn't mentioned the events in the cave with a single word, so the dark-haired man didn't bring up the topic either.

It had felt good.

In his normal form, he had never allowed this kind of arousal to go that far. Whenever a feeling of excitement had arisen within him, he could crush it like embers beneath his will.

He had never sought out a partner, and feelings like arousal or attraction had been so weak that they had washed over him with a single breath.

Crowley watched Adam as he guided them back onto the right path along the river.

Slowly, the sun began to set, bathing the fields in an orange light. The storm had cost them half a day. The dark-haired man studied the young man ahead of him, the way the evening sun reflected in his blonde curls, giving them a warm glow.

"We should find a place to camp for the night. The sun will set soon. Preferably a cave or something similar—the ground is completely soaked from the rain, and I'd rather not sleep in the mud," Crowley addressed the other, who flinched in surprise.

Apparently, Adam had been so lost in thought that he hadn't expected the dragon to speak. If Crowley tried to decipher every thought in the blonde's head, his own would explode.

Over the past few days, he had grown accustomed to a constant hum in his mind, and whenever Adam directed a thought at him, it was clear and distinct amidst the buzzing background noise. How could a human think so loudly?

Only when Adam was asleep was it quiet. The dragon could enter his subconscious, but he didn't want to.

"There's an empty stable." With one hand, Adam pointed to a small hut with a crooked entrance gate, standing lonely and abandoned on a small hill.

Somehow, Crowley had a bad feeling about it, but the prospect of another night in the dirt wasn't appealing either. A small, deserted barn seemed like the far better option. Having spent a few days with Adam now, Crowley noticed the slight tremble in the blonde's hand, though he didn't think much of it.

The old barn had clearly been unused for a long time but seemed stable enough to shelter them from the wind and weather for the night. The wooden planks were blackened with soot, but the frame looked as though it had been rein-forced with new beams.

The closer they got, the slower Adam walked. Out of the corner of his eye, Crowley saw the blonde's blue eyes beco-me slightly misty, but Adam blinked away the tears before they could fall. Confused, Crowley furrowed his brows. The blonde's entire posture suggested he was forcing himself to approach the barn.

The dragon focused on their surroundings but sensed no danger. It was just an empty stable.

Crowley had enough tact not to bombard the other with questions through their mental connection.

Instead, he turned his attention to their shelter. Adam pushed aside the large wooden latch of the gate as if he knew exactly how to open it in the easiest way. Maybe he had been here before—Crowley knew Adam lived nearby.

As if the wooden beam would burn him, Adam shoved it aside and hesitated before stepping inside.

Inside, the barn smelled of old wood and faintly of coal. The walls were dark, and a hole in the roof had been crudely patched with planks.

From the looks of it, the barn had once caught fire. That would explain why it had been abandoned. The wooden boards over the roof weren't blackened by soot, suggesting that the repairs hadn't been made too long ago.

Crowley took one last glance through the open stable door just as the sun disappeared beyond the horizon.

They would reach the capital soon. Once he got rid of the ring, he would be free and could return to his cave. If he had traveled alone, flying the whole way, he would already be in Vitris by now.

Crowley felt the ring in his chest pulsing as if laughing mockingly.

He shot a quick glance over his shoulder to ensure Adam was preoccupied with setting up a sleeping spot before raising his hand and shifting it into a dragon's claw.

The scales appeared in patches, and one claw was entirely missing. That confirmed Crowley's suspicions and left him in a sour mood.

Over the past few days, he had noticed something sapping his strength. At first, he thought it was just the unfamiliarity of a human body. But now it was clear—his powers were fading.

It could only be the work of the ring in his chest. Since leaving his cave, the ring had been silent, yet his dragon powers had grown weaker by the day. He had to get rid of it as soon as possible.

Swiftly, he reverted his hand back to normal and turned away from the entrance to follow Adam's example, trying to find a comfortable spot on the ground. That was when he noticed Adam's tense posture and panicked expression.

"You don't have to be afraid," Crowley tried to reassure him. "It still smells like smoke, but the fire was years ago. No one else is here, and I'll stay awake for most of the night, as always."

But his words seemed to have the opposite effect, and Adam's expression twisted into something pained. Crowley couldn't figure him out.

"Let's leave the door open. Maybe the smell of smoke will fade faster that way," Crowley suggested before sighing and settling down a respectful distance from Adam.

Adam, still trembling but with a somewhat calmer gaze, curled onto his side, resting his head on a bent arm. His wide eyes fixed on Crowley.

In the darkness of the barn, now without the sun's glow, Crowley's figure must have appeared only as a shadowy silhouette.

"Are you okay?" the dark-haired man asked into the quiet.

For a long moment, there was nothing but the familiar hum in Adam's mind before an answer finally took shape:

"I've been here before."

Crowley had figured as much. But he held back any comment. This seemed to be something weighing heavily on the blonde's mind, so he waited to see if Adam would say more.

Instead, Adam turned away in silence, making it clear he wouldn't share anything else.

As he heard the quiet pattering of rain beginning again outside, Crowley was inwardly grateful for the shelter. But other than a low grumble, he said nothing and closed his eyes.

Dragons were naturally paranoid creatures who never slept first or revealed weakness in slumber, but somehow, Crowley felt... calm.

He hadn't felt this at ease in a long time, perhaps ever. Maybe that should have concerned him, but sleep claimed him faster than his paranoia could.

Crowley awoke in the middle of the night, roused by sounds in the darkness.

His eyes quickly adjusted, but this was not his cave, the one he knew inside and out. Another faint noise tore him from his thoughts, and the small ridges along his spine bristled. At least those little traces of his dragon self were still there, reacting in anticipation of an attack from the dark—but nothing happened.

Frowning in confusion, Crowley raised an eyebrow and slowly pushed himself into a sitting position. Had he imagined it? No, there it was again.

"Adam?"

The moment he spoke the other's name, he bit his tongue. He had been with this mortal for quite a while now, yet he kept forgetting that Adam couldn't hear him.

"Adam?"

Crowley tried again, this time through their telepathic link, but it was like calling into an empty well. Delving into someone else's mind while they slept felt... wrong. Whether they were one of his own kind or a human, it didn't matter.

The sound in the darkness grew louder. Crowley exhaled sharply through his nose, a dissatisfied grumble vibrating in his chest. His core flared briefly, casting the stable in a warm red glow. Just enough for his eyes to make out the curled-up figure at the far end of the small stall.

His dark eyes widened. Did Adam have another nightmare?

The blonde's posture was tense, his knees drawn up to his chest. Slowly, Crowley shifted into a crouch, his core pulsing brighter. The stable seemed larger now, bathed in the deep red light. Outside, the rain continued its steady drumming against the wooden roof.

"Adam?"

Crowley made another attempt to reach him through their bond. Moving cautiously, as if afraid of startling him, he edged closer. The nearer he got, the louder the sound became—it was a faint whimper. So he hadn't imagined it after all. The ridges along his spine trembled with tension.

Perhaps Adam sensed him subconsciously. As Crowley slid close enough, he raised a careful hand, watching the broad tremor in Adam's back.

He was finally close enough to see the source of the strange noise that had woken him.

Crowley's nostrils flared once in anticipation.

Adam's face was contorted in pain, his mouth slightly open, a weak, rattling sound escaping from his lips. His breathing was labored, his eyes open yet unfocused, glassy. But he didn't seem fully awake.

"Adam?"

If Crowley didn't get him to calm down, he was going to suffocate. Adam was having an attack—he was hyperventilating, and judging by the trail of saliva on his chin, he had been struggling for air for some time.

"Adam, calm down! Breathe in deep and slow," Crowley urged, both through their bond and aloud. But his words dissolved into the small stable, unheard.

Uneasily, Crowley's hand twitched upward, but before he could touch Adam, he hesitated. His fingers curled into a fist. If he startled him now, he might scare him into suffocating completely.

He was running out of ideas.

A fresh, choked sound tore him from his thoughts.

"By the mother's flame...", the dragon sighed.

Impatiently, Crowley glanced around, searching for anything useful—but there was nothing. This stable was truly abandoned.

They had found a quiet place to rest for the night, but it was far from any other farmhouses.

He couldn't leave Adam alone. And even if he wanted to, there was no one to call for help.

"Adam, hey, look at me... please", Crowley heard himself whisper. The young man in front of him couldn't just die here, in this cursed, forsaken barn.

Yes, he knew Adam couldn't hear him, but what else was he supposed to do with a suffocating and barely concious human?

"Crow-ley."

The moment Crowley heard Adam attempt to say his name, his entire focus sharpened on him.

"Adam, I'm here. You have to relax, or you'll suffocate. Try to breathe slowly."

"Crowley, I... can't... breathe..." Adam's voice rasped, missing some consonants, but Crowley was close enough to understand him with some effort.

It took him a second to register that he had just heard Adam's voice properly. It sounded foreign to him—so different from the voice he was used to hearing in his mind.

Crowley shook his head. That wasn't important now.

"What do I do?" he asked through their telepathic bond.

Adam's gaze flickered from one spot to another, as if searching for something. But at Crowley's words, his eyes focused on the dragon's face.

Good. He understood him.

That was at least something. Now they could talk. He could talk the blonde man through whatever was happening right now.

"Help me..."

Crowley saw the first hot tears slip down Adam's cheeks, his chest trembling with each ragged, gasping breath.

Help him. How?

Uncertain, Crowley slowly raised his hand again, but when he noticed the panic in Adam's expression, he hesitated.

"It's okay. I won't hurt you," he reassured him.

If Crowley waited any longer, Adam would suffocate. And Crowley would be trapped with this cursed golden ring in his chest forever.

Without Adam, he would never find the witch who had cursed him.

Yes, he had her name, but who was to say she had even given Adam the real one?

For a fleeting moment, Crowley remembered their scuffle in the riverbed. The emotions in his chest confused him.

Frustrated, he furrowed his brows and growled: "I'm going to try to help you, but you have to let me, okay?"

Adam's expression was uncertain, but he nodded briefly before another painful gasp tensed his whole body.

His gaze darted from Crowley's hand to an invisible point on the opposite stable wall. That was permission enough.

Another tear slipped down Adam's cheek. They had to hurry.

Gently, Crowley placed a hand on Adam's shoulder, careful not to startle him. With the other, he cupped Adam's chin, tilting his head back.

"Deep breaths!"

By forcing him out of his curled-up position, Crowley gave Adam's lungs room to expand.

The mortal immediately coughed—a ragged, wheezing fit—before finally gasping for air.

Crowley withdrew his hands.

Slowly, Adam's breathing evened out. His hands, arms, and legs still trembled like leaves in the wind. A thin sheen of sweat coated his forehead, sticking his blonde curls to his temples.

Adam avoided Crowley's gaze as he struggled to sit up. Choking down so much air at once made the human retch a few times. It took a long time for him to fully calm down.

Crowley grimaced when he noticed Adam's running nose and tear-streaked face. The blonde's body still trembled slightly, but Crowley remained seated close by, waiting for it to pass.

He gave Adam all the time he needed to reorient himself.

Hesitantly, Crowley placed an arm around the human's shoulders, unsure if it was the right thing to do. Dragons comforted each other differently.

Silently, he watched as Adam wiped his hot, drying tears away with the heel of his palm.

In the darkness, Crowley noticed faint red marks along Adam's neck. The blonde seemed embarrassed that Crowley had seen him like this, which explained his restless fidgeting.

"Thank you…" Adam murmured, rubbing a slow fist over his chest before closing his eyes in exhaustion.

Crowley relaxed his expression, shifting away slightly once he decided Adam had calmed down enough.

"You should clean your face," was all he said before returning to his spot.

He had stopped Adam from suffocating himself, yet the only thought in his mind was what could have driven him to such fear and panic.

For the rest of the night, Crowley kept his back turned to Adam, lost in thought. He could feel the human's warmth behind him, but Adam did not move any closer.

Maybe he needed space.

Sleep was out of the question now.

If Adam had suffered another nightmare, was it the same one from the forest?

Despite everything they had experienced—at the river, in the earth cavern—did Adam still see him as a monster? During the day, he didn't seem afraid. But his subconscious…

Crowley stared at the dark stable wall. The scent of old, charred wood around him grew stronger—or maybe he was just imagining it.

Irritated, he closed his eyes and forced himself to sleep.

Even though he needed far less rest than a human, the ring in his chest drained his strength.

For the first time since they had set out, Crowley felt something like exhaustion. He surrendered to it at last and fell into a dreamless sleep.

ADAM

The next morning, Adam's throat burned. For a moment, images from the previous night flickered in his mind, but he pushed them away just as quickly as they had come.

He swallowed the sour taste on his tongue. After his panic attack last night, nausea had overtaken him when his lungs could finally draw in air again. First, he needed something to drink.

The memory of his dream was still so vivid that the room seemed to spin around him. It took him two tries before he managed to push himself into a sitting position, glancing around. His body trembled.

It wasn't exactly cold; the barn had kept out most of the night's chill and the rain. Still, Adam's tunic was drenched in sweat, clinging uncomfortably to his damp skin.

His head pounded as if someone had struck him. With a deep groan, the blonde closed his eyes for a brief moment— only to see the burning barn again and smell the ash. Panic shot through him, and he snapped his eyes open, struggling to breathe once more.

He wouldn't fall into that hell again.

This old barn, their current hiding place, had reopened wounds he had tried to forget. Memories of things long past, things Adam wished would remain buried.

At first, he thought he could endure it.

The barn had been repaired for the most part, smelling only of aged wood and scattered straw. And yet, this was the closest he had been to a barn since the accident, and it had dragged him straight into the abyss of his memories.

He pressed his palms firmly against his eyes until stars danced behind his eyelids, focusing on his breathing. Only then did he allow himself to take in his surroundings.

Crowley was nowhere in sight.

A sinking feeling settled in Adam's stomach. Had the dragon left him behind?

He swallowed against the nausea. Crowley had helped him last night—why would he abandon him now?

With some effort and still slightly unsteady legs, Adam rose, brushing dust and straw from his clothes. He reached out to Crowley with his thoughts, but minutes passed without an answer.

Panic surged through him again.

Shoving the stable door open with his shoulder, Adam was immediately blinded by the glaring sunlight. How long had he slept?

"Crowley?"

He tried calling out the other's name in case their telepathic link wasn't working. Nothing.

He waited a moment longer before trying again.

The rising sun was so bright that he nearly stepped into a basket of fruit sitting beside the stable door.

"That's not quite what I gathered those for, but if you'd rather step on them, be my guest."

Adam flinched as Crowley's familiar voice echoed in his mind. He had genuinely feared, for a brief moment, that Crowley had disappeared.

Turning away from the basket, Adam searched for the dragon.

"Where are—" The words died on his lips as a tall figure emerged from around the barn.

Adam's eyes widened as Crowley approached—shirtless.

Droplets of water clung to his pale skin like scattered diamonds, tracing a slow path from his throat, over his sternum, down toward his navel. The blonde followed one particularly large drop all the way down before his ears burned, and he quickly averted his gaze.

Crowley was naked, his tunic hanging loosely from one hand.

Immediately, images from the cave back then surfaced in Adam's mind, replacing the cold and painful memories the barn had stirred. Heat crept into his cheeks—and further south. He prayed nothing was visible through his clothes.

He was still staring when Crowley finally pulled his tunic over his head.

Even after everything he had done, Adam's body was a traitor. One moment of selfish indulgence, and now all it took was a glimpse of Crowley's bare skin to make him hard.

He's a dragon, Adam reminded himself, over and over. But it did little to change his current predicament.

With burning cheeks, he forced his gaze onto the fruit basket by the barn door.

If Crowley noticed his staring, he said nothing, instead changing the subject.

"I went looking for fresh water. There's an old mill down there with a small stream—I used the time while you slept to wash up."

Adam nodded. The mill and stream belonged to the village elder. He was surprised no one had spotted Crowley, though maybe he was worrying for nothing.

Now that he knew what Crowley truly was, every interaction with humans felt like a potential threat.

What if someone noticed Crowley wasn't fully human? He didn't want to put the villagers in danger.

Adam had chosen this old barn because it was far enough from the farmhouses to keep them hidden. And if Crowley had even managed to go to the mill unnoticed, maybe luck was on their side.

He only looked up when the taller man suddenly held out a clay jug of water.

"Drink."

With slightly trembling hands, Adam took it, forcing his body to remain calm as he gulped down the cool liquid.

Once his immediate thirst was quenched, he lowered the jug, watching as Crowley tied a strip of fabric—likely once a tunic belt—around his forehead, concealing his slightly pointed ears.

Adam realized he was staring again and cleared his throat awkwardly.

The cold water had soothed his throat, and he already felt more refreshed.

When he inhaled deeply, he smelled only the fields and the clean air washed by the rain.

Just as he was about to ask when they should leave, he caught Crowley's gaze—fixed on something in the distance.

Before Adam could turn to see what had drawn his attention, Crowley's voice interrupted his thoughts.

"We should leave. I doubt the owners will be pleased that we spent the night in their barn without permission. Doesn't matter if it's abandoned or not."

Without another word, Crowley moved as if to flee.

Adam let the water jug fall and grabbed his wrist. The skin under his fingers was cool, still damp from the stream's water.

"Wait! I know the owners of this barn," Adam said quickly.

A glance over his shoulder confirmed his suspicion — Cain was approaching on his gentle mare, Bella.

Adam had hoped to avoid running into anyone from his village, but Cain had already spotted them.

Running now would only raise more questions.

Cain was his uncle's friend. If Adam told him the same story he had told his uncle before leaving for Crowley's cave, everything should be fine.

Still, talking to Cain was difficult. Ever since he lost his son — Adam's best friend — guilt had gnawed at him. He hadn't been able to visit Cain or speak more than two words to him since then.

Not only because of a language barrier, but because of the weight of the past.

Now, with Crowley at his back, Adam's heart still pounded in his chest, but he couldn't run anymore.

As Cain raised a hand in greeting, Adam slowly released Crowley's wrist to return the gesture.

CROWLEY

The first conversation with another human besides Adam seemed inevitable. Crowley felt the ridge of scales along his spine rise in nervousness.

When they lay flat against his skin, they blended almost perfectly with his human flesh. But whenever something agitated him, this part of his body reacted almost instantly. The small spikes stood up and pressed against the inside of his tunic.

He forced himself to calm down, and slowly, the ridge settled back against his spine.

He wouldn't stand out.

Many of his kind had lived among humans for years, and as far as Crowley knew, no one had ever been exposed. Dragons guarded their abilities carefully—for they were what protected them from hunters and greedy men.

The man on the brown horse carried no visible weapons. His hair was cropped short, and his roughly woven linen shirt and faded trousers reminded Crowley of the clothing Adam had worn when they first met.

With a step to the side, Adam positioned himself in front of Crowley, drawing attention to himself. His body wasn't large enough to fully obscure the taller man behind him.

Crowley watched as the horse flared its nostrils and began to prance nervously. The black-haired man sighed softly. He couldn't suppress his true nature—animals always saw right through him.

Adam pulled away from him and took a few steps toward the rider, keeping the horse from having to get closer to Crowley than necessary.

"Adam, is that you? What are you doing here? Is something wrong with Theodore?"

The rider's hands formed the words slowly, as if he wasn't particularly practiced in speaking with Adam this way.

Crowley recalled a conversation he'd had with Adam a few days earlier. When the dragon had asked how human settlements in the countryside functioned, Adam had explained that there were various clans living together, much like villages.

When Crowley flew over these lands, he had often seen such villages but had never given much thought to the scattered buildings.

That day, the mood between them had been lighthearted, so Adam had continued, telling him about his life with his uncle, Theodore. Since the two had left the village where Adam grew up years ago, he and his uncle rarely saw this Cain and his family.

They still tended the fields together, but given the vast size of the farmland, it was rare for the two older men to cross paths during the day.

Theodore had never left the village community and still fulfilled the duties of a clan elder. Adam had never asked why they had moved away.

Crowley glanced up at the man on horseback. So this must be this Cain.

Out of the corner of his eye, he saw Adam's hand once again reach for the necklace that hung beneath his tunic.

"No, don't worry."

Adam used the simplest hand gestures and shook his head. He cast a somewhat helpless glance over his shoulder toward Crowley.

The dragon tried to shake the tension from his shoulders and raised his hand in greeting. He forced a slight smile but remained where he was.

Either Cain didn't notice that his mare was anxiously dancing on the spot because of Crowley, or he was deliberately ignoring the animal's unease.

Best not to make any sudden movements.

"My friend Adam has agreed to take me to the capital. My family is from Vitris, but I'm unfamiliar with this region," Crowley lied, saying the first thing that came to mind.

His words were stiff, and for a moment, it seemed as if Cain wouldn't believe him. But then the older man's expression softened.

"Adam never mentioned having friends in Vitris. Come along—my wife has, as always, cooked far too much, and you both look like you could use a warm meal," the farmer invited them.

The words were spoken without hand gestures.

Perhaps the man only knew the bare essentials of signing.

Adam could read lips—that explained the faintly hurt look that flashed across his face for a brief moment.

Even a dragon like Crowley knew it wasn't kind to speak that way about the son of one's best friend.

With a single hand movement, Cain turned his horse and gestured with a nod for them to follow.

Uncertain, Crowley shot Adam a sideways glance, but the blonde only gave him an apologetic look before directing a thought his way:

"I was hoping he'd just leave us alone once he saw it was only the two of us in the barn. Let's go, eat, and then continue our journey. Your lie was good—though calling us friends might've been a bit much," Adam explained before setting off. People hardly believed he could make any friends at all.

Crowley felt an unpleasant tug in his chest as he processed Adam's thoughts. He was about to press further when the blonde continued speaking.

"My uncle and Cain worry about me because I have trouble fitting in… because of the whole being deaf thing," Adam explained, trying to sound nonchalant. But Crowley could see the tension in his posture through the light fabric of his tunic.

Slowly, the dragon started walking as well, always careful to maintain a safe distance from Cain and his horse so he wouldn't startle the animal by accident.

"What should I say if he asks how we met?" Crowley wanted to know.

Adam thought for a brief moment before answering.

"Tell him we once worked together at one of the barracks along the trade route. I used to earn a gold coin here and there by going from barrack to barrack, scrubbing floors and washing dishes. He should believe that."

Crowley's concern that Cain might realize he was being deceived turned out to be unfounded. The farmer didn't probe any further after hearing the explanation about the barracks, which Adam had suggested.

Curious about Cain's relationship to Adam, Crowley decided this was a good moment to ask. After all, the older man had seemed almost relieved when Crowley had told him their little lie.

"Adam always struggles so terribly to meet new people, but that's understandable. Not everyone has the time or interest to write things down for him," Cain remarked as he set a steaming cup of tea in front of each of his guests.

Crowley recognized the scent and took a grateful sip of the herbal tea. Though he remained alert, he reminded himself again and again that this was a farmer and not some ghost from his past hunting him.

He attempted a charming smile.

"Not being able to hear certainly makes life unnecessarily complicated. You're right about that, Sir."

Crowley adapted by using words he heard other people say to strangers. This was the first interaction he had with a human besides Adam. And in his humble opinion he did exeptionally well.

"Oh, just call me Cain," the farmer offered before running a hand over his short brown stubble and pulling a cap onto his head.

"My name is Crowley. Excuse my bluntness, but what exactly is your relationship to Adam?"

The dark-haired man hoped he hadn't overdone it. Cain only seemed slightly puzzled by his question, not suspicious.

Out of the corner of his eye, Crowley saw Adam watching Cain's lips. Occasionally, the blonde averted his gaze, letting the words pass him by.

He didn't seem to mind that Cain had been speaking only to Crowley since they had entered the house.

Adam traced the rim of his teacup with his fingers, staring out of the open kitchen window. Since Crowley was sitting beside him, Adam couldn't read his lips, so the dragon made sure to repeat at least the key parts of their conversation through their link for him to follow along.

It was only proper, given that they were discussing him as well.

When Crowley asked about Cain's connection to Adam, the blonde's fingers abruptly stopped moving.

"Oh, that's easy to explain," Cain began, apparently unaware of the tension in Adam's posture.

"Adam is the nephew of my oldest friend, Theodore. I watched him grow up, and I see him as something like my own child."

Slowly, a strange sadness settled over Cain's face, and he lowered his gaze.

"I had a son. His name was Silas. Adam and he understood each other without words from the very start."

A sorrowful smile crossed the older man's lips before he continued.

"They were inseparable, like brothers. I tried to be a father figure to Adam alongside Theodore. As you may know, he was orphaned and raised by his uncle."

Crowley kept his eyes on Cain, but as soon as the name Silas was spoken, he felt Adam's leg trembling beneath the table.

Apparently, he had been able to read the name from Cain's lips.

Carefully, the dark-haired man pressed his knee against Adam's in reassurance, but the blonde flinched away from his touch.

Curious as he was, Crowley wanted to ask more about this Silas, but the blonde man's reaction held him back.

"Crowley—that's quite an unusual name for someone from Altos," Cain remarked with a warm smile, still pouring tea for his guests.

Crowley was grateful for the change in subject, as the air in the small farmhouse kitchen had already grown heavy.

Perhaps later, when they were traveling alone again, he could ask Adam who Silas was and why even the mention of his name hung so unpleasantly in the air.

Out of the corner of his eye, Crowley saw Adam quickly blink away the tears that had gathered in his eyes.

"It's an old name. My family has a fondness for antiquity," Crowley replied. He tried not to lie more than necessary—otherwise, they would get tangled in a web of their own deceptions.

Glancing at Adam once more, he sent a thought directly to his companion without looking at him.

"Are you alright?"

Adam gave only a brief nod in response.

"Antique? Yes, that fits well," Cain chuckled softly, unaware that his conversation partner was holding two conversations at once.

Cain tilted his head slightly, and for the first time, he looked at Adam. His gaze fell on the teacup in front of the blonde, which remained almost untouched.

Surprised, the farmer raised an eyebrow, and Crowley held his breath. Had they somehow given themselves away?

The older man took Adam's hand between his rough palms, his thumb brushing over the ring-shaped scar on the younger man's finger.

Startled, Adam pulled his hand back and stared at Theodore with wide eyes.

While Crowley was still thinking of a way to defuse the situation, Adam quickly formed the word "burn" with his hands. A burn scar.

"Good explanation," Crowley praised Adam for his quick thinking.

Cain's gaze flickered briefly to Crowley, and for a moment, the dragon felt accused. He was already preparing to explain himself, but there was nothing he could say about the ring in his chest without revealing too much. So, he remained silent.

"Adam always has bad luck when it comes to fire. Apparently, that's a recurring theme for him," Cain said with a pitying shake of his head.

It was bizarre how Cain spoke to Crowley as if Adam weren't even in the room.

The blonde didn't seem bothered by the conversation happening about him, as though he was used to being spoken around rather than spoken to. Perhaps he didn't even realize people were talking about him at all.

With each new discovery about the blonde, Crowley became increasingly aware of just how little he actually knew about the man sitting beside him.

The sudden opening of the front door broke the tense atmosphere.

Adam looked up, surprised, at the woman who had just entered the kitchen. His expression immediately shifted to joy—he knew her.

In just a few steps, the tall woman reached the table and pulled Adam into her arms.

"Let me look at you, boy! You're a rare sight these days!" she exclaimed in a booming voice.

Cain covered his mouth with his hand to hide a laugh. Crowley deliberately held back.

"You barely come to festivals anymore, and you only help out in the fields when things get really tough. Ever since you and Theodore moved further south, we hardly see you. I still spot your uncle from time to time—either in the fields or at council meetings—but you? I haven't seen you in ages."

The woman spoke so quickly that even Crowley, who could hear, struggled to keep up. Adam, on the other hand, couldn't have had the slightest idea what she had just said.

But her expression radiated concern, and Crowley didn't need to be a genius to realize that she was someone important in Adam's life.

The blonde, however, only grinned and gently pulled himself free from her enthusiastic embrace.

Even though Crowley currently looked like a human, he still felt out of place in this situation. Three people in one room was already overwhelming.

The woman's embrace had been so warm, so natural—it was as if she were Adam's real mother.

"Sofia, love, you know Adam can't hear you," Cain said gently. "Why don't you take him outside? I left my notebook out there. He can write down whatever you want to ask him."

Cain and his wife seemed to complement each other well—where she stormed into a room like a whirlwind, he stood steady like an old tree.

It was a kind suggestion, but Crowley couldn't stop himself from casting a quick glance at Adam.

What if they got separated? They needed to keep moving toward the capital.

Adam noticed the look and smiled slightly.

"It's alright," he reassured Crowley. "I haven't seen them in ages. I'll help her prepare the meal, and then we can head out again—I promise."

A human's promise meant about as much to Crowley as the flutter of a butterfly's wings.

And yet, he silently watched as the tall blonde woman took Adam's arm and led him outside. That left Crowley alone at the kitchen table with Cain.

Technically, their conversation hadn't changed—after all, Adam had never been an active participant.

And yet, something about Cain suddenly felt much more serious.

"Please don't think I was trying to set you up," the farmer said calmly. "Sofia's return wasn't planned, but I'm glad my wife pulled Adam away. He may not hear what we're saying, but don't think for a second that he doesn't notice when people are talking about him."

There was something hidden in Cain's voice—something Crowley couldn't quite decipher.

The dragon gave a curt nod, but his entire body tensed further.

Thanks to their telepathic connection, Adam had heard their conversation this time.

But of course, Cain had no way of knowing that.

"So, does this mean you want to talk about Adam directly now?" Crowley asked bluntly.

Cain nodded and crossed his arms on the table, resting his elbows on the surface.

"I'd like to know—how well do you think you actually know him?"

The question caught Crowley off guard.

He had expected Cain to interrogate him about where he had really met Adam or what they were truly doing in Vitris.

"I think... I don't understand," Crowley said hesitantly.

He was about to reach out to Adam through their connection when the older man let out a quiet sigh, and his entire posture shifted.

"Adam doesn't have friends," Cain said, his voice softer now. "Especially after losing Silas. I don't think either I or his uncle Theo have ever met a single one of his so-called 'friends' since then. And suddenly, I find you both at the old barn."

A cold shiver ran down Crowley's spine.

Had they been caught in a lie simply because of the word "friends"? Who could have guessed that Adam wasn't the type to bring friends along? And wasn't it him who had come up with the little white lie about the barracks? The dark-haired man tried to work with the few pieces of information he had.

"We really did meet while working in one of the barracks and got along right away. We also share a common goal. So I don't quite understand how I ended up being interrogated like this," he defended himself, unable to hide the threatening undertone in his voice. The small ceramic cup between his fingers cracked ominously.

Taking a deep breath, Crowley tried to loosen his grip on the cup before his nerves caused him to shatter it.

"No need to get so worked up. I don't believe this resembles an interrogation in the slightest." Cain's calm voice was probably meant to be reassuring, but for Crowley's already tense posture, it only had the opposite effect. He could feel the scales along his spine begin to vibrate.

"I simply asked if you and Adam are close?" the older farmer repeated his question.

Crowley immediately knew the answer: Of course not. They had known each other for only a few weeks. Briefly, he recalled that rainy afternoon in the cave, and he felt that familiar pull just below his navel.

They didn't know each other well enough, but there was an undeniable attraction—he couldn't deny that.

But he would sooner bite into his own hand than admit that to a human he had only had one proper conversation with.

Before Crowley could respond, Cain continued: "Adam's uncle and I, we often worry about him. Ever since the death of my only child—his best friend—he hasn't been the same boy he once was."

Slowly, Cain poured himself and Crowley more tea. Crowley's eyes widened in surprise.

"So Silas was—" he began.

"The two of them were inseparable until Silas died."

Crowley didn't know what to say. It felt as if Cain was letting him in on something deeply personal, and Crowley didn't think it was his place to know.

Of course, he had been curious about who Silas was, but it felt wrong to hear about it from someone other than Adam—even if it was from his father.

Cain continued in a calm voice: "To this day, Adam blames himself for Silas' death. I have to admit, at first, I blamed him too—for the fire in the barn. But over the years, my heart learned to forgive. He wouldn't want to hear it from me, but I have forgiven him. The pain won't ever go away, but it has become easier to bear. And I think it would be easier for Adam, too, if he finally forgave himself."

Crowley stared at the older man with wide eyes.

"Why are you telling me all of this?" His question came out almost as a whisper.

"Because you're the first person Adam has let close to him since Silas died. You two were in the barn where Silas lost his life. Since that day, Adam hasn't been able to come within fifty meters of it. I myself could only resume renovations on it a few years ago," the farmer explained as he stood up with a quiet groan—his way of signaling that he had said all he needed to.

Crowley's heart pounded in his chest. That was why Adam had had such a panic attack last night, and yet, he had been the one to suggest the barn as their shelter.

"You're giving me too much credit. Adam and I just happened to cross paths. We're not really friends," Crowley tried to downplay the situation. This wasn't his business. He was bound to Adam by a curse and had only followed him for that reason in the beginning.

"That may be," Cain replied with a slight shrug. The weight of his deceased son's memory hung heavily in the air, and it was clear the older man had said what he needed to.

"Let's go check how much of my notebook is still intact," Cain said with a small smile, though his eyes had turned glassy during their conversation. Crowley didn't need to pry further to know that this loss would haunt the farmer long after he and Adam were gone.

But why had Cain told a stranger something so deeply personal? What if Crowley used this information against Adam? The amount of trust Cain placed in him was unexpected.

Crowley's feet moved on their own, his thoughts still swirling around everything he had just learned. He felt strange, as if he had been given a secret he wasn't sure he was supposed to know.

He gave his head a small shake. Maybe he would ask Adam about it someday, but if their paths were to part soon, there was no point in digging deeper. He and Adam weren't friends.

Once he got rid of the ring and regained his full power, he would probably never see the blonde again. Somehow, that thought had seemed more appealing a few days ago.

Outside, Sofia and Adam sat together at a small table, a well-worn notebook open in front of them. Adam was in the middle of signing something when he looked up and met Crowley's gaze.

"Everything alright?"

It was strange that Adam's first thought upon seeing Crowley was to ask how he was doing.

For now, Crowley decided to push his conversation with Cain aside and simply nodded. It wasn't a lie—he really was fine.

He would let the heavy topic of Silas rest. The old farmer's request still gnawed at him a little, but he wasn't going to get involved in things that weren't his concern.

Instead, he leaned slightly over the well-worn notebook.

"Shouldn't I be the one asking you that? Cain thought you might need help—unless, of course, you'd like to finish your oh-so-important conversation first", answered Crowley through their bond and bit a smirk back to show on his aloof face.

Adam rolled his eyes at Crowley's attempt at humor. With a bit too much haste, he got up from the bench, almost as if he couldn't wait to get away from Cain's wife.

Sofia looked up at Crowley before she also stood. She wiped her ink-stained hands on her apron and squared her shoulders in front of him.

She was a few centimeters taller than Adam, so she only had to tilt her head slightly to look up at Crowley. With a friendly smile, she extended her hand.

"My name is Sofia. Adam told me a little about you, young man."

For a brief moment, panic shot through the dragon.

What had Adam told her?

But he quickly masked his unease and shook her hand briefly. Her palm was warm, calloused from work, yet felt entirely different from Adam's hands.

Unbothered by Crowley's lack of words, Sofia patted his shoulder. "You look like you could lend us a hand," she stated firmly.

She struck Crowley as a woman who always got what she wanted, no matter what. He raised an eyebrow skeptically.

Meanwhile, Cain placed a hand on Adam's shoulder, gave it a gentle squeeze, then reached for the quill and wrote something on an empty section of his notebook.

From the corner of his eye, Crowley observed the shaky handwriting and read along:

"Do you remember Evangeline? She returned to the village a few days ago after receiving a piece of jewelry. Tonight is her Darshin Devi—she would surely want her old friend to be there."

Crowley could barely decipher the trembling letters, and some of the words were unfamiliar to him. Only because

Adam read the words and repeated them in his mind was the dragon able to understand.

"Can we stay one more night? There's an important festival in the village tonight. I promise, at sunrise, we'll head straight to the capital," Adam directed his favour at the black-haired man after finishing the note.

A Darshin Devi was a festival. And festivals meant large crowds.

Crowley wanted to refuse immediately. He had no intention of staying among humans in his mortal form for even a day longer than necessary.

"I thought you didn't want to draw any more attention to us than necessary? We're lucky Cain and his wife didn't ask too many questions," the dragon countered while still half-listening to Sofia, who was telling him something about Evangeline.

"Your disguise is perfect, and we can come up with a shared story by tonight in case anyone asks. A Darshin Devi is very important to people in the countryside, Crowley. Please. Evangeline is a girl from my youth—I knew her well."

As Crowley thought about a younger Adam, he was reminded of Adam's deceased friend. Cain had told him that after Silas' death, Adam had struggled to form new bonds. A deep sigh escaped him.

What was one more night? As long as he still felt some of his dragon power coursing through him, he could be at ease.

"Alright. But at sunrise, we leave," the dark-haired man stated firmly—he would allow no arguments.

Turning to Cain, he asked, "So, there's a festival tonight?"

A gentle smile appeared on the farmer's face.

"Evangeline, a girl around Adam's age, received a piece of jewelry from the gods a few days ago. In our village, it's tradition to thank the gods for their gift with a ceremony. That's why Evangeline has returned home—to celebrate with all of us. Her Darshin is a ring, though she hasn't revealed what element it holds yet."

As Cain spoke, he helped his wife transfer peeled potatoes into a large bucket.

Crowley didn't know much about the human gods. He only knew that after the death of the All-King, the old gods had faded further into obscurity. Dragons had no gods.

He watched the couple as they, with Adam's help, cleared the wooden table outside and set it for a meal.

Whatever Crowley had expected, he was surprised by how much he enjoyed Sofia's home-cooked food.

ADAM

After their meal, Sofia took care of the dishes while Cain settled comfortably in the shade of a tree, stuffing his pipe. Adam had repeatedly tried to offer his help, but Sofia had simply shooed him away with a wave of her hand.

As soon as Adam turned his back on Crowley, the dragon had disappeared. After the scare he'd had that morning, he now only felt mildly uneasy. Crowley was surely somewhere nearby.

"Looking for me?" Crowley's voice had become so familiar in his head that Adam no longer flinched when he heard it without seeing a matching face. He tilted his head back, squinting against the sunlight, until he spotted Crowley sitting on the roof.

"What are you doing up there?" he asked, puzzled.

"Sitting. What does it look like to you?" the dragon replied, tilting his face toward the sun.

Very funny.

Adam's lips twitched slightly as he watched the other's striking profile for a moment longer. Then, with quick steps, he walked around the small house, climbing onto the stacked firewood at the back to reach the roof. He settled down beside Crowley.

"They are quite kind and seem very worried about you," Crowley observed, eyes still closed as he basked in the sunlight.

Adam looked down at his hands.

"Cain and Sofia mean well. He watched me grow up, and in his eyes, I'll always be the child I once was," the blonde explained.

"Because you can't hear?" the dark-haired man asked, cracking one eye open to glance at Adam from the side. He noticed Adam's raised eyebrow but averted his gaze, looking up at the brilliant blue sky instead.

"He told you about Silas, didn't he?" the younger man sighed.

He had expected the topic to come up—after all, he had set foot in the barn for the first time in years. But the fact that Cain trusted Crowley enough to speak about his deceased son still surprised Adam.

"Not much," the dark-haired man admitted with a shrug.

Adam could feel Crowley turn toward him, his gaze burning into his side. But he continued staring up at the clouds until the sun stung his eyes so much that he had to blink away a few tears.

"What happened back then?"

Crowley's question made nausea churn in Adam's stomach. A deep flush crept onto his tanned cheeks, as if he'd been caught doing something forbidden.

He shifted his position, pulling one knee to his chest. Slowly, Adam closed his eyes to steady himself. He trusted Crowley, after the short time they had spent together. And what would the dragon even do with the knowledge of Silas?

No, the real pain came from having to actively recall that terrible day.

"Can I ask you something first? What exactly did Cain say to you while you were alone?" Adam opened his eyes and turned his head to look directly at Crowley.

"He told me the barn we stayed in once burned down, and he lost his son in the fire. He also said you two were very close friends."

Cain had told Crowley far more than Adam had expected. His eyebrows briefly drew together in disbelief. He couldn't lie about their connection.

If he started telling Crowley about Silas, the dragon would figure out the truth—what Adam had done.

Apparently, Crowley noticed his confusion, because he only gave a helpless shrug.

"I was just as surprised as you. He said it was remarkable that you could even step inside the barn again and thought I had something to do with it."

The way they communicated required no eye contact, and that made it easier. Adam let his gaze wander across the fields.

From their spot on the roof, they had a clear view of the vast stretches of land that belonged to their clan. He could see the communal gathering place and the scattered farmhouses dotted around it like freckles.

Cain and Sofia's village—where Adam had grown up with his uncle—wasn't a village in the traditional sense. The fields overlapped or started in one place, paused, and then continued elsewhere. Several families tended multiple fields together.

There was a village elder who kept track of which families belonged to the community and which did not. Many rural people had formed such communities, organizing themselves into clans that came together for celebrations or conflicts.

Since many people in the countryside still followed the old religion, it was easier to build communities with like-minded individuals and celebrate their traditions together. Their unity kept their faith alive, and they had always outnumbered those from the larger cities. Because of that, the townsfolk tolerated their small festivals and Darshin Devis dedicated to the old gods.

Occasionally, there were disputes with travelers, but nothing had escalated into an outright rebellion.

"And what did you tell him?" Adam asked after a brief hesitation.

"That we needed a place to stay, and you were the one who suggested the barn. Don't worry—I didn't tell him what actually happened there."

For a long moment, there was silence.

Adam was grateful that Crowley had only shared the bare minimum. He knew that Cain still suffered greatly from the loss of his son. Wounds like that didn't heal—you simply learned to live with them.

But for Adam, the guilt had been eating away at him for ten years. It gnawed at his chest, hollowing him out from the inside, haunting even his dreams.

"So, you really want to know what happened back then?"

Adam clenched his hands into the thatched roof beneath him. The small strands of straw pricked his palms, but the pain helped ground him, stopping him from getting lost in the memories.

"Cain said he forgave you long ago."

That had to be a lie.

Adam knew the dragon couldn't lie to him like this.

A part of him believed it—believed that Cain had truly forgiven him. But that didn't change the fact that Adam could never forgive himself.

His eyes glistened with unshed tears, but his expression was filled with something else—hatred.

Hatred for himself.

Hatred for the old gods.

Hatred for them chosing Silas to recieve his Darshin.

With sudden fury, he pressed his palms into his eyesockets, hard enough to hurt.

His voice was nearly a scream in their shared thoughts:

"I know Cain means well, but it's not true! It was my fault—Silas died because of me. The barn burned because I was a selfish bastard!"

It had been Silas' fifteenth birthday.

CROWLEY

The dark-haired man hadn't interrupted Adam. He had seen the memories—so clearly, it was as if he had been there himself. Adam's entire posture had changed as he allowed Crowley to witness a memory he felt unworthy of.

At this moment, Adam wasn't in his mid-twenties. Right now, he was thirteen again, reliving the moment he lost his only and best friend in the flames.

And he had loved this Silas—Crowley could feel it through their connection, so heavy and overwhelming were those emotions between them. Adam blamed himself for the accident, which had been triggered by nothing more than a harmless kiss.

Crowley had remained silent when the first tear rolled down Adam's flushed cheek, quickly followed by a second and a third.

Only when the memories and thoughts Adam had just shared with him began to fade did Crowley finally direct a thought toward him.

"Blink, Adam."

"What?" That was enough to pull the blonde man out of his memories and back into the present.

"You haven't blinked in several minutes," the dark-haired man stated matter-of-factly, slowly raising a hand to wipe one of the hot tears from Adam's cheek with his knuckle. Adam didn't flinch; his entire posture seemed frozen.

As if he needed to make up for lost time, Adam blinked several times in quick succession, and movement gradually returned to his body. He wiped his face with the sleeve of his shirt.

"You didn't have to show me all of that."

"But Cain told you to talk some sense into me, to make me see that it wasn't my fault, didn't he? Now you know that it was."

"Guilt is something that's easily assigned. You didn't set the barn on fire on purpose."

Adam remained silent, still staring into the distance.

"Do you think Silas would blame you for it?"

Adam's eyes snapped to him immediately.

For a long moment, it seemed like Adam wanted to respond.

But in the end, he bit his lip and rubbed his burning eyes. Eventually, Adam shook his head in answer, and with that, their conversation about the past ended — for now.

Crowley averted his gaze but remained seated beside Adam. He didn't know how to comfort a human, so he simply let Adam cry beside him.

Perhaps that was what he needed.

After some time, he felt a weight against his shoulder.

The blonde had slumped against him in exhaustion, his tears now trailing down his cheeks in thin streams.

Crowley felt like an observer in a play where he didn't know his role. In this moment, Adam reminded the dark-haired man of his own small, wounded self. It hurt to see him like this.

They sat together in silence for a while, until the preparations for the ceremony began.

After they left the roof, not another word was spoken about Silas. Adam had washed his face and thrown himself into work immediately, leaving Crowley alone to continue exploring the village.

Away from all the noise and the preparations, Crowley found himself a good spot to watch from a distance. Even though this village consisted only of a few families and their fields, when they gathered for a festival like this, quite a few people came together. Too many for Crowley's taste.

He watched as Adam helped an elderly woman knead a massive piece of dough.

The houses were built from lightweight yet sturdy materials such as teakwood and clay. At the very center of the open space stood a large house, adorned with intricate wood carvings and vibrant paintings. It seemed to be an important building for the villagers.

The villagers themselves were dressed in bright, colorful garments. The men wore airy tunics and trousers embroidered with intricate designs—just like the tunic Crowley himself was currently wearing.

That was probably why the men and women of the village ignored him. To their eyes, he didn't look like a stranger.

The women wore saris or wrap dresses made of shimmering silk, dyed in vivid colors and woven with gold or silver threads. Their bodies were adorned with jewelry made of pearls and small, carved wooden beads.

All Crowley knew about this festival—what had Adam called it again? Darshin Devi—was that it was a ceremony of gratitude to the old gods.

The people thanked them for bestowing elemental magic upon a person in the form of an enchanted piece of jewelry. Crowley furrowed his brows and shook his head in disbelief.

After he had seen enough, he found himself a quiet spot to sit in the sun and wait. He would let Adam have the day to celebrate with an old friend. Besides, he wasn't familiar with the customs and preferred to stay in the background.

He had chosen a secluded place to avoid unnecessary contact with other humans, but apparently, his expression wasn't intimidating enough.

When he turned his head, he saw her.

Short brown curls and a round, freckled face. A young girl. Crowley would have guessed she was around Adam's age—maybe a little younger.

"You came here with Adam, didn't you?" she asked openly, offering the dragon a warm smile.

His silence didn't deter her from sitting down beside him. She didn't seem to mind that he didn't respond.

"It's funny, you know? After all these years, I'm back here just because I received a Darshin."

Ah, so that explained who she was.

"Then you must be Evangeline."

"So you can talk when you want to!" she beamed at the dark-haired man, her smile making her round face appear even fuller.

Crowley rolled his eyes and turned his gaze back to the busy villagers.

"What's your role in this ceremony?" he asked, not wanting to alienate her too quickly. The less attention he drew to himself, the easier it would be for them to leave tomorrow morning. He would be nice to these people, if only for Adam's sake.

Evangeline leaned back against the tree trunk, her shoulder brushing against his. Instinctively, Crowley turned to the side, looking directly at her. He wouldn't allow a stranger to touch him. For a brief moment, he thought he saw confusion in her brown eyes before she answered.

"I'm thanking the gods, of course, silly."

Now, the dark-haired man felt the corners of his mouth twitch slightly. Would she still call him that if she knew what he was?

"This is the first time I'm attending such a ceremony. I can't really imagine why it's necessary if all you have to do is give thanks. Can't you just do that on your own? Forgive me, I live in Vitris and have never been to a ceremony for the old gods," Crowley explained, grateful for the fabricated backstory of his origins.

Evangeline laughed brightly.

"The dean of the academy in Oboros is a strict follower of the All-King, and they say he can't stand Darshins. If he even hears that someone has received a gift from the gods, all hell breaks loose. I don't want to lose my position at the academy, so I came home to celebrate here, among my family and friends."

From what she told him, the dean of Oboros sounded to Crowley like a paranoid coward — either afraid of elemental magic or simply envious of it.

He studied the woman in front of him as she spoke. She wasn't a small woman, but he had imagined an academy student to look very different. In her colorful dress, she fit perfectly into this village, not the bleak desert landscape that made up Oboros.

For years, war had raged along the border, as no one could quite agree on where one land began and another ended. But that didn't seem to stop people from living their lives—just like this girl, born in Altos, who now studied at the academy in Oboros.

The brown-haired girl noticed his gaze, and her cheeks turned red.

"When the sun sets, I gather all the village's offerings in a small basket and make my way to the altar of the old gods. There's a small stone slab in the middle of a natural labyrinth."

She pointed behind Crowley toward a densely overgrown clearing at the edge of a small grove. From their elevated position on one of the few hills in the village, it did indeed look like a maze.

"I have to choose someone of the opposite gender to ac-company me. At first, I thought about asking my neighbor, but when I heard Adam would be here again, I wanted to ask him. After all, we've known each other for quite a while."

Something about the idea of Adam disappearing into a labyrinth with this girl didn't sit right in his stomach. When he thought back to Adam's memory of his friend's Darshin Devi—the one Adam had shown him just hours ago—he could guess what happened inside that garden.

"But, now that I think about it… I'd rather have you come with me," the young woman suddenly pulled the dragon from his thoughts.

"Me?" Crowley couldn't quite hide his surprise. But he wasn't stupid—he had noticed the way she had been inching closer throughout their conversation. She was beautiful, no doubt. But still a stranger.

Maybe she was trying to make advances on the dragon. He had seen many people courting each other in the past.

But unlike with Adam, his heartbeat didn't quicken, and nothing in his body reacted to the young woman in front of him.

Evangeline nodded, her cheeks darkening even more.

"I used to have a crush on Adam when I was a child. I thought it was interesting that he couldn't hear. I even tried to learn a bit of sign language, but I never got very far."

She laughed as if she had told a joke and continued, "To study at the academy, I moved to Oboros and only came home for the ceremony. A few days ago, I found out that Adam and his uncle had moved south years ago. I thought I'd never see him again. But then he's here, for my ceremony, and he has you by his side."

Her smile shifted from shy to alluring, and Crowley leaned away slightly.

"I've realized that back then, I didn't really know what love was. Who really understands love as a child?"

Crowley was tempted to answer with Adam's name. But he wasn't sure if anyone else knew that the blonde had been hopelessly in love with that Silas-boy.

"As an adult woman, I know now that love is a feeling that fades. Besides, Adam wouldn't be much help in the labyrinth, you know," she explained, leaning even closer.

"The companion of the jewelry bearer has their eyes blindfolded, and the bearer must guide them through the cornfield to the altar. It's a test of trust for the gods."

Gods this, gods that—these people seemed willing to do anything for their deities.

Adam had asked him to stay here for the ceremony of an old friend. Would it complicate things if he declined her answer?

Not sure how to get out of this, Crowley was just about to come up with a lie—just like he had done with Cain—when he heard approaching footsteps.

Not another human, he thought, already preparing to direct his pent-up frustration at the newcomer—until he saw familiar blue eyes.

"Everything okay?" This time, it was Adam who spoke to him through their connection.

As if caught doing something forbidden, Evangeline immediately backed away and stood up. Uncertain, she raised her hands as if she wanted to form words—but then let them drop again.

Apparently, she wasn't confident enough to attempt the little sign language she claimed to have learned for Adam.

The blonde smiled gently and pulled a small notepad from the satchel slung over his shoulder.

In elegant handwriting, he wrote: "Crowley is just a little shy. Forgive him."

Crowley only rolled his eyes—shy, yeah, right—but didn't argue. Adam wrote quickly, clearly used to having to jot down his thoughts for others to read.

Evangeline glanced at the dark-haired man, but his gaze remained fixed on Adam.

"So, your name is Crowley." She grinned at him. "You're not much of a talker, but that only makes me more curious to learn more about you. So, will you be my ceremony partner?"

She wasn't going to give up easily.

Evangeline had turned fully toward Crowley, speaking to him directly as if Adam wasn't even there. Everyone here seemed to think it was normal to exclude the blonde from conversations.

Crowley was just about to ask Adam how he should handle this when Adam interrupted his thoughts:

"What's wrong? Did she insult you? Don't take it the wrong way—she just speaks her mind directly. She doesn't mean any harm."

How could Adam remain so calm?

Slowly, Crowley realized that Adam was used to not knowing whether conversations were about him. The blonde man didn't seem to mind when discussions took place around him, leaving him standing there like a ghost in the group.

While Adam remained composed, waiting for their conversation to end, it made Crowley furious. How could someone treat another person as if they were invisible—especially after claiming they had once been friends?

Crowley had never seen anyone besides Cain communicate using hand signs. Even Sofia used a notebook to write down what she wanted to say to Adam.

"She wants me to go into that labyrinth with her," Crowley explained curtly.

That elicited a reaction from Adam—a brief shadow flickering in his usually clear blue eyes.

"That's part of the tradition. The one wearing the ceremonial jewelry can choose a companion of the opposite gender to enter with them. It's nothing unusual. You can go with her. Once you reach the altar, you just have to pray together, and then you can leave," Adam explained through their connection.

Crowley still wasn't fond of the idea, but he had promised Adam they would participate in the ceremony. And if it had to happen, he'd rather go into the labyrinth with

Evangeline than let Adam do it. He didn't like how she so openly ignored Adam.

Turning to Evangeline, he gave her a small nod. "Fine. I'll go into the labyrinth with you."

As if Crowley had just handed her a second piece of ceremonial jewelry, she beamed with delight.

"Then I'll see you tonight. And who knows? Maybe a little gift from me will be waiting for you inside the labyrinth," she said, giving Adam only a small wave before walking down the hill.

Crowley stared after her, bewildered, feeling the ridge of scales along his spine vibrate.

"Well, would you look at that? Seems like I worried for nothing about asking you to stay for the Darshin Devi. You're exactly her type," Adam said with a smile. Yet, his gaze remained fixed on the shrinking silhouette of the woman.

Crowley narrowed his eyes. "I don't want to be anyone's type," he growled, crossing his arms over his chest.

Surprised by his defensive stance, Adam turned his head to him. "You don't like her?" he asked curiously.

Crowley wrinkled his nose and shook his head. "She's quite pretty, but she's still human. I'm only going into that labyrinth for your sake, that's all."

Frustrated, he stood up and left Adam behind. He'd find another spot to wait for this stupid ceremony to start. This time, he sought out a higher place where no human girl could approach him and persuade him into anything else.

About an hour before sunset, the villagers began lighting lanterns.

Sofia had found Crowley's hiding spot on one of the intricately woven straw roofs and dragged him away under the pretense of dressing him for the ceremony.

"We were quite surprised when we heard that Evangeline wanted to go into the labyrinth with you," she said as she ushered the tall man into the farmhouse kitchen.

Inside, Crowley saw a neatly folded pile of fabric on the table. What was wrong with his tunic?

"What's this?" he asked sharply, pointing at the stack of clothes.

Sofia's expression softened into that of a concerned mother.

"You can't step before the altar of our gods in regular clothing. Normally, people in the clans choose their potential companion long in advance. If it then comes to a Darshin Devi, many already have their ceremonial attire prepared or have saved up for it. We don't have that luxury, but we'll make do, right?"

Crowley hesitated. Without Adam, it was difficult to find the right words.

"What if it doesn't fit? And I don't feel comfortable changing in front of others."

"Don't worry, we'll find something for you tonight. And our clothing isn't complicated; you can put it on yourself if you'd like."

The tall woman smiled reassuringly and began assembling an outfit for the evening.

It could have been worse. Instead of his simple dark blue tunic, he now wore a cream-colored kurta that reached his ankles. Around his upper arms were leather bands adorned with golden accents.

He had removed the makeshift headband and let his hair fall freely instead, allowing it to cover his ears.

Crowley couldn't understand these people. He had lied his way through every moment since he arrived, yet Cain and Sofia had welcomed him so warmly.

He ignored the bronze mirror Sofia had brought into the kitchen—he still couldn't bear to look at his own reflection.

Instead, he glanced down at himself, at his body wrapped in soft silk, at his legs covered by loose black trousers that tapered at the ankles.

His hand brushed the wide belt around his waist, made of heavy embroidered fabric, decorated with small stitchings and metal plates.

According to Sofia, the belt symbolized the wearer's devotion and spiritual commitment to the gods. But Crowley knew no gods. He felt like a wolf thrown into a flock of sheep, forced to pretend he was one of them.

Yet, his heart had stopped racing the moment Adam had approached. Instead, it started beating in a different way.

That was a good start, wasn't it?

It was strange how differently a single village treated him when he wasn't towering several meters tall and breathing fire.

"Are you ready?" Sofia's voice pulled him from his thoughts.

He stepped outside and took a moment to take in his surroundings.

The fields looked like black scales on the back of a massive sleeping beast in the darkness, but the lanterns cast everything in warm shades of yellow and red, like a thousand tiny butterflies.

He heard music and singing. The drums rumbled like thunder across the land, accompanied by the soft sounds of flutes and fiddles.

The melodies were lively and cheerful, fast-paced and playful. The drums set a steady, rhythmic beat that invited people to dance and clap along. The tones were clear, bright, and simple—without intricate harmonies, yet full of energy.

"The others have already started eating and drinking. Adam is waiting for you."

Curious, Crowley followed Sofia down the hill to where the others had gathered. With each step, the small metal plates on his belt jingled softly.

Children ran wildly through the crowd, and the scent of wine and grilled meat filled the air.

This time, Crowley felt his heart pounding loudly in his chest again.

Adam was easier to spot in the crowd than expected. He sat away from the bustle, next to a small, unlit hearth, peeling a baked potato for a young child. He tossed the peels into the still-smoking embers beside him.

Unlike Crowley, Adam wasn't wearing a ceremonial outfit. But instead of his usual short white tunic, he now wore a long robe in deep red. The wooden jewelry and embroidery looked foreign on the dragon—but on Adam, they were beautiful.

Only then did Crowley realize he had been staring. He shook his head, trying to cool the heat rising in his cheeks.

The blonde man looked so peaceful, so happy to be in this familiar environment, even after sharing the darkness of his past with Crowley. It felt unfair to have to tear him away from this again tomorrow. But they still had unfinished business.

And Crowley wanted to go home, too—even if his cave would never feel as much like a home to him as this village seemed to be for Adam.

Slowly, the dragon approached the blonde man as the child, now clutching the steaming potato, ran off.

ADAM

Even without hearing, the blonde noticed how Crowley was approaching and put down the small knife before looking up.

Their gazes met, and immediately Adam's heart started beating faster. The ceremonial clothing looked good on the dark-haired man. Of course, it wasn't a perfect fit; Sofia must have pieced it together from old clothes.

Still, Crowley looked like one of them. For a brief moment, Adam imagined what the dragon might have looked like as a child. What would it have been like to grow up together? Surely, Silas and he would have started a small rivalry, they were very similar in Adam's eyes.

Adam smiled slightly before lowering his gaze and turning over another potato in the embers to prevent it from burning.

"How exactly does a ceremony like this work?" Crowley asked before sitting next to the younger man on the small wooden bench. There was just enough space for two grown people.

The blonde could feel Crowley's leg press against his, and he started to feel warm again. He swallowed his excitement, practiced at suppressing it. He had allowed himself once, but no more.

Crowley was a dragon, even if he had enjoyed it, they couldn't let it go that far again. Especially not in Adam's old village. He didn't want to imagine how his uncle, Cain, or Sofia would react if they found out Adam liked men. No, this secret would go to his grave with him.

"During such ceremonies, a lot of drinking happens. Then there's dancing, and in the end, the two Azizi go into the labyrinth, offer food and drink to the gods, pray, and come out again. The prayer is silent, so you don't have to say anything. Afterwards, the Azizi are welcomed back at the entrance of the labyrinth, and the whole village celebrates together," the blonde explained with a shrug, before picking up a wooden cup from the ground and holding it in front of Crowley's nose.

At the confused look from the dark-haired man, he only grinned and explained, "Rice wine. Evangeline's father made it. You don't have to look at me like that, it's not poisoned."

As proof, he took a sip himself and held the cup out to Crowley again. Still skeptical, the dragon took the vessel and sniffed the contents. It burned his nose. Still, he took a small sip and made a face.

"It's not disgusting, but it's not good either."

Adam laughed his soundless laugh, only the trembling of his shoulders showing that he was enjoying himself. He had always laughed without sound after losing his hearing.

"Welcome to the world of alcohol, where it doesn't have to taste good as long as it's drinkable," the blonde grinned at his seatmate. He took the cup from Crowley's hand, raised it in a toast, and emptied it in one go.

"You look good in our clothes. Normally, the Azizi wear much more jewelry and ornaments, they really dress up to go to the altar of the gods."

"Will Evangeline wear special clothes too?"

The question about his old acquaintance made Adam avert his gaze, and his face turned red. He knew that Evangeline had liked him when they were younger. But it was difficult to talk to children who had no patience for him when it came to writing words or learning to form them with hands.

Besides, she had gone to Oboros Academy right after Silas' death. Since then, he hadn't seen her again. Their lives had become too different.

He worked on the fields or in the local barracks to earn a few gold coins. Every year, he tried to participate in the selection exams for the Knights' Guard, but he was never allowed. Thanks to his impairment, no one expected him to marry or start a family anytime soon.

Thinking about a family, the blonde briefly wondered if Crowley might have an interest in Evangeline, but he hadn't seemed particularly enthusiastic when they first met.

The dark-haired man had even said he was only going into the labyrinth with her because he had asked the dragon to stay one more night for Evangeline's Darshin Devi.

"Of course, she will be dressed up too, it's her Darshin Devi, after all," Adam explained to the other man while watching the warm light of the lanterns around them reflect in Crowley's eyes. Maybe it was just the reflection, but the colors in his eyes looked like molten gold. He was beautiful in a way Adam couldn't explain.

Over the next few hours, Crowley was asked to dance several times, but he declined each time. Adam watched the game with quiet amusement. Crowley was a new face, and apparently very attractive to others as well, but it was clear how uncomfortable the dragon was.

After a few attempts, the girls looked questioningly at Adam. He felt sorry for the dark-haired man and just shook his head at the girls. He then took Crowley's hand and pulled him along. He had no specific destination, but he felt somewhat responsible for making sure the dragon also had an enjoyable celebration.

Most of the people had gathered in the large square in front of the clan elder's house. Adam led the dark-haired man along a small trail until they reached an old weeping willow.

The lanterns and small fires illuminated the surroundings just enough, but there were no running children and, hopefully, no girls or women without dance partners would approach them here.

Leaning his back against the wide trunk of the tree, Adam closed his eyes for a moment.

"Thanks, I really didn't feel like going with strangers, let alone dancing in this body," Crowley said, crossing his arms over his chest. Adam glanced at the leather arm cuffs that accentuated the dark-haired man's strong forearms.

"Yeah, I could see that," the blonde agreed. "But you're doing really well. Don't worry, the ceremony will start soon. In the labyrinth, you'll be alone with Evangeline, and after that, the rest will celebrate with her so carefree that you'll be able to disappear in peace. You don't have to stay after that. I'm already grateful that you're taking on the role of an Azizi," Adam confessed, lowering his gaze to the grass between his sandals. He wiggled his toes slightly.

"And where will you be?" Crowley's question surprised him.

"What do you mean?" Adam looked up, furrowing his brow in curiosity. Crowley lowered his arms and looked the blonde directly in the eye.

"When I'm with Evangeline in the labyrinth, we can talk to each other, but I don't know the customs and norms. What if I make a mistake and put us in danger?"

Adam hadn't really thought about it, but the dark-haired man was right. Though he doubted Crowley would ruin everything immediately, he didn't want anything to go wrong either.

Sending a dragon and a human woman alone into a labyrinth was reckless.

"Okay, I'll follow you. The cornfield is off-limits during the Darshin Devi, but Silas and I used to sneak in and play hide-and-seek. I'll try to stay far enough away so Evangeline can't hear me, and if something happens, I'll be there. Don't worry, they forgive a boy with a disability more quickly than a stranger," Adam suggested, trying for a smile, though after all these years, it still hurt to be seen that way.

It was both a curse and a blessing.

For a moment, Crowley looked like he might take a step toward Adam. The blonde held his breath in anticipation.

CROWLEY

A loud gong made him whip his head around. Adam must have noticed his confused look, as he followed Crowley's gaze. Understanding settled on the blonde man's face.

"Apparently, everything is ready now. Come, I'll take you to the labyrinth, we'll wait for Evangeline there," Adam suggested, reaching for the black-haired man's hand.

This was the second time that evening he let himself be led by the blonde. Adam's hand was cool in his.

Without turning around, Adam continued in his thoughts: "There's a part of this ceremony you won't like. It's tradition that one of the two Azizis has their eyes bound, and the other isn't allowed to speak."

Crowley didn't like the direction Adam's explanation was heading.

"The one who can't speak has to guide the blind one through the labyrinth. I ask you, if they tie your eyes, please don't just rip the blindfold off. This tradition is very important to the people here. I'll be nearby in case anything happens. You can take off the blindfold after the prayer if it gets unbearable."

Although Evangeline had already explained the rough outline of the ceremony to him, the nervousness still gnawed at his veins.

"So you want me to go in there, blindfolded with this girl, and hope she leads me to the altar?" Crowley asked skeptically, stopping in his tracks.

Adam also stopped and turned his torso toward the other.

"You may be Evangeline's type, but this is still a ceremony of the gods. She would never do anything to sabotage her Darshin Devi. Trust me. The path into the labyrinth isn't that long, just follow her, and once the prayer is done, you can quickly come back out with her."

Crowley hated that he didn't immediately object and cancel the whole thing. He hated that he had agreed just so he wouldn't stand out.

She was a sweet girl, and it seemed like she had taken a liking to his human disguise. Once they were inside the labyrinth, he'd make it clear that they would never see each other again.

Besides, Adam had promised to follow them. If Crowley made a mistake, the blonde would do something about it.

For Crowley, being able to travel to Vitris tomorrow without any trouble was just as important as it was for Adam. Crowley nodded and let Adam lead him on.

Still, nervousness surged through Crowley's nervous system. The blonde seemed to sense his tension. Without slowing his pace, he changed his grip on Crowley's hand, interlocking their fingers and giving his hand a gentle squeeze. A warm feeling began to spread in Crowley's chest.

Just before they reached the labyrinth and the already waiting crowd, Adam let go of Crowley's hand. The black-haired man lingered in the warmth for a moment longer before his gaze fell on the tall arch marking the entrance to the labyrinth.

It was covered with ivy, and Crowley could feel that the land before him was glowing with magical energy. Nature had claimed this piece of earth for itself. The sound of bells rang in the beginning of the ceremony. The gong had probably just been a sign to gather at the entrance to the cornfield. Once the silver bells rang, the atmosphere changed.

With one last glance over his shoulder, Adam looked up at him. His smile calmed the dragon's heart.

Crowley looked back over his shoulder, and there she was, Evangeline.

As she approached, golden chains and small bells jingled around her hips with each step. She was dressed entirely in white, with a high-neck white blouse richly adorned with pearls and embroidery. The long flowing skirt was made of such light material that it fluttered in the wind, brushing against the young woman's legs.

A broad silver chain adorned her neck. She also wore delicate earrings and bracelets that sparkled in the light of the lanterns around her. A special headpiece crowned her head, a colorful band decorated with symbols and signs. The band was the only color in her ceremonial outfit. The young woman wore her brown hair the same way as Crowley, loose.

She was pretty, no doubt, but the black-haired man just wanted to get the ceremony over with as quickly as possible.

The brown-haired woman stopped directly in front of the dragon and looked up at him.

"You look good, our clothes suit you. Maybe you actually belong more to the country than the city," she greeted him with a soft laugh.

Crowley had to grin slightly at the absurdity of her statement. It brought a slight blush to Evangeline's cheeks. With careful fingers, she took a black silk ribbon from an older woman standing behind her.

"You're too tall, bend down a bit," she ordered, still with a smile on her lips. Crowley hesitated, but he felt Adam's eyes on his back.

"Don't worry, nothing will happen to you. Just focus on my voice," the blonde tried to calm him through their telepathic connection.

If Adam had only had four senses his whole life, he would probably be able to endure a few minutes. Slowly, he leaned forward.

For a moment, he felt dizzy as his eyes were covered. Her gloved fingers tying the blindfold around him tickled Crowley's temples. He tried to stand as still as possible. His mind started to spiral, and he thought he could feel the cold bars of a cage pressing against his back again.

But before his mind could fully sink, Adam's voice returned to him in his head.

"You're trembling. Don't worry, Evangeline will take your hand in a moment." Almost simultaneously, the black-haired man felt the gloved hand reach for his.

Crowley focused on the familiar voice and let himself be guided by the brown-haired woman under the cheers of the surrounding people.

With the words, "May the ancient gods guide you," they were sent into the labyrinth.

Without resistance, he followed the pull of her hand through the archway into the overgrown maze. His ears twitched slightly under the blindfold, trying to hear Adam somewhere, but all he could make out was the rustling of the leaves and the sound of their clothes.

"You're doing great, Crowley," the blonde suddenly praised him, and the dragon had to suppress the urge to look for Adam. The blonde had promised to follow them. He better keep that promise. Reluctantly, he followed his jewelry-bearer.

"Smile a little, Evangeline keeps looking at you," Adam admonished, and Crowley imagined hearing a soft laugh behind him. With a deep breath, he tried to relax.

It smelled like corn and the scents of the festival behind them, the smell of grilled meat and something sweet in the air.

If he focused, he could still faintly taste the rice wine on his tongue that Adam had given him. Surprisingly, it was eerily silent around them, as if the labyrinth absorbed all sounds from the outside world.

Only the faint chime of wind chimes broke the unnatural silence. Apparently, this was meant to be a small help for the two of them. Evangeline guided them safely through the narrow passages, and Crowley's heart began to calm with each meter they ventured deeper into the labyrinth without anything happening.

He wasn't in a cage.

The small leaves brushing his cheeks and shoulders weren't cold metal bars. It helped that Adam kept sending him short words of praise or small corrections through their connection.

Crowley felt Evangeline's steps slow down, and she squeezed his hand.

"You've reached the altar. Keep the blindfold on for a moment longer. She'll place her offerings on the altar and pray, you don't need to do anything else. After that, the official part of the ceremony is over, and you can take off the blindfold," the blonde explained.

Shortly after, Adam said something that almost made the black-haired man tear the stupid cloth from his eyes.

"I should hurry back before it's noticed that I snuck into the cornfield. I'll wait for you at the entrance."

Just as Crowley was about to respond, he heard Evangeline's voice in front of him: "Thank you for coming with me."

The black-haired man's head jerked forward in surprise. He hadn't expected the brown-haired woman to address him so soon. On one hand, he wanted to stop Adam from leaving him alone; on the other, he couldn't just leave Evangeline behind.

"You asked me to come. Besides, I honestly expected worse. When you're done with your prayer, we should go back. The others are probably waiting for us." As he spoke, he raised his hand and reached for the blindfold to finally remove it.

As soon as the cloth loosened, Crowley blinked in relief. His gaze fell on the altar, where candles and small bowls of sugar-coated baked goods were arranged.

Out of the corner of his eye, he saw Evangeline approaching him. Completely unexpectedly, the brown-haired woman grabbed his shoulders, stood on her tiptoes, and kissed him.

It took him a moment to understand what had just happened before he roughly pushed the young woman away from him.

"What the—" the black-haired man was about to hiss, but Evangeline started laughing loudly.

Now, he was completely confused. Why was she laughing suddenly?

The brown-haired woman wiped her eyes with her knuckles.

"Sorry, but I didn't want to let the chance for a kiss slip by. Honestly, I guess I'm not your type." Her brown eyes were glassy, and her face had taken on a reddish hue.

"I'm so stupid, I should have realized it, the way you look at Adam," she said, her voice strange as she crossed her arms in front of her chest. Confused, Crowley furrowed his brow and looked at the woman before him. How did he look at Adam?

"Evangeline," he tried to speak to her, but she only shook her head, clearly fighting back tears.

"Anyway, I had hoped my kiss might change something, but let's just forget about it and disappear from here," she said, her voice cracking slightly.

She tried to sound strong, not wanting to show how much it hurt, but her face betrayed her. Crowley watched as Evangeline grabbed the basket she had brought with her and turned to leave the cornfield without another word.

He didn't understand what was happening. He had done what had been asked of him. But he hadn't agreed to be kissed like that.

"Adam?" Crowley asked through their connection. "Are you still in the labyrinth?" But he received no answer. Now that he could see again, the way out of the labyrinth was easy. He caught up to Evangeline just before they passed through the gate.

The people from the village greeted them with cheers and singing, but Crowley ignored it all. His eyes were searching for a certain blonde man. A heavy hand on his shoulder made him jump, but it was just Cain, smiling warmly at him.

"You must be looking for Adam. He went back to the house; he said he forgot something. Go get him, and then come celebrate with us. Evangeline will show us some of her magic," explained the older man, patting Crowley on the shoulder.

Crowley wasn't interested in the magic of the brown-haired woman, but he was grateful that Cain had told him where Adam was. He nodded at the farmer and ran back to his house.

ADAM

Adam hadn't left the labyrinth immediately. He wanted to make sure Crowley took off the blindfold and the two would make their way back to the entrance.

After what he had witnessed then, he had fled. He didn't want to know whether Crowley had reciprocated the kiss.

Why did it bother him so much?

The blonde's lungs burned as he closed the heavy wooden door behind him and leaned against it. In the darkness of the farmhouse, he took a short breath and closed his eyes.

He fought against the nausea, but the image of the couple had reminded him of Silas Darshin Devi. He had gone into the cornfield for nothing. Had he known that Crowley and Evangeline would kiss there, he would have stayed back at the entrance with the others.

But the dragon had seemed somehow frightened at first, and Adam hadn't wanted to leave him alone and blind in the labyrinth. Crowley had only agreed so the evening could go smoothly.

In Adam's eyes, they were the accepted couple, just like Silas and Katharina and Crowley and Evangeline. Not that he ever imagined he and Crowley could have been a couple, yet both situations hurt like a hot knife on the skin.

He knew he could never be normal. That his life would be a secret dance on a tightrope if he ever wanted to farm fields and remain within the village community.

Angrily, Adam wiped his eyes and stepped toward the kitchen window. From here, he could look down at the gathering place. He watched the people dancing and leaned his forehead against the cool glass. He had lived here for half his life, had been born here, knew the people, had celebrated with them.

And yet, it felt as though he didn't truly belong. He couldn't hear the music, couldn't join in their songs, and would never be able to live the life expected of him here in the countryside. He sighed deeply, closing his eyes.

"Do you mind if I hide here with you?" Crowley's voice in his thoughts startled him so much that he spun around and knocked one of the chairs at the kitchen table over.

But he was still alone. Confused, he looked out the window and saw Crowley standing near the entrance door, watching him. His eyes glowed gold, the brown had faded, replaced by his true eye color, making him look menacing as he stood there in the cool night air.

"Cain said you'd forgotten something. Have you found whatever you were looking for?" The dark-haired man asked, but didn't take a step closer.

Adam watched him through the glass, feeling somehow braver. He lifted his chin and stared directly at Crowley.

"I thought I'd use the time while you and Evangeline were kissing." The words came out without a filter. Adam knew Crowley hadn't done anything wrong, yet his thoughts flowed out of him like a burst dam.

"Without the blindfold, it must have been easy for you to find your way out of the field. You've managed all day without me, maybe it wasn't necessary for me to sneak into the labyrinth with you," the blonde man hissed through his thoughts.

It would probably have been an amusing sight for an outsider to hear the two of them silently arguing. If it weren't for the look in the dragon's eyes.

Adam saw the gold in Crowley's eyes darken, and a cold shiver ran down his back.

Slowly, the dragon took a step toward him.

"You thought you'd use the time while we were kissing? Adam, she kissed me!" Crowley retorted, showing the sharp fangs.

The younger man didn't want to hear who kissed whom first. Upset, Adam pushed away from the window and opened the front door to face the other man. He already felt shame and self-hatred creeping up his chest, choking him.

This Darshin Devi had awakened old memories and reopened wounds Adam had inflicted on himself. Adam hated some parts of himself, but especially hated his temper when he could feel it slipping through his fingers.

Tonight, the image of the two kissing, both of them, had torn open his chest and exposed his wounded heart, helplessly.

He struck out at everything that came near, like a frightened animal in a cage. He didn't want to feel this way, knowing it was foolish and unreasonable to think that Crowley could be more to him than just his companion on the way back to Dominique.

"Save it, Crowley." Adam was surprised that his eyes hadn't begun to burn yet.

"I don't care who you have experiences with as a person. I just want to be alone, do you understand?"

The dark-haired man was with him in two large steps and grabbed the soft fabric of his kurta at the chest.

"You left me alone!" Crowley hissed. Suddenly his sharp teeth were way too close for comfort. Adam's eyes widened in surprise.

The tension between them was palpable, the air thick with static and pent-up emotions.

"You just don't get it, do you?" Crowley growled, letting go of the other's clothes. "You told me you wouldn't leave me."

Adam knew the dragon was right. And he wanted to apologize for running away, but his shame over this ugly part of himself lodged itself in his throat.

Shame that he would never have a woman, as Theodore wished. The hatred that he was broken through and through. The gods had punished him over and over, leaving the blonde bleeding.

His frustration ate through him like fire, inflaming his chest and showing him the ugly side of himself, as he snapped at the bigger man: "Should I have stayed? I thought you had no interest in Evangeline. But apparently, you don't care who touches you."

Adam didn't want to poison her memory of the earth cave, didn't want to take away the pleasant warmth that came when he thought back to Crowley's image.

Now his chest was cold, and his nails were already dug in, tearing it open. Crowley's gaze grew angry, and he clenched his fists at his sides. Adam crossed his arms over his chest and bit his lip to hold back the tears his anger threatened to bring.

"Watch your thoughts. I went into that cornfield with her because of you," the dark-haired man reminded him bitterly.

Of course, Adam knew that, but his feelings had gotten the better of him, and he didn't know how to rein them in without destroying everything around him.

His jaw muscles twitched as he tried to control his surging feelings. Black spots began to dance at the edges of his vision.

A moment of silence passed, where both just stood there, staring at each other, before Adam lowered his gaze first and pressed his palms against his eyelids with a frustrated groan. The pain helped him calm down a little.

"I hate all of this," the blonde admitted, without lowering his hands.

"You didn't seem like you hated all of it," Crowley replied. Adam could feel that Crowley hadn't moved and his voice seemed to have lost some of its sharpness. The blonde groaned and lowered his hands.

"Because I've lived my whole life the way people expected me to! And every time I wanted something, it was cruelly denied. Silas, the Order of Knights, my own hearing, and tonight—" Adam left the sentence open, shaking his head before lifting it again and looking directly at Crowley.

The gold in the dragon's irises had faded and shimmered through the brown like tiny stars.

The distance that their sharp words had created seemed to shrink, and an unexpected understanding flickered between them. The tension transformed into a different kind of intensity, one that ran much deeper than anger or frustration.

"Why does it seem like you keep coming back to this place in your head, where it hurts? If you hate it so much?" Crowley asked, tilting his head slightly.

Adam sighed. It seemed so easy for Crowley to leave everything behind, everything he knew and loved.

"I can't. I can't just let the past rest. Every time I come back to the village, I'm reminded of what I've done. But I can't just leave forever. My family is here, Theodore, Cain, and Sofia. Where should I go? To the city where I don't know anyone except Dominique? Or maybe to Oboros, to the Academy, where I'd just despair over the textbooks? I can't even get into one of the barracks to be trained as a knight, Crowley!"

The blonde furrowed his brows. Of course, he had considered just leaving, but he couldn't do that to his uncle. He had no choice in how he wanted to live his life.

Adam's breath grew heavier, and his eyes searched the dragon's for something he couldn't name himself.

For a long moment, it was silent, both men breathing heavily, but the anger had dissipated. The simmering emotions had already turned to smoke in the dark night around them.

Crowley was the first to break their silence in their thoughts. "I know it's not easy. You got one of the hardest fates I can imagine. And yet, over the past few weeks, you've shown me again and again that you'd manage without difficulty. I've watched many people in my life, and I've never met anyone who fascinated me as much as you."

Crowley's words were like balm to Adam's heart.

"I didn't mean it like that…" the blonde tried helplessly to salvage what he had broken. Crowley shook his head.

"Forget it, but for the future, never again portray me as a monster who willingly opens up to every person, understood?", Crowley snarled.

"I have boundaries, even though I still need to get to know this body better. Evangeline may have wished for something I couldn't and didn't want to give her. She doesn't stir anything in me. At least not the same way your touches have affected me."

Adam looked at the other man in surprise, fighting the heat rising in his cheeks. How could this humanized lizard say something like that without batting an eye? Did Crowley have no shame?

The sudden eruption of fireworks startled the blonde as they lit up the dark night sky behind Crowley. Both men tilted their heads back, watching the play of colors. Occasionally, an unnaturally violet flash interrupted the scene.

"She must have gotten light as her element," Adam mused. "I'll go back and congratulate her again. Tomorrow morning, we'll continue our journey as soon as the sun rises, alright?"

Adam's chest had stopped tightening. He had feared for a moment that Crowley's anger toward him might have been enough to end their journey.

The blonde wouldn't have even blamed the dragon.

The taller man nodded briefly and after watching another colorful explosion lighting up the nightsky, he also started moving.

Together, they walked back to the gathering place, their palms brushing against each other every so often.

Adam congratulated Evangeline, and his smile was sincere. He was happy for her and glad she received a piece of jewelry. He declined her invitation to dance. His feelings were still too turbulent, and he just wanted to go to bed.

But the gods weren't done with him yet that night. Just as he was about to tell Crowley that he was heading to bed, he saw a man approaching. Adam's eyes widened in surprise as he walked toward the man, who was hunched slightly.

"Uncle?" The blonde looked at his foster father, confused. "Where have you been? I didn't see you all afternoon."

The brown-haired man laughed and raised his trembling hands, forming his slow answer.

"This morning, I went hunting with a few other men from the village for Evangeline's Darshin Devi. I got injured and slept the entire afternoon. I've handed over my duties as clan leader to Cain for the day to recover from my accident."

At Adam's concerned expression, he waved his hands dismissively.

"Don't worry, I just fell off my horse. A little rest and my old bones will be as good as new."

Then Theodore's face suddenly became serious.

"Tell me, is it true you came here with a young man from Vitris?"

That's exactly what Adam had feared. He'd have to lie to his uncle. But it was safer to tell him this lie than the truth about Dominique and Crowley.

Since explaining the whole story would take more than just a few words, Adam pulled out his small notebook from his shoulder bag and began writing.

"I told you about the errand I got. I'm on my way to Vitris. On the way, I met Crowley, who was also heading there, but since he had never left the city before, he got lost. I offered to accompany him since we had the same destination."

It hurt to write this down. Not a complete lie, but it was far from the truth.

"That's why I brought him along. We were just passing through and learned from Cain that tonight was Evangeline's Darshin Devi. I couldn't continue right away, so I invited him to join the celebration. If it hadn't been so spontaneous, I would've definitely informed you."

Adam held out the notebook to his uncle, feeling his heart pounding up to his throat. He really didn't want to lie to Theodore, but it was best if he knew as little as possible about Crowley.

After tonight, Theodore and the dragon would probably never meet again.

Adam loved his foster father more than anything else. Theodore had taught him everything he knew: how to walk, fish, shoot a bow, predict the weather from the smell of the air. The blonde owed Theodore a lot. His lie would protect his uncle. Adam didn't want Theodore to worry unnecessarily. It was enough that he would never live the life his uncle had envisioned for his foster son.

Theodore had tried to arrange a marriage for Adam three times, and three times Adam had been able to prevent it. He didn't want to bind an impoverished woman to him, someone he couldn't give what she deserved. Instead, he was the crippled boy of the old Theo, and even though it gnawed at him some days, it was better this way. He would care for his uncle until his death so he could give back everything his uncle had done for him.

Adam put the notebook away, and a real yawn crept onto his face.

"He was Evangeline's companion in the labyrinth. He's probably celebrating with her now, otherwise, I'd introduce him to you. Maybe tomorrow. It's been a long day for me too, I'm going to head to bed."

It was cowardly to avoid a situation between Crowley and his uncle like that, but he felt the exhaustion now more than ever. So, tonight, he would be a coward. He had already been many things.

For a moment, it looked like Theodore was about to say something, but instead, he patted Adam on the shoulder and nodded. Adam could feel his uncle's gaze on his back as he walked to the house he would spend the night in.

Theodore, as the clan leader, had the largest house. Even after they moved south, it had remained his home whenever he had to travel for village matters. The estate was arranged around a central courtyard, surrounded by buildings on all four sides.

The main buildings were aligned along a north-south axis, with the most important rooms, like the reception hall and the family leader's living space, in the northern part. The buildings were made of wood and brick, with curved rooflines.

Adam entered the courtyard through the large entrance gate. Above the gate hung an intricately carved beam with calligraphic inscriptions. The clan leader's house at the gathering place was the largest in their community, but as clan leader, Theodore had merged several houses into one estate.

Adam was thankful for this, as he and Crowley could stay in one of the side houses and maybe escape his foster father's eyes. To prevent the dragon from wandering aimlessly around the village, the blonde informed his companion where they could sleep that night.

CROWLEY

It took a good hour after he had last heard from Adam before he could leave the festival behind.

The people had all been friendly and open-hearted toward him. Men and women had danced extensively to the sound of drums and flutes. For the dragon, it had felt a bit like the old days when he could observe humans.

The curiosity inherent in all dragons had shown him the darker sides of humanity, but tonight he had also felt their warmth.

With slightly unsteady legs, he followed the scent of Adam to the large estate. The scent was easy to recognize.

Among the various sharp smells from the campfires and the remnants of the burned fireworks, the blonde smelled like a forest after a summer thunderstorm. Fresh and cool, a stark contrast to the heavy smells that usually lingered in the night air.

Leaning against one of the intricately decorated support beams to take a deep breath, Crowley had drunk more of the bitter drink Adam had given him. After the third cup, he had stopped caring about the taste.

Exhausted, he trudged across the courtyard to the smallest of the side houses and pushed open the wooden door with his shoulder.

Inside, it was dark, but Crowley's eyes didn't need light to see the blonde man lying asleep in a bed. The black-haired man lingered a moment longer in the doorframe, leaning his shoulder against the dark wood.

He watched as Adam's chest rose and fell slowly. Tonight, it seemed that no nightmares were troubling the young man. Crowley wondered if this was Adam's bedroom and if that's why he could sleep so peacefully.

The dark-haired man's gaze fell on a second bed in the otherwise simply furnished room. Before heading to his own sleeping spot, he carefully walked over to Adam's bed and looked down at the sleeping figure.

His gaze traced the blonde's features, taking in every small detail. The delicate eyelashes that rested on his cheeks, the gentle curve of his cheekbones, and the soft curls spreading out over the pillow.

Carefully, Crowley reached up and brushed a strand of blonde hair from Adam's face, being careful not to wake him. His touch was light, almost reverent.

Of all the people he had observed, Adam was the most interesting. A warm smile spread across the black-haired man's face as he looked at him lying so peacefully. His heart was filled with a warmth that almost overwhelmed him.

Perhaps it was the drink that sat warmly in his stomach, but he felt bold enough to caress the smaller man's body further.

Crowley's fingers traced the contour of the tanned cheek, following the gentle lines of his face. He couldn't stop looking at him, lying there so trustfully and unaware of his presence.

The memory of Adam's anger-contorted face, when he had snapped at the dragon a few hours earlier, sent a small sting through him. Something must have deeply hurt the blonde. Crowley wanted to know more, more about the young man sleeping before him as if there were no world around him.

Slowly, Crowley touched the blonde's ear with his thumb, trailing along the ear's edge. Although Adam couldn't hear, Crowley found his way, and it was admirable. At the quiet moan he heard, the small scales along his spine tingled with interest. As though burned, Crowley pulled his hand back quickly and stepped back.

He didn't want to wake Adam.

The dragon's body hummed lightly; he had probably drunk too much of the rice wine. Without moving a muscle, he stared at the sleeping man before him, but Adam hadn't woken. He rolled onto his other side, turning his back to the larger man.

For a moment, Crowley considered lying next to Adam in the bed, wrapping his body around the smaller one, just as dragons did.

Dragons protected what they loved with everything they had. Orion had fought with all his strength to protect Crowley back then and had saved him. Dragons were solitary creatures, they lived with their parents for a time until they moved on, leaving their offspring to fend for themselves. That was the way of things.

Crowley's mother had stayed with him and Orion for a long time. Now, as an adult, the black-haired man could understand why. They had been on the run, though from what, he still didn't know. Maybe it had been the man who had captured Crowley as a young dragon.

The man who wore the symbol of the Academy Dynas on his chest. The emblem had burned itself into his mind on the night Crowley had escaped. The crest was so vivid in his inner vision that it felt as though it were right before him.

His captivity had been so many years ago that the man was likely nothing but dust by now. But should he ever see that symbol again, or hear the family name Nachtgrim just once more, he would claim the blood debt, no matter the cost.

He turned away from the sleeping man and walked to his own bed. Before falling into the sheets, he removed the belt with the metal plate and let it fall carelessly to the floor, before settling in for the night.

The next morning, the two were awoken by bright sunlight streaming into the room. Neither had thought to draw the curtains the previous night.

Adam seemed quite amused by the fact that Crowley had drunk more of Cain's rice wine, to which the black-haired man responded with an eye-roll. The blonde didn't mean anything by it and informed the larger man that he should wash out his mouth with some clear water if he wanted to get rid of the fuzzy feeling.

While Crowley did exactly that, Adam opened a room divider and placed it in the center of the room before starting to change on his side. The robe he had slept in was hung over the bamboo wall, and he put on a tunic that looked similar to the one he had taken two days ago. Only the ornaments on the hem were more carefully stitched.

Crowley raised an eyebrow. He had already seen the young man's naked body when they had bathed in the river—so where did this newfound modesty come from? Puzzled, the black-haired man removed his ritual clothing and saw the dark blue tunic Adam had stolen for him lying at the foot of his bed. It looked brand new; perhaps it had been washed for him. The fabric was warm against his skin from the strong sunlight pouring through the window.

Adam had insisted on going to his uncle alone. Crowley didn't fully understand why he shouldn't meet Adam's own uncle when he had already met Silas's parents. But this was the blonde's world. So, Crowley waited for the other to return so they could continue their journey as quickly as possible.

Crowley had imagined their goodbye would be more complicated. Adam had packed his provisions, the leather shoulder bag at his hip bursting with food, drink, and everything else they might need for their journey to Vitris.

Evangeline and Sofia had seen them off on behalf of the village. Apparently, even after such a raucous celebration, normalcy had returned, and everyone went back to their work. It was impressive, considering that Crowley could still feel the throbbing in his temples from the previous night.

The young woman avoided the dragon's gaze but didn't seem angry. Sofia embraced both men warmly and then addressed the black-haired one, "If you ever get lost outside your city walls again, you know where to find our village. Feel free to come to us, we always have a spot for you."

Crowley felt a tug in his chest. Her warmth hurt, so he could only nod slightly.

Back on the road, Crowley tied his hair into a high ponytail and used the belt from his tunic as a headband again. Adam watched him from the side. Amused, the dragon raised an eyebrow.

"Everything alright?" he asked through their connection, grinning. Adam's cheeks flushed slightly, and he turned his gaze away to the distance.

"I hope you slept well in a human bed. The next three days to the capital, we can only sleep in the barracks along the way," the blonde changed the subject.

As they continued their journey, Crowley looked up at the sky and watched a group of migratory birds rush past the clouds. Subconsciously, he rolled his shoulders.

He would have preferred to shift back into his dragon form and fly through the air as well. His gaze followed a family of birds, and his heart suddenly became heavy as he thought of his own family.

FLEDGLING

As a child, he hadn't understood.

Why he wasn't allowed to travel alone, why it had been so important that no one knew where they were.

Young dragons remained under the protection of the older ones until the latter decided it was time to move on and leave their offspring to fend for themselves.

But Crowley had found his mother's watchful eyes to be overly cautious. And after she had disappeared, Orion had taken over the task of looking out for him. If Crowley wanted to find out why they never stayed in one place for more than a year or two, his brother never gave him an answer.

Crowley had been naive – just a child. Now he knew that his family had been so wary in order to protect themselves. Whenever they were in danger of being hunted or pursued, they moved on.

Hundreds of years ago, a family had started hunting dragons on purpose. Crowley didn't remember exactly when it had begun, the attacks, the ambushes – he must have been very young. Eventually, the nets came, the smoke, and they lost more and more members of their family.

The poisonous smoke, the smell had burned itself into Crowley's soul; he would recognize it anywhere. Now, he knew which family was behind these atrocities. He would find every Nachtgrim and tear them apart in the air with his own teeth for what they had done to him back then.

Crowley's curiosity had once brought him almost to the southeast coast of the continent. From afar, he had begun to observe the humans there.

At first, they were nothing more than animals that liked to wear the skin or fur of other animals, but the longer Crowley watched them, the more interesting they seemed to him. Again and again, he had returned to the harbor and ignored Orion's warnings.

"The humans are getting smarter and they're getting more dangerous. Stay away from them, Crowley!" His older brother's words made no sense. If humans really attacked him, he could easily defend himself.

A deep breath could set an entire fleet of ships on fire. Perhaps only half a fleet, since Crowley wasn't a fully matured dragon at that time.

For several weeks, he had been watching the harbor. Large wooden structures came and went, some richly decorated, others so old that Crowley wondered how these things didn't sink in the sea. They carried pressed iron pieces with them that they exchanged for other goods, and powder to create colors that Crowley had never heard of.

He listened to the sailors when they told stories. He especially enjoyed the tales about the Island of the Beyond, Isla Bula. The humans seemed to be afraid of the island, many sailors said it was a stroke of luck to leave it behind.

Crowley couldn't understand that; he and his family had been to the Island of the Beyond many times. The island was surrounded by a veil of mist, but if one stuck to a direction and flew high enough, it wasn't impossible to find one's way out of the fog.

Moreover, the people told ghost stories about the island. Crowley had never encountered a ghost there, not even a nature spirit.

The young dragon should have stopped at merely watching and listening, but his curiosity drove him closer to the harbor. Crowley didn't remember exactly the day of his capture, only the time that came after, which had burned itself into his memory. The only thing he remembered were the greedy looks of the men who locked him in a tiny cage and loaded him onto a ship.

And his screams, his calls for his brother, which went unheard in the darkness.

He had been careless and had gotten too close to one of the ships. Even as a young dragon, he had been larger than the horses the humans kept.

A small boy in dirty rags had spotted him and cried for help. Even before Crowley could take off, a heavy net had been thrown over him. After that, his memories became blurred.

CROWLEY

When Crowley opened his eyes the next time, the sun blinded him as it shone into his face. A cold shiver ran down his spine, and he felt the ridge of scales along his back rise.

He was no longer at the harbor, no longer on the ship; instead, he was on the way to Vitris. Crowley's golden eyes landed on the back of the blonde man in front of him. He had been so lost in his own world that he had blindly followed a deaf man.

Shaking his head, the dragon suppressed a laugh and casually crossed his arms behind his head.

Adam had made them follow the trade road for several days, the one he and his uncle had taken both times when they traveled to Vitris.

In the first nights, they hadn't passed any barracks, and when they finally found one, there were no rooms left. After sleeping under the open sky for several nights, it was clear how much Adam was looking forward to the first barracks with a room available.

Crowley had been content with the ground, but after experiencing a real bed in Adam's village, he was obviously not opposed to the barracks anymore.

This time, Adam took charge of the conversation. Even without hearing, he knew better how to get a room and had the necessary coins to pay for it.

Crowley watched as the innkeeper almost casually placed a small brass key on the table in front of them.

Addressing Crowley, he said, "I'm really sorry, but we only have one room left that's big enough for two people. It should be enough for one night, and you're welcome to have breakfast with us in the morning." Perhaps the dragon had been mistaken, and people preferred choosing him before they had to speak with a deaf man. Somehow, this fact weighed on the dark-haired man's stomach.

Crowley passed the information and the key to the blonde, who gave the innkeeper a grateful nod and led them upstairs.

Crowley suppressed a grin. Apparently, Adam had gotten so used to his voice in his thoughts that he had forgotten others couldn't hear it. His nod to the innkeeper must have seemed very strange, but they were quick enough to disappear upstairs.

With a soft click, the heavy wooden door opened. Both men stopped in the doorway and stared at the very lonely-looking bed that almost filled the entire room. Crowley stood a little behind and could see how the blonde's ears turned red.

"We can take turns sleeping in the bed," the blonde suggested, dropping his bag next to the bed. The dark-haired man raised an eyebrow questioningly.

"Why don't we just both sleep in the bed? We were lying next to each other on the hard ground." Crowley shrugged once and sighed as he dropped onto the bed.

For him, there was no visible problem here. The bed was spacious and soft, and it had been the blonde who had complained about sleeping on the hard earth.

Besides, this was their last night before reaching Vitris. Then he would meet Adam's witch. Learning such an old form of magic twisted his stomach, but he had no other choice. The ring in his chest had to disappear, and the longer he waited, the more he felt his own powers waning.

Exhausted, the dragon closed his eyes.

ADAM

He was going to sleep in the same bed as Crowley.

Of course, they had already slept next to each other on the ground, but a proper bed was something else entirely. He didn't even want to imagine what the owner of the barracks was thinking.

What if he put two and two together? Adam didn't want one of his old workplaces to know that he was gay. He would never be able to return here, and this was the last barracks before the capital if you came from the east.

But maybe he was worrying for nothing. It was just one night, and no one in the barracks had given them strange looks.

The only problem—one that Adam only became fully aware of when he put on his thin robe for sleeping—was Crowley himself. The dark-haired man slept in his clothes, which, while not reeking, still bore small stains from two nights on earthy ground.

For the sake of his own peace of mind, Adam should have kept quiet, simply laid down beside the larger man, and gone to sleep.

But instead, he directed his thoughts toward the other: "Isn't it uncomfortable to sleep in the same clothes you wore all day?"

Crowley opened one eye, already lying on his side of the bed, and looked at the blonde. His "headband" had been removed and now rested on the nightstand beside him.

"It's a little warm in here, but I don't have spare clothes like you do," the dark-haired man replied, closing his eye again.

Adam should have left it at that, but instead, a single suggestion burned itself to the front of his mind: "You could take off your tunic, and I could open the window. It's only going to get hotter and more humid the closer we get to Vitris."

The blonde bit his tongue, but now that the thought had escaped, he couldn't take it back.

Crowley didn't notice the internal turmoil of the other man as he sat up and pulled the dark fabric over his head.

Adam focused on the window and on whatever was happening outside in the darkness, but he could only do that for so long. Eventually, he had to turn back to the bed.

The dark-haired man had pulled the thin cotton blanket up to his waist and looked as though he was already asleep. Adam quietly extinguished the candle on the small dresser beside the bed before lying down next to him. In the safe darkness of the room, Adam allowed himself to observe the other man.

He could only make out vague outlines, but he had never been this close to the sleeping dragon before. Only a hand's width separated them, making Adam too aware of his own breathing. And so they lay there.

Adam noticed how relaxed Crowley looked in his sleep. The way he rested, one could almost believe he was just an ordinary human. His long black hair spread out beneath him like a carpet of dark silk.

It was in that moment, as he studied the details of Crowley's face—the long eyelashes, the slight bend in his nose, the harmony of his features—that Adam felt a warm sensation in his chest. A feeling he couldn't quite place, a mix of affection and admiration that stole his breath.

Suddenly, he felt incredibly vulnerable, his thoughts spinning.

All day, his mind had been in turmoil. He was surprised that Crowley hadn't confronted him about it. For the most part, they had both been lost in their own thoughts, traveling in silence. Adam didn't complain; it had given him time to deal with the storm of emotions raging inside him.

At first, his attraction to the older man had been purely physical—nothing had changed about that. Crowley was a handsome man, but he was also a dragon currently residing in a human body.

Even so, that familiar desire coiled in his stomach. But Crowley wasn't the first man Adam had wanted but couldn't have. And he certainly wouldn't be the last.

Yet ever since he had seen the look in Crowley's eyes when the dragon had found him in Cain's house—when he had hurled all those terrible words at him, lashing out because he had felt vulnerable, because he hated being reminded over and over again that the things he desired would never truly be his—something had shifted.

Silas. Becoming a knight. Crowley.

When had he started yearning for those brown eyes to soften when they looked at him? How long had he harbored these feelings without recognizing them?

Adam swallowed, his throat dry, and he noticed how his hand trembled slightly as he cautiously slid it across the sheets, closer to Crowley. He hesitated, then gently touched the dark-haired man's hand where it rested atop the blanket.

The touch was light, almost like a whisper.

As if he were doing something forbidden, Adam held his breath and hooked his pinky finger around Crowley's.

The dragon stirred in his sleep but didn't wake. Adam quickly pulled his hand back as if burned.

His heart pounded faster, and heat crawled up his ears. The realization that he might be falling for Crowley hit him like lightning.

It was a sudden, overwhelming moment of clarity that terrified him.

How could he have been so blind?

All those shared moments—the times Crowley had made him laugh in a way he hadn't since Silas died. The deep conversations, where he had been forced to lay everything bare through their connection. It all appeared in a new light now.

Since Silas, he hadn't allowed himself to open up to another person like this.

And now, he had met a dragon in human form who had burned his way through every wall Adam had built. Torn them down to their very foundation, leaving nothing but smoldering embers in his wake.

Crowley had carved through Adam's self-loathing like fire through dry brush in a wildfire.

Fire burned. It hurt. It destroyed when one wasn't careful.

Adam had lost his first love to fire, and now, the gods were cruel enough to place a man in his path whose fire burned so hot that it threatened to consume him whole.

Crowley's skin was warm, inviting. It took every ounce of Adam's willpower to sink back into the pillows and close his eyes.

He took a deep breath and let the realization settle in.

His emotions were still a chaotic storm, but never before had he been so willing to surrender to the flames within him as he was tonight.

He felt as though he were standing at the edge of a cliff, unsure of what lay beyond.

Squeezing his eyes shut, he tried to calm himself, but his racing heart and Crowley's presence beside him made it impossible to fall asleep for a long, long time.

The first rays of sunlight filtered through the thin curtains of the small room, casting a faint glow over the two sleeping figures in the only bed.

Half-asleep, Adam shifted slightly. His arm brushed against something warm—someone. It took him a moment to remember where he was. He blinked drowsily and glanced to the side.

Crowley lay right next to him, and the warm thing he had touched was the dark-haired man's arm, wrapped around his waist.

At some point, Adam must have drifted off, but now, all the thoughts from last night came rushing back in an instant. He prayed he wouldn't wake the other man because his thoughts weren't the only thing making his face flush.

There was also another feeling, further south, that made him hope Crowley would stay asleep just a little longer.

Trying not to think about it, he turned onto his back and stared awkwardly at the ceiling. If he moved Crowley's arm now, the dragon would surely wake up.

After a long moment, Adam sneaked a glance to the side—only to find that Crowley had already opened his eyes and was watching him warmly.

Their gazes met, and for the briefest second, absolute silence stretched between them.

Crowley furrowed his brows slightly and murmured, still thick with sleep, "Morning."

Adam's eyes lingered on the dark-haired man's beautifully shaped lips as they formed that simple word. His gaze instinctively drifted downward, just enough to notice the faint outline beneath the blanket.

He swallowed hard.

Before Crowley could notice that he was dealing with the same problem, Adam hurriedly sat up—only to be reminded of the heavy arm still draped around him.

Before it could brush against anything that would betray him completely, he quickly pushed it off.

The thin blanket offered no real cover. Adam could feel the heat creeping up his face. How the hell was he supposed to get out of this situation?

Crowley, in contrast, seemed far less tense as he sat up as well, the light fabric slipping down from his hips.

Before the dragon could say anything, Adam was already on his feet, clutching his own blanket tightly around himself.

"I saw a small washroom across the hall yesterday. I'll go freshen up, and then we can head down for breakfast."

Before Crowley could get a single word out, the blond had already fled the room.

He hadn't lied—there really was a small room meant for washing up. But today, Adam had another reason for using it.

He slipped into one of the narrow stalls, pulling the curtain shut behind him.

Shielded from view, he scooped up the cold water from a nearby bucket and poured it over his head. But no matter how much he tried, his arousal refused to subside.

Frustrated, he had no choice but to take matters into his own hands.

This had never happened to him before—so why now?

His irritated thoughts slowly melted into something hazier, something warmer, as pleasure flooded his senses, his focus narrowing to that aching heat low in his stomach.

His eyes fluttered shut, and without meaning to, his mind conjured an image of Crowley—stretched out naked in the sheets they had slept in last night.

Touching himself.

Bringing them both to the edge together.

Biting down on his fist to stifle any sound, Adam leaned against the wall, breath shuddering as he worked through his release.

This was his downfall.

It couldn't possibly get any more humiliating.

He took a few moments to collect himself before daring to return to the room.

By then, Crowley was already dressed, his arousal completely gone.

Either he had dealt with it the same way Adam had, or dragons really could control their urges.

If it was the latter, then life was just unnecessarily unfair to Adam.

CROWLEY

Arousal ran like warm honey through his veins. Where Adam had felt panic, Crowley only felt a simmering heat beneath his skin.

His mind wandered back to the cave, as often the past days. He remembered how Adam's hand had felt around his pulsing member.

This time the heat was no all-consuming monster. As if he had had to feed the first wave of craving, now it was a welcome feeling. Crowley embraced the hunger this time and even leaned into the touch.

With a satisfied growl he reached between his own legs and wrapped a hand around his flesh. He had never touched himself like this before, but he had watched the blonde man. Watched him closely, how his hand had moved so it was easy to remember how to work himself.

The whole room smelled like Adam.

When Crowley closed his eyes, the image of those blue eyes and the dirty, blonde locks was so clear before his eyes as if he was truly right before him.

There was still the draconic urge to reproduce beneath the heat in his belly, but it wasn't as strong as it had been the first time.

If he had held Adam back when he fled, would he have offered his help again? Maybe he should follow him into this washroom...

Through their telepathic bond he didn't hear anything, besides the static Adam always seemed to have clouding his mind.

Their experiences in that earth cave had set his nerve endings ablaze and left him burned in its wake.

With his eyes closed, he moved his hand up and down, just as Adam had. His breathing grew heavier, and the heat in his body swelled like a kettle on the verge of boiling over.

Where there had been confusion last time, there was now a familiar mix of pain and anticipation.

His body sank back into the pillows as if on its own, his hand moving faster. The bedsheets smelled like Adam.

A low growl escaped his lips.

Mine.

Crowley's eyes flew open in shock just as he came, hot and shuddering into his own hand.

Quickly, he wiped the evidence away on the sheets and pushed himself up from the pillow.

Where had that thought come from? A dragon like him would never choose a human as a mate.

He liked Adam—more than liked him—but they still belonged to two different races.

His heart pounded as he reached for his clothes, hastily making himself presentable before Adam returned.

The next day, when they could finally make out the city walls in the distance, they took one last break before reaching their destination. Crowley took a large sip of the rice wine Cain had given them.

"Crowley, what's it like to fly?" Adam asked, directing the question to the older man.

The dragon was so surprised by the question that he almost choked on his drink.

That was like asking what it felt like to breathe.

Flying was as natural to dragons as it was to birds, so Crowley simply shrugged. "It's just… what makes us dragons who we are."

How did one explain something like that to someone without wings?

For a brief moment, Crowley considered offering to take Adam on a flight, but he quickly dismissed the thought. Carrying Adam on his back in his true form would be far too conspicuous. Besides, he wasn't a horse. And who knew how much strength the ring in his chest had drained from him?

Adam hopped down from the stone wall where they had been resting, signaling that he had rested enough and they could continue their journey. Had Crowley answered his question to his satisfaction?

They reached the city walls of Vitris just before sunset. Despite that, the heavy wooden gates were already sealed shut, and the torches outside had been lit. Adam's gaze trailed up along the towering gates to the stone walls above, but no guards were in sight.

"Should we knock?" Crowley asked, almost amused.

Adam shot him his best *Are you serious?* look. Crowley found himself very funny at the moment.

"I thought they only closed the gates after sunset," the blond murmured, crossing his arms over his chest.

"We can't just stand out here until sunrise."

There had to be another way in.

Crowley tilted his head back, studying the stone walls and wooden gate for a moment. No guards or archers were stationed along the wall. Vitris must have felt very secure if they had already withdrawn their sentries before nightfall.

"There's another way in," Crowley said, glancing at Adam. It was almost ironic that they had been talking about flying just hours ago.

A slight shiver ran through Adam, and both of them noticed the thin veil of mist rising from the warm earth beneath their feet. If they waited just a little longer, the fog would climb up the city walls, cloaking their approach.

"We can use the mist," the dragon suggested. "I'll carry us over the wall."

At least, he would try. He rolled his shoulders once, testing his strength. If he only summoned his wings, it should be enough to get them both over the barrier.

It was a little ironic. If someone had asked Crowley a mere month ago if he would ever let a human touch him, even the thought of carrying one through the air, would have made the old dragon scoff. Now he was offering this absurd idea himself.

Ignoring Adam's questioning look, Crowley waited as the mist began gathering around them. Then, he took a calculating step back from the city wall.

He wasn't sure of his limits in this form, so he could only hope he hadn't been too bold with his plan. It wouldn't take long—maybe ten beats with his wings at most.

He pulled off his dark blue tunic and tied it around his waist. He didn't want to tear it; he would need it later.

A sharp burning sensation spread across his back, and his expression twisted slightly in discomfort as his wings broke through his skin.

Adam's eyes widened in shock.

Crowley simply smiled. "What? Didn't you want to know what flying feels like just a few hours ago?"

With that, he spread his wings to their full span.

Adam, however, only looked even more panicked.

"You're not afraid of heights, are you?" Crowley asked, tilting his head. "Don't worry, I won't drop you."

As if that settled everything, he reached out to grab Adam's shirt—but the blond took a panicked step back. Crowley immediately let his hand drop.

"You're making this harder than it is. You just need to hold on to me." Maybe he had been too hasty with this plan.

"…Are you going to carry me piggyback?" Adam asked, his fear evident in his wide eyes.

"My wings are right here, Adam. Trust me, I've got you."

To demonstrate, Crowley gave his wings a slow, deliberate flap before folding them back against his back.

Adam still looked uncertain.

With a sigh, Crowley crouched slightly. "I'm going to pick you up now," he warned.

Since Adam didn't step back this time, Crowley scooped him up over his shoulder in one smooth motion. A startled squawk left Adam's lips as the ground vanished from under his feet—literally.

Crowley adjusted his stance, testing his balance with the added weight. Adam was light; carrying him was hardly a challenge.

Taking a deep breath—both to steady himself and to re-assure Adam—he murmured, "I told you I wouldn't drop you."

Why was that so hard to believe?

He could carry an entire calf in his claws with ease.

Admittedly, most of the time, the cargo he transported was already dead. But as long as Adam didn't move, fly-ing over the wall just once shouldn't be a problem—even if Crowley wasn't in his normal form.

For a brief moment, it seemed like Adam was about to struggle against Crowley's grip, trying to free himself from his shoulder.

The dark-haired man could feel the younger one digging his fingers into his back. Adam's blunt nails left crescent-shaped imprints on his skin—was he holding on that tightly out of fear, or was he trying to push himself away?

Crowley wasn't entirely sure what the blond was at-tempting, but if they wanted to use the mist as cover, they had to act now.

Had Adam truly resisted, Crowley would have released him immediately. But after a few tense seconds, despite the stiffness in his body, Adam remained relatively still on his shoulder.

Crowley braced one hand against Adam's back to keep him steady before spreading his wings again.

Taking off in this form was different from launching himself in his dragon shape, but the muscles in his wings were strong enough to lift them both off the ground.

Unfortunately, he didn't get far.

The moment they were airborne, fresh panic surged through Adam's body.

So he was afraid of heights.

Crowley had barely risen three meters when Adam started thrashing again, squirming and fighting against his grip. Wasn't this practically self-sabotage?

Crowley was the only thing keeping him from falling, and yet Adam was using every ounce of his strength to struggle against him.

ADAM

When Crowley actually lost his grip around Adam's waist, real panic surged through the blond's body.

As Adam nearly slipped from his shoulder, Crowley grabbed him firmly with both arms, pressing him tightly against his chest.

It might have bordered on self-sabotage, but Adam's instincts had taken over, making him flail wildly.

He was human. Humans weren't meant to fly. Without the ground beneath his feet, Adam had nothing to anchor himself to.

His fingers grasped at anything they could find.

It took a long moment before he finally felt Crowley lowering him down again. Even then, the taller man kept his hands on Adam's hips, as if letting go completely might cause him to collapse.

"Are we on the other side?" Adam asked, his vision still spinning, dark spots dancing at the edges of his sight.

"Hardly," came the dragon's response. "Before you got yourself killed, I landed again."

It took a second for the words to fully register. Slowly, Adam released the other man and took a step back.

"I'm sorry, I—" Adam started to explain, but Crowley simply raised a hand.

"Fear of heights. Fine. We'll just wait until sunrise."

Adam felt ashamed for being such a coward, but no matter how hard he tried, he couldn't bring himself to attempt it again.

Silently, he watched Crowley as the man's wings folded back into his back.

The dark-haired man pulled his tunic back on and sat down against the wall. The rising mist gave his figure something otherworldly. As if he didn't belong to this world at all. And maybe he didn't. Once they got rid of the ring, he never would be part of Adam's world at least again.

"Could we… maybe practice?" Adam spoke again after nearly an hour of quiet waiting. He had walked along the wall, searching, but there was no other way inside. Vitris was impenetrable at night—unless you could fly.

Crowley opened one eye and looked at him. The dragon had been sitting so still, almost in a meditative state, that Adam had assumed he was sleeping.

"Practice? Flying?" Crowley asked.

Adam nodded. Was that a stupid idea?

Crowley rolled his shoulders and stood up.

"It would be easier to just wait. The sun will rise in a few hours, and shifting, even partially, drains my energy."

Was Adam imagining it, or did Crowley's voice sound angry?

"I'll be sure to personally thank your witch for that," the dragon muttered.

Adam resisted the urge to correct him—Dominique wasn't his witch. He had stated that before, but he also didn't want to argue again.

Adam had to admit, Crowley did look exhausted.

"Do you think it's because of the ring?", Adam asked, almost reaching out to touch Crowley's chest before stopping himself.

"Maybe. I've never taken on a human form before. Maybe I just need to adjust." Crowley's posture relaxed slightly.

They were both exhausted, and Crowley was probably irritated that flying over the wall wasn't as simple as he had assumed.

"Let's try one more time," Adam asked cautiously. "Just once. I swear I won't move. If we wait until sunrise, the city will be packed, and it might take another whole day to find Dominique in the chaos."

"You don't know where she lives?" Crowley sounded surprised.

Adam's face felt like it should have burst into flames by now. The taller man must think him utterly idiotic by now.

"I met her at the market. I didn't think to ask where she lived. She just said we'd find her when we returned."

Crowley clearly wasn't thrilled with that answer. He snorted in frustration, the mist swirling at the sudden burst of air.

Only then did Adam notice that the ground they stood on, just outside the gates, was covered in poppies.

The last time he had been here with his uncle, summer had just begun. These poppies only bloomed in autumn, when the air grew colder. Had it really been that long since he had met Dominique? Since he had set out to find a dragon?

"Fine. We'll try again," Crowley interrupted his thoughts.

Adam swallowed hard. This was happening. Crowley noticed his hesitation but said nothing. Adam had agreed to try again on his own.

"What exactly are you afraid of?" the dragon asked.

It was obvious that Adam would rather just wait until sunrise. And yet, he had suggested trying again.

"If it's the height, just close your eyes. I won't let you fall."

Adam took a deep breath, brushing his hair from his forehead.

"Are you kidding? My whole life, dragons, fairies, and unicorns were just stories," he admitted.

Crowley metaphorically bit his tongue—he didn't interrupt to inform Adam that everything he had just listed did exist. They even met a unicorn and will-o-wisps on their journey so far.

"I knew magic was real, even before I met Domi," Adam continued.

"But that kind of magic was only given to those chosen by the gods, those rewarded with a magically charged artifact."

Slowly, he sank to the ground and gripped the chain around his neck. He clutched the pendant so tightly that his knuckles turned white.

"The necklace you wear… it belonged to Silas, didn't it?" Crowley asked bluntly before sitting beside him.

Adam instantly released the pendant as if it had burned him. But there was no point in lying. So, he nodded.

"After the accident in the barn, I took the necklace to remember my best friend. That day, the pendant's light went out. But I can still feel Silas's warmth in it." A soft smile tugged at his lips. He would never love anyone the way he had loved his best friend.

Slowly, he lifted his gaze, meeting Crowley's golden eyes.

There was a warmth behind that gold that made Adam's heart beat faster.

Maybe his heart could still love someone.

But then, his gaze drifted to Crowley's chest, to the golden ring nestled there, and he almost imagined it laughing at him.

That ring was the only reason Crowley had come with him at all.

And yet, so much had changed on this journey. They had changed.

Maybe Crowley would stay with him, even after they got rid of the ring.

The thought sent a swarm of butterflies loose in Adam's stomach, ones he couldn't contain even if he wanted to.

His feelings threatened to tear down the walls he had built around his heart for years.

He was scared. Scared of losing the ground beneath his feet. But even more terrifying was the realization that his heart had finally let go of Silas…

…to make space for a great, black dragon.

If that dragon wanted him.

"I grew up in a normal world, without a hint of fantasy," Adam said at last, circling back to Crowley's original question.

"Then I met you."

CROWLEY

Their entire conversation took place in their minds, yet Adam still lifted his gaze to meet Crowley's eyes directly.

"That made me think. Yes, by the old gods, I'm afraid, because all of this is unknown to me! I've never been beyond the border, let alone with a witch and a dragon, and now you expect me to climb onto your back without batting an eye and soar through the skies with joy?"

Tears had begun to well up in Adam's eyes, and he didn't blink them away, even as they threatened to spill down his heated cheeks.

Crowley hadn't expected such honesty, and now that it was laid out so openly before him, he suddenly realized that this openness was what made Adam so brave.

The mortal displayed a vulnerability that frightened Crowley. Adam was one of the strangest humans he had ever met—and one of the bravest.

"When I was a child, I didn't believe that humans had consciousness." He didn't know why, but this old, buried memory had surfaced during Adam's monologue.

"I thought they were like animals. That's what I had been taught. So, I didn't think much about it. But then another, older dragon and I were captured, and I watched as they coldly beheaded him and laughed afterward. Right before my eyes. That was a deliberate act. You can't accidentally cut off someone's head and then take pleasure in it."

He wasn't sure if Adam even wanted to hear this story, but those deep blue eyes remained fixed on him. A part of Crowley wished he could say these words aloud—his voice would carry the emotions better than his thoughts. But perhaps it was better this way.

Crowley didn't trust himself when it came to these memories. Rage, shame, hatred—all these emotions resurfaced when he thought back to that time in the cage.

His entire life since his imprisonment, he had despised humans. He had been afraid, and that fear had made him vigilant. He hadn't let a single human get close to him—he had killed before he could be killed.

Then he had met Adam.

This young man had somehow slipped through his walls, found his way beneath his scales.

Without realizing it, Crowley had exposed his core and, metaphorically, placed it into Adam's open hands. When had that happened? Since when had the hatred, the anger, the fear, and the sorrow inside him been replaced by this warm feeling of safety?

How could a single human change his entire perception so drastically? Dragons were proud beings, the mighty lords of flame, water, ice, or thunder.

For all these years, the memory of his capture had filled him with terror, but for the first time, it no longer threatened to consume him. Adam was like a small flame in the darkness—something Crowley could hold on to.

"I've been absolutely terrified of humans ever since. Hard to believe, I know." A cold snort left his throat, and he would have preferred to end the conversation here.

"A mighty dragon, afraid of humans." A wisp of smoke escaped his nostrils, drifting into the cool night air.

"I don't know how your fear feels when you're faced with magic or about to fly for the first time. But your fear is only of the situation itself. Back then, I was paralyzed with terror. A child who didn't know if he would survive."

Cautiously, Crowley raised one of his hands, palm facing upward toward the other. In his human form, they were more alike than he had expected. Adam's hand was warm as he pressed his palm against Crowley's.

"And just as I was afraid, you're allowed to be afraid too. But I promise you, you don't have to fear when you're with me. On this journey, you'll encounter many things you thought only existed in stories. You will be afraid. But I can promise you that for as long as we're together, I won't let you fall."

The words came easier and faster than Crowley had expected. To lighten their weight, he cleared his throat and stood up.

"So, come on. The sooner we're in the air, the sooner we can land again."

Adam bit his lip, but a small smile still broke through as he rose to his feet as well.

"I think I'm ready to learn how to fly."

Crowley looked down at the younger man, and something like pride began to stir in his chest.

"I know I can't expect you to trust me blindly after such a short time."

Adam didn't respond to that. Instead, he asked something else.

"Why did you decide to tell me about your imprisonment?"

The question caught the dragon off guard.

"You don't have to tell me more. If you'd rather, we can pretend this conversation never happened," Adam offered after Crowley hesitated.

"I've never felt so weak and helpless." Crowley's honest answer seemed to surprise Adam.

"You were a child back then."

Adam's words wrapped around the wounded part of Crowley's heart like a flower, as if the delicate petals could shield the broken dragon boy inside him from the world and its pain.

"That's not what I mean," the black dragon said, turning his head away, his cheeks flushed. It was obvious how uncomfortable he felt, but he didn't want to leave his words hanging.

"Yes, I was captured as a child, and I watched a family member die. That memory will stay with me forever. But what I mean is, I've never felt so weak and inferior as when I compare myself to you."

Adam furrowed his brows in confusion, letting the words sink in.

"What… do you mean by that?"

Slowly, Crowley lifted his gaze to meet the blonde's once more, and his golden eyes had never looked so vulnerable.

"For ages, I tried to show nothing but strength. The dragon no one could hurt. I was ruthless and cruel. I hurt others before they could hurt me. I always struck first. Before they could see how much I trembled when a human so much as pointed a blade at me. And then I met you."

Using the same words back at him made Crowley smile despite the heaviness of their conversation.

He watched the younger man tremble slightly under his words, his eyes widening.

"But back then, in the forest, when we fought the knights together—you were fearless. Even if you didn't realize it, I was trembling all over. Especially since I had never fought as a human before. The form I had to take just to accompany you on this journey terrifies me whenever I see my reflection in the water."

Crowley's nails dug into his own palms as he opened up so completely.

Adam looked at the great dragon before him, then slowly raised his hand, placing it gently against Crowley's cheek. At the touch, the core within the dragon's chest flared for a brief moment.

"Why are you telling me all of this now?" the younger man asked, tilting his head.

For a moment, his gaze flickered to the red, pulsing light before they locked eyes again. Crowley's heart pounded so loudly that even without enhanced hearing, Adam must have been able to notice it.

"Because I want you to know that I understand your fear. And yet, in every moment I spend with you, you show a strength and courage that someone like me can only dream of."

ADAM

Crowley's words wrapped around Adam from the inside, leaving behind a warm sensation. His heart pounded slowly and heavily in his chest as he replayed Crowley's words over and over in his mind.

He knew the black dragon's words weren't lies, yet it was so difficult to believe them.

"You paint me bigger than I am," the blonde man murmured before lowering his gaze to the ground between them.

A single poppy bloomed between them, as if it were eavesdropping on their conversation. The thought made Adam smile, and when he looked up again, Crowley mirrored his expression, tilting his head slightly.

"You seem quite big to me," the taller man teased in return, lowering his head so they were at eye level. Adam's hand remained resting on his cheek.

Adam's heart no longer pounded wildly from excitement but rather from the knowledge that Crowley had let him close enough to share a piece of himself. He had stepped out of his comfort zone to help Adam, so Adam could be the brave knight Crowley described him as.

It took every spark of courage Crowley had just granted him to ask the question without backing down — without running from an answer he might not be able to bear.

"Do you think the ring is playing with your emotions, Crowley? We've done things… things you wouldn't normally do with just anyone." Adam bit his tongue.

His choice of words was terrible, but he didn't know how else to confess his worries of the past few days.

"I mean, do you think you would kiss me if the ring wasn't inside your chest?" the blonde asked as straightforwardly as he could.

Time seemed to stand still. Adam didn't even allow himself to breathe, holding his breath as Crowley's large eye roamed his face, as if searching for something.

"Where is this question coming from?"

How could Adam explain that this question had been haunting him for a while?

He didn't know if the ring had any magical influence. But he couldn't imagine someone like Crowley ever choosing someone like him — at least, not willingly.

It was easier to destroy it himself now before he fell too deep and lost himself in something unattainable.

After a moment that felt like an eternity to Adam, Crowley finally added, "I would very much like to kiss you."

The blonde's chest filled, as if a waterfall had suddenly washed away the cold inside him.

His brain was filled with static, more than usually and it took his hazy mind a moment to react.

Blinking rapidly, Adam fought back the tears before the dragon could see them. Crowley's words wrapped around his heart like a protective embrace.

Maybe, just maybe, he could allow himself a moment of weakness. Slowly, he rocked onto his toes, their noses brushing against each other.

But before their lips could meet, the blonde took a cautious step back. They were still right outside the capital's gates. Just because they were tightly shut and guard was in sight didn't mean that there weren't eyes watching. Years of hiding couldn't be ignored so easily.

"I want to kiss you too," Adam admitted, "but let's first get me used to not having solid ground beneath my feet."

He didn't want to kill the mood, but he knew that if Crowley kissed him now, they would never make it over that damn wall before sunrise. Images of a stormy night and a desperate shower swirled in his head. Adam's cheeks burned. If his heart beat any faster, he might just throw up right here in front of Crowley.

"So… for now, I'll just hold on to you?" the blonde asked, watching as Crowley raised a brow. Adam felt his face heat up. How else could he have phrased that?

Crowley gave a small nod before stepping back and pulling his tunic over his head again. Adam had long since given up trying not to stare.

His imagination was simply too strong. As was his excitement.

And Crowley's human form was unfairly breathtaking.

The dark-haired man staggered slightly, breaking Adam from his not-so-innocent thoughts.

It was understandable—this constant shifting had to be exhausting for him. Adam felt a pang of sympathy and reached out to steady him, but the dragon merely shook his head and pushed his hands aside.

"I'm fine. My body just tires much faster," Crowley explained before black wings once again burst from his back. No matter what the dark-haired man said, it looked painful.

The older man rolled his shoulders once and stretched his wings experimentally. With a slight grimace, the blonde asked: "Are you sure that doesn't hurt?"

His companion just shook his head and spread the leathery wings to their full extent.

"Not really. The balance shifts a bit, but you get used to it after a while."

Adam's eyes studied the outstretched wings, and for the first time, he noticed the same scars and markings that covered Crowley's neck and sides.

"Alright, then hold on to me. Once you're comfortable with the height, we can clear the wall in three easy wingbeats. Think we can manage that?" the dark-haired man asked, extending a hand.

It made sense. Still, Adam hesitated for a moment before taking the final step toward Crowley.

The instant he took Crowley's hand, he felt tiny sparks racing through him at the simple touch.

The dragon's chest was warm, the red light pulsing gently beneath his skin.

It was unfair—how beautiful this man was. And even more unfair that he had taken off his tunic for their flying lesson. Crowley merely smiled and pulled the blonde against him.

"You didn't seem to mind me being undressed when we bathed together. Besides, I think we're long past the point of embarrassment, don't you?" the dark-haired man remarked with a grin, his long, loose hair falling forward and tickling Adam's collarbone.

Of course, he had to bring that up again. The blonde's face burned, but there was no escaping it now.

"Let's just fly, okay?" he muttered in defeat, biting his lip.

Slowly, he wrapped his arms around the dark-haired man's neck.

Their journey would be interesting—whatever happened next, he'd deal with later. For now, he had to face his second fear: plummeting from an inhuman height.

He refocused on the wings sprouting from Crowley's back. One arm remained looped around the taller man's neck while the other reached out, fingertips brushing against the thin membranes. The velvety skin stretched over the wings was soft beneath his cool fingers. Adam couldn't believe something so thin and almost fragile could keep a creature as large as a dragon aloft.

His heart pounded as he traced the intricate structure of muscles and bones, feeling them twitch beneath his touch. Maybe Crowley was ticklish there.

Next, his fingers found the ridge running down Crowley's spine between his outspread wings.

He had never noticed this part of the dragon's human form before. Curious, he rose onto his toes to peer over Crowley's shoulder. Dark scales lined his spine, fading as they blended seamlessly into his pale skin.

Just as he was about to ask about them, he felt Crowley's warm breath right against his ear. A shiver ran through him—from the smaller man to the larger, or maybe the other way around.

A heat coiled low in Adam's stomach, and he was about to pull away when Crowley's arm wrapped around his waist.

Even though he only heard the words in his mind, the dragon's breath against his temple felt as if he were whispering them directly into his ear.

"I thought we were flying."

Crowley's body was so warm against his.

Adam swallowed hard and nodded obediently. He'd leave his fingers right where they were and continue his exploration another time—if he ever got the chance again.

"Okay, you know how it feels when I lift us off the ground. Just try not to look down," the dark-haired man advised, giving his wings a test beat, stirring a cloud of mist around them.

Easier said than done, but Adam would try.

As soon as he felt himself lose contact with the ground, his body tensed.

"Hey, relax. I've got you. I won't let you fall."

The words were too warm, too close.

"Look at me," Crowley commanded, tightening his grip. As if entranced, Adam tilted his head back, meeting the glowing gold eyes.

"Don't forget to breathe, and as long as you don't fight my grip, I won't let you fall."

Adam nodded, doing his best not to look down. Crowley's wings were proportional to his body, which meant that in his human form, it took far more wingbeats to get them over the wall than Adam had expected.

He had buried his face in the crook of Crowley's neck again, but as soon as the dragon spread his wings wide, allowing them to glide through the thin mist, Adam dared to lift his gaze.

They were above the wall now, and it took him a moment to get his bearings. From up here, he had a perfect view of the houses and streets of Vitris.

A brief wave of dizziness washed over him at the sight, but as promised, Crowley's grip around his waist didn't loosen.

The dragon wouldn't let him fall.

CROWLEY

The dragon's silken wings made no sound in the cool night air. Crowley relished the warmth of Adam's body in his arms.

He wasn't heavy, and with the right weight distribution, their flight remained smooth and steady. Little by little, the blond relaxed in his grip, even daring to curiously glance down at the houses below.

"Do you think we could spot your witch from up here?" Crowley allowed himself to ask.

Adam merely shook his head in response. "I have no idea what her house looks like. But I recognize that well over there, and that's a statue of the All-King."

Crowley followed Adam's pointing finger and studied a stone figure. He recognized the face. Statues like these were scattered throughout the land, but he had never seen one this large before.

"I'm going to bring us down slowly, okay?" the dark-haired man warned, and on a whim, he placed a hand on the back of Adam's head, fingers threading through soft blond curls.

A slight tilt of his body was all it took for them to start descending.

Crowley glanced down at the young man in his arms, watching as Adam turned his head from left to right, as if trying to judge exactly when his feet would touch solid ground again. The sight was rather endearing, drawing a chuckle from Crowley.

"And you see this every time you fly?" Adam asked, clearly impressed.

Crowley laughed again, the sound reverberating in his chest—something Adam noticed more from the vibration than the actual sound.

"I told you, flying is the best way to travel," Crowley replied, giving another strong beat of his wings to ensure they didn't lose altitude too quickly. He wasn't about to ruin Adam's hard-earned trust by making the landing too rough.

"It's beautiful," Adam whispered, reaching out toward a paper lantern hanging from the roof of one of the houses below.

"Yeah… quite beautiful," Crowley murmured, though his gaze never left Adam.

The younger man turned his head, meeting Crowley's stare. His blue eyes shimmered softly in the warm lantern light. A smile spread across his lips, and for a moment, time itself seemed to pause.

Everything around them—the city, their journey, the vast sky—faded into insignificance as their gazes locked.

Slowly, almost hesitantly, Adam lifted his hand, his fingers grazing Crowley's cheek in a gentle touch that spoke volumes more than words ever could.

Crowley held him close with one arm, while the other smoothed the curls the wind had tousled.

Adam closed his eyes, leaning slightly into Crowley's palm—an unspoken agreement, a silent permission to embrace the feeling growing between them.

Crowley beat his wings on instinct alone, his entire focus centered on the breathtaking man in his arms. Their hearts pounded in sync, a quiet but unyielding rhythm guiding this moment.

He lowered his head, pressing his forehead against Adam's. For the first time, Crowley's mind was utterly blank.

There was so much he felt, so much he wanted to say, but instead, he breathed in the scent of the man before him and concentrated on his wingbeats.

Adam's eyes fluttered open, his lashes brushing lightly against his skin as he looked up. He leaned in closer, their lips mere inches apart, and then—

The space between them vanished as they finally kissed. It was a kiss filled with tenderness and longing, soft yet so intense that the world around them ceased to exist.

Crowley, completely lost in the moment, failed to notice their altitude slipping until—

CRASH.

They tumbled into an empty horse cart, set aside for the night.

Crowley groaned in pain, but he hadn't let go of Adam.

Luckily for them, no one had been near the wall at this hour. If the crashing of the cart hadn't already drawn attention, then the startled whinnies of nearby horses surely would.

Adam let out a pained hiss as he rolled off the dark-haired man, emerging from the wreckage with a wince.

Crowley pushed a wooden plank off his shoulder before forcing himself upright. Surprisingly, his wings were unharmed as he folded them neatly against his back.

A glance at Adam, who was struggling to stay upright on trembling legs, made it clear just how unexpected the fall had been. Thankfully, they hadn't crashed from too dangerous a height.

Crowley's lips tingled, and all he wanted was to grab Adam and kiss him again.

Could human kisses be addictive?

Adam shook his head before looking at Crowley—then, unexpectedly, he started laughing.

Caught off guard, he quickly clapped a hand over his mouth as if to stifle the sound, but it was too late.

Crowley liked Adam's laughter—it was genuine, full.

Grinning, he pressed a finger to his lips, listening carefully to the night. A dog barked in the distance, but other than that, it seemed no one had noticed their little crash landing. The wrecked wooden cart, however, would definitely be discovered come sunrise.

With a quiet groan of discomfort, Crowley retracted his wings into his body. Once done, he wiped a bead of sweat from his chin before stepping toward Adam, reaching for his arm.

"Sorry, are you hurt?" Crowley asked cautiously.

Adam took a moment before answering.

"I'm fine. I just—thought I was about to pass out. The impact made me see stars."

Relieved, Crowley exhaled and plucked a stray splinter from Adam's shoulder.

"I swear, I usually land better than that," Crowley joked. It worked—Adam grinned, shaking his head.

"Come on, let's make use of the night and find Dominique's house before the streets get too crowded."

Thankfully, they hadn't crashed near the city gates. The buildings surrounding them looked run-down—perhaps they had landed in a quieter district with fewer people. That would certainly make their nighttime search easier.

ADAM

The flight had lasted a full 20 minutes, but Adam had thought he was going to die. Never before had he been so far from the ground. For a moment, everything had spun, and it had been unclear which way was up or down.

Though Adam's uncle had told him that Vitris had no guards posted overnight, the blonde had expected at least someone.

His knees were still shaking, but he hadn't died. He looked around to figure out where in the capital they had ended up at.

Crowley had landed them in an abandoned horse cart. The decaying wood around them clearly indicated that they were in the poorer district, a good distance south of the main gate.

The marketplace lay to the west of the city. If they made it to the main street, they could follow it easily to the market.

Adam's gaze wandered curiously over the houses, which was a generous term. Many of the buildings around them appeared dilapidated and hardly seemed to fit the image of a capital city the blonde had in mind.

The house adjacent to theirs seemed to be the only sign of life. All the other buildings were dark or appeared abandoned. Well, they had infiltrated the area in the middle of the night.

Through the dim light from the cloudy windows of one house, Adam could see a small clay figure placed on a windowsill. It was a depiction of the large statue he had recognized from the air.

There were small figures or representations of the All-King scattered throughout the city, and a shiver ran down the blonde's spine. It felt like a completely different world to see this face everywhere in Vitris, as if the city were isolated from the lands around it.

Neither in Adam's village nor in the barracks he had visited was the All-King as prevalent as here. Through the cloudy windows, he noticed several people inside the large house next to the decaying cart stop.

The flickering lights inside made the building look like a giant heart. On the opposite side of the street, rows of old houses stood with darkened windows.

The streets were intermittently lit by lanterns, but aside from a stray cat, the blonde could see nothing. Vitris seemed to feel secure behind its thick walls, as even their crash hadn't raised an alarm. The dragon had largely cushioned their fall.

Adam's gaze returned to the dark-haired man who stood with his eyes closed. Maybe he was listening to see if anyone else was nearby or if they'd been seen. Another brief wave of jealousy passed through the blonde's heart.

In his normal life, Adam managed just fine without his hearing, but the longer he traveled with Crowley, the more he realized how much he wished he could get it back.

At first, he had just wanted to hear so he could join the King's Guard for his friend Silas. As he neared his goal, his wish hadn't changed much. But in addition to his knighthood, Adam longed to hear, just as Crowley did with his eyes closed, the sound of the wind.

He wondered what Vitris must sound like during the day.

And how Crowley's human voice would sound. If it would be anything like the voice he heard in his head.

Adam was about to ask if they could move on when the light from a lantern spilled into the alley where they stood. A rather scantily dressed woman was standing in the doorway, letting the beam of light sweep through the alley.

Panicked, Adam grabbed Crowley's arm and pulled him close, with the back of his head and his back hitting the hard wood of the cart behind them. This way, Crowley's body shielded the blonde enough that the light didn't reach him.

The sweet smells wafting from the open door made it clear that it was a brothel. Adam had never been to one before.

There was nothing like that in the countryside, and the blonde wasn't sure if there would be anything for someone like him inside worth a visit. Asking about it wasn't an option. The woman on the stairs didn't seem interested in them. Enough customers were taking their ladies outside.

Adam's thoughts took off at that moment. Crowley's bare chest pressed against his.

Right, the dark-haired man still had his clothes tied around his waist.

Before his thoughts could betray him, Adam focused on the smells around them. The mix of sweet smoke, perfumes, and sweat made Adam feel slightly nauseous, and he squinted his eyes. He was startled as he felt Crowley's nose brush against his neck.

The light dimmed, but the door remained open. Adam cursed inwardly and briefly considered pushing the larger man away. His hands hovered just above Crowley's chest, but what really made his knees weak was Crowley's breath caressing his skin. Had he said something?

Frustrated, the blonde placed his hand over Crowley's mouth, pushing him away slightly.

"What's that about?" Adam asked, indignant.

He knew he probably didn't look presentable right now. He hoped it was dark enough that his burning face and what was happening between his legs wouldn't be too obvious.

"I could ask you the same," Crowley replied, raising an eyebrow. Adam could feel the other man grin against his palm.

Damn, he couldn't stop Crowley's words like this, especially since he could still hear his smoky voice in his thoughts.

"There's a brothel back there. The way we look now, we won't stand out. Let's wait until the door closes, then we can disappear," the blonde suggested, trying not to think about how Crowley's warm breath brushed against his palm like a caress.

Maybe something in his eyes had betrayed his feelings, because he could feel Crowley's mouth moving behind his hand. But what happened next, he never expected.

The larger man's lips and teeth slowly closed around Adam's ring finger, right where the burn scar was. With a dangerous golden gleam in his brown eyes, Crowley bit down lightly.

It didn't hurt, yet the sharp teeth of the dragon sank into his skin, sending little shockwaves straight between his legs. Adam leaned weakly against the wooden wall behind him, a soft moan escaping him.

With a bright red face, he yanked his hand away from Crowley and ducked under his arm, running away.

To hell with the open door; he couldn't take another second with the other like this.

His heart pounded so hard, it felt like it might burst from his chest. But only when they reached the next street corner did he allow himself to breathe again. His thoughts were in turmoil, but at least they had entered the city unseen.

From the corner of his eye, he saw Crowley coming around the corner. With a cheeky grin on his lips, he came to a stop next to the blonde man.

Meanwhile, the dragon had put his clothes back on properly. Adam just rolled his eyes but was secretly relieved that Crowley's presence no longer threatened to make his heart fail.

Before Crowley could comment on what had just happened, he made his suggestion: "I don't know which house Dominique lives in, and it's too late to ask around. We could see if we find anyone at the marketplace? Maybe someone got up early."

Either Crowley hadn't noticed Adam's embarrassment or was kind enough not to comment on it, because he replied directly, "Let's search the places where you were with her, maybe we'll find a clue."

Together, they headed toward the large marble stairs that led up to the market. Adam took the time to check the small side streets to see if any house looked like it could belong to a witch.

It had sounded like Dominique's house would be easy to find. Through one of the long alleys, he spotted the fountain she had led him to.

"Wait, Crowley! Let's check by the fountain," the blonde suggested, leading them to the stone basin.

The moon had emerged from behind the clouds and reflected on the surface of the water.

From here, Adam could already see the stairs leading up to the market. When he stood at the edge of the fountain and looked into it, he recognized his own reflection.

Surprised that Crowley wasn't behind him, he turned around.

The dark-haired man had remained at a distance. Could he not see himself in the reflection of the fountain's water?

Adam already figured something like this back when they took their break for a quick bath. Since then whenever there was the dragon's reflection somewhere, Crowley distinctively looked the other way.

The blonde man didn't want to push him into anything and instead walked back to the taller man.

"She offered me her help here. We could rest on one of the benches until the sun comes up and then ask around?" Adam suggested.

Though they were in the city, without knowing which house Dominique lived in, they were likely stuck waiting for the sunrise. At least they would save some time by not waiting for the guards to open up the doors.

Just as the blonde was about to approach one of the benches, he felt Crowley's hand around his arm.

"Do you still remember what she smelled like?" Crowley asked unexpectedly. Adam looked up at the older man, frowning.

"What?" he asked, confused.

"I asked if you remember—"

"I understood the question, but why are you asking me this now, out of the blue?"

Adam didn't understand what Crowley was getting at. The larger man sighed slightly.

"If you tell me what she smelled like, maybe I can find her. It's worth a try, and better than sitting here doing nothing."

That would certainly be worth a try. Adam tried to remember.

Vitris had been filled with all sorts of different smells the day he met Dominique. The dominant scent in the air had been that of exotic spices. It had smelled of incense, perfume, and various animals. Adam tried to block out all those scents he associated with the capital until only a faint floral note remained.

"I think it was something with jasmine," Adam began, describing hesitantly.

He struggled to assign names to flowers and herbs. His foster father had taught him how to read and write, but the books on the country's floral diversity had been lacking, so he hadn't been able to learn about them. The scent in his memory had been floral, warm, and sweet, like honey.

CROWLEY

Adam's description hadn't been the best, but it was at least something. And Crowley would rather run around looking for a floral, honey-like scent then sit around and wait for the sun to rise.

After sunrise the streets would be filled with more and more people. The dragon had met enough humans first hand for this decade.

When they finally walked through Vitris, the cool night air met him, but it was different—denser, heavier.

The high walls and narrow alleys seemed to trap the wind, and each breath was filled with foreign smells: damp cobblestone, old wood, a hint of burnt oil.

The streets were empty. No one in sight. Only the dull echo of their own footsteps.

It was strange, almost eerie, because as large as the city was, at that moment it felt completely abandoned.

The windows of the houses were shut as if the inhabitants were hiding behind them from something known only to the night.

The scattered street lamps flickered erratically, casting long, eerie shadows on the pavement. Something was wrong, and he couldn't name it.

It was too quiet.

Too empty.

The dark-haired man inhaled the air again, but among all the smells, he found nothing that smelled like jasmine.

The buildings around them stood close together, towering so high that they seemed like teeth biting into the darkness.

There were no familiar sounds of night birds or insects, no animals creeping through the underbrush. Just this strange, oppressive silence, broken only by isolated, unsettling noises that gave him the feeling of being watched.

His eyes wandered over the scattered statues on window sills and along the streets. It was as if the people here placed everything on this All-God. Crowley's gaze fell on Adam's back, who was walking just ahead of him, looking around just as he was. Without Adam noticing, Crowley kicked one of the small statues over. He expected something to happen, but the night remained still.

"I knew it!" the dragon thought, disillusioned.

"A human can't become a god."

The figures were superstitious nonsense, likely providing comfort to the people in the city without truly protecting them.

Every window, every dark corner seemed to hide a secret, as if a figure might suddenly emerge from it. It wasn't the kind of silence that brought peace, but a silence that caused discomfort — the kind that made you perk up and feel a tingling on your neck because you felt you weren't alone, even though you couldn't see anyone.

As they continued walking, Crowley's sense grew stronger that this city was more than just walls and streets. As crazy as the many statues were, they gave Vitris at night the feeling that the streets were filled even without people.

Since they had left the slums and started heading west through the city, the dragon kept hearing fragments of Adam's thoughts. The blonde was pondering what kind of jasmine he knew and how it smelled. Good idea, maybe the witch had chosen a special kind.

"Could it be night jasmine?" the dark-haired man asked directly. Crowley had encountered night jasmine before, back at the Oboros harbor. The flowers had been sold in bunches. By day, they were inconspicuous plants, but at night their scent grew ten times stronger.

Crowley closed his eyes and focused on the scent. The honey-like note melted on his tongue. He led Adam past a fountain into another dark alley. This time, he stopped the man when he saw two guards turning the corner from the darkness.

So Vitris wasn't completely deserted at night. With his body, he pressed Adam against the stone wall, deeper into the shadows, and waited for the guards to pass. The scene was playing out for the second time that night.

Maybe he was imagining it, but Adam pressed against him before running out of the narrow alley. Crowley's hand twitched forward as if wanting to pull Adam back, but quickly closed into a fist, pressing his nails into his palm before following Adam.

A stone staircase led deeper into the city. For a moment, the high city walls seemed as though they would crush the two visitors from below. But then Crowley's gaze fell on a small house hidden between two tall buildings. Above the door, a small fire burned in a brass bowl, emitting a strong scent of night jasmine.

"I think we've found your witch's house," Crowley stated. Adam sniffed the air briefly.

"Yes, that's the scent. It's coming directly from the bowl above the door," the blonde confirmed and stepped cautiously toward the house. Should they knock? It was the middle of the night. But they had come this far.

Crowley watched the blonde as he knocked with his knuckles on the wooden door. It took a moment before the door opened a crack, and a young woman poked her head out. When she recognized Adam, her face immediately brightened, and she opened the door fully. She formed words with her hands, but in the middle of her movement, she noticed the dark-haired man and stared at him for a long moment.

"You're the dragon I sent for," she stated with a bright voice.

"And you're the witch who's going to take this gold ring out of my chest," Crowley replied. The girl before him belonged to the witches' lineage, something his father had warned him about. Yet she didn't seem to pose any real danger—she appeared very... exhausted.

"Come in first," the light-blonde woman offered with both words and hands, stepping aside to allow her guests to enter. Adam followed her without hesitation.

Crowley's gaze lingered on the brass bowl above the door for a moment.

"Why are you burning night jasmine?" he asked her.

"You know what plant this is? I'm impressed. Night jasmine mostly grows along the coasts of Oboros. You can make very good perfumes from it, but I burn it to keep the evil gaze of the gods away."

She smiled, and Crowley couldn't tell if she was just teasing him or if the scent truly kept the old gods at bay. Crowley knew too little about the old gods that people worshipped. So, the witch's words could be true—or not.

He followed Dominique and Adam inside. It smelled of damp herbs and various sweet spices, lavender, and a hint of cinnamon. Somewhere, a fire crackled, and it smelled of a fireplace. Nothing in the witch's home eased the tension in Crowley's body.

"Would you like something to drink?" she offered after unlacing her boots.

Adam nodded at the same time Crowley shook his head. Dominique casually filled three goblets, as if she had only asked out of politeness.

The liquid steamed lightly, and when Crowley smelled the drink, he was surprised to find that it was just herbal tea. He had expected something else from a witch.

His kind had warned him about the ancient magic that witches possessed, and his imagination had likely run wild.

While Dominique and Adam used their hands to converse, the dragon glanced around the witch's house. The blonde was kind enough to convey the most important parts of their conversation to Crowley through their connection.

Dominique asked about their first meeting and whether they had found their way here easily—no new information for the dark-haired man. The same questions they had answered Theodore and this time Adam's counterpart even understood sign language.

Therefore, he let his eyes wander around the room. It didn't look special. Dried herbs hung everywhere, and there were jars and bottles filled with various powders and liquids.

A faint smell of magic lingered in the whole house. The air felt slightly electrically charged. His father had explained to him that the magic of witches was so powerful that it smelled like a storm and could destroy everything in its path.

Crowley studied the little woman before him. She didn't even look like she could fend off the two men in her house if Crowley and Adam decided to attack her.

"And then Crowley and I followed the scent of jasmine and found your house," Adam's final thought brought the dragon's attention back to the conversation.

The dark-haired man set his goblet down on the kitchen table and looked at the light-blonde woman before him.

"You speak very well with your hands, what a coinciden-ce. Did you learn that just for Adam?" Crowley addressed the witch, looking at her skeptically. She pressed her lips together but tried to stay friendly.

"No, I enjoy learning new things and met a young wo-man many years ago who also couldn't hear. To understand her, she taught me to speak with my hands. As you may know, witches age very slowly; I've had plenty of time to constantly improve my abilities. I'm glad I can finally use them actively again."

Her smile didn't seem forced, yet Crowley struggled to hold back his hostility.

Dominique formed her words as she spoke, simultaneously with her hands.

Hesitantly, Adam slid his sandals off his feet, and Crow-ley gave him only a brief glance from the corner of his eye before folding his arms across his chest. A heartbeat later, he did the same as the blonde. After all, he was a guest in the witch's house.

"I want to get straight to the point, free me from the ring," Crowley ordered in the friendliest tone he could muster. He didn't like being caged, but being in a real witch's house was the second worst place he could be.

Dragons were great, powerful rulers of the skies. They were at the top of the food chain and only feared two things: being hunted and killed for the greed of humans and the boundless power of witch blood.

No one except a witch herself knew how their magic worked. This secret had been guarded for millennia. A witch, thanks to her magic, was so powerful that, in the eyes of many, she seemed like a god. It made sense that Dominique was trying to keep the right gods at bay.

"Slow down with the young horses, Dragon. I'd like to tell you and Adam first why I brought you here. I already know Adam's name, so how should I address you?"

Dominique asked her question without hesitation, lifting her gaze. Her eyes shone in the faint candlelight.

Crowley's golden eyes like the sun, Dominique's silver like the moon.

"It's enough that you look at me like that, and I know you're addressing me, witch," Crowley replied sharply. He felt Adam's hand on his forearm.

Apparently, even for someone who couldn't hear his words, it was clear how uncomfortable he was here. Sighing, the dragon rolled his shoulders.

"Call me Crowley."

Dominique's gaze briefly moved to Adam before returning to the dark-haired man. There was a spark in her eyes, but it vanished as quickly as it appeared.

"I'm Dominique, but you can call me Domi," the witch offered kindly. She spoke her next words at the same time as she formed them with her hands, so they were directed to both Adam and Crowley.

"Before I can help Adam fulfill his wish, you both need to help me. There's a small matter you should know about."

Her words were slow and measured. It seemed as though she didn't dare speak the next part. Finally, Dominique lifted her gaze, locking her clear eyes on Adam's, as if Crowley didn't exist. However, her next words made the dragon's senses sharpen.

"I need your help because I don't currently have access to the full extent of my powers—"

That was all Crowley needed to hear.

A witch without her full powers was just a mortal, nothing more. With one hand, he pushed Adam protectively behind him, then reached for the young woman with his other hand.

Dominique was briefly surprised by the attack, but it seemed she had been expecting it. Crowley's hand was diverted by an invisible force and pulled downward.

When his hand hit the ground, he lost all feeling in his fingers and couldn't lift them from the floor. Despite all clear thoughts, he tried to strike at the witch with his second hand, but that hand was also pushed to the ground by the same force, draining it of all sensation.

On all fours, he knelt before Dominique and Adam on the floor.

Panic shot through his body immediately. He wouldn't let himself be caught again.

His gaze must have betrayed his panic, because Adam's expression changed instantly. With an almost angry look, the blonde reached for the pale woman's wrist.

Crowley glared at the young woman from below and bared his teeth. He may have appeared human, but his behavior would always remain that of a dragon.

The fury in his eyes only dissipated when he saw the surprised and also frightened look from the blonde.

The dark-haired man lowered his gaze and took a deep breath. His impulsive behavior had gotten him into this situation, and he would think twice before attacking Dominique again. For now.

"You don't really think I would invite a dragon into my home, knowing that I lack the power to defend myself, without taking precautions, do you?" He should have known that if he'd just thought for one second.

"What do you want, witch?" he snarled at the young woman in front of him.

"If you had let me finish, we would already be done and perhaps one step closer to the solution," explained the light-haired woman. As she spoke, she used both her hands and her voice.

Defeated, Crowley swallowed the rest of his pride and listened to Dominique, who had taken a seat at her small wooden table, her legs dangling at the same level as Crowley's face. The temptation to simply bite her leg was strong.

Dominique was a small, curvy woman who, despite her size, did not lose any of her confidence. She sat with a straight back on the wooden table, looking between the dragon and Adam.

"To fulfill Adam's wish, I need my full powers back. In Oboros, there is the Dynas Academy of Magic. I want you to help me destroy it.

I don't know how they did it, but the scholars and wizards there managed to weaken me to the point where my magic only obeys me under duress. What once came as naturally as breathing now only happens by force."

Dominique's eyes began to gleam suspiciously, but she blinked the oncoming tears away quickly.

Crowley's entire posture shifted, and his head jerked toward the witch. Had he heard that right? The Academy in Oboros was her target. The same academy whose emblem had been burned into Crowley's mind, just like the hot irons had once burned into his flesh.

Slowly, Adam raised his hands, but before he could form anything, Crowley leaned forward and addressed Dominique directly. He tried to make his voice sound as calm as possible, but his gaze was sharp and cold as he asked his questions.

"You know the academy? How? What do you know about those who oversee the academy?" This time, he didn't repeat his question for the blonde in his thoughts; he needed to conduct this conversation alone.

The blonde woman hesitated for a moment. It was clear she didn't know how much to reveal. The academy was directly under the control of the King of Oboros. If she attacked the magic school directly, it could have repercussions across all of Altos. This could spark a far greater war between the two kingdoms than the ridiculous squabble over the borderlands.

But for Crowley, only one thing mattered: he would find the Nachtgrim family, and he would burn every last one of them to the ground until only ash remained. Slowly, Dominique began her explanation.

Her hands trembled slightly as she formed the words: "I used to study there myself. I know how the people there are when they don't understand something. They dig and dig until they get to the bottom of it, regardless of others. They want to know how witch magic works. For years, I tried to make them understand that there's nothing to explain. This magic doesn't follow a system, and it can't be written down. They wouldn't listen to me."

For the briefest of moments, pain flashed in the witch's gaze.

"I left the academy years ago and came to Altos, but apparently, they found me. I don't know exactly how they did it, but I can feel myself growing weaker with each passing day."

In the end, her voice cracked, and her chest rose with shallow breaths. "Help me get it back, and I'll fulfill your greatest dream—" she turned to Adam as she said this.

She had avoided Crowley's question. He only growled in annoyance, but from his position, he couldn't do much about it. He felt trapped again, but this time, he fought against the panic rising in his chest. He wasn't helpless, and her spell would eventually wear off if she was truly as weak as she claimed to be.

"And I'll free you from my ring and whatever else you want, as long as you help me," she said, addressing Crowley.

There was a sense of understanding in her gaze, and her unnaturally white eyes glowed in the candlelight. Then, he would question her later. She had already forced him here with the ring.

It would be a pleasure for him to set the academy and all the Nachtgrims within it on fire. And in return, she would answer his questions.

Crowley only growled in response, but his arms were still numb. If these were her weakened powers, then the magic scholars weren't fools for having successfully weakened her.

With her full strength, she could have easily destroyed the academy and anything else that existed in Oboros.

"Why us?" asked the dark-haired man. He repeated the question for Adam in his thoughts. The blonde woman looked back and forth between the two men.

"Now it's my turn to ask a question: How is it that Adam can follow our conversation when he can't hear you?"

Crowley rolled his eyes, but he knew that his dismissive attitude would only make his situation worse. He would reveal as much as necessary.

"He can hear my thoughts. Otherwise, I would have never figured out what he, a deaf man, wanted from me. It was brave of you to send someone without hearing," the dark-haired man noted. Dominique flushed slightly, and that alone gave Crowley a sense of satisfaction.

"I knew Adam wouldn't have any problems. That's why I gave him my cursed ring. It binds you both together. You would have come back to me with him, whether you wanted to or not. So I can only take the ring off you once you've helped me," she stated matter-of-factly, gracefully hopping off the table she had been sitting on.

Crowley watched the witch, feeling his core pulse in his chest. This wasn't about negotiating what she could offer the dragon for his help. She had already entangled him so deeply that he had no choice but to help her.

The dark-haired man bared his teeth, but a gentle touch on his neck made the growl die in his throat. Adam pressed his thumb lightly into the tense muscles of his neck, massaging in gentle circles.

Turning to the blonde man, she continued, "Adam, I need you for your knowledge and for your courage. Also, my ring binds the dragon to you. Wherever you go, he will follow you." As Dominique lowered her gaze to the dragon before her, some of the enthusiasm faded from her face. Crowley could clearly feel the sensation slowly returning to his hands.

"I admit, I sent Adam with the idea of finding a dragon. It may have seemed malicious, but I had to make sure he'd come back with one. I need you for the sake of your fire-" Her gaze dropped to Crowley's chest, not on the ring, but on the reddish glow hidden beneath. The dragon almost wanted to place a hand over his chest to interrupt the witch's greedy stare at his core.

"I want to see the academy burn. It must never be rebuilt, and no sister of mine must ever be in danger again. The wizards there become arrogant. Only a fire as hot as a fire dragon's can destroy the academy. I have no army, and I serve no king, so it must be done quickly," explained the white-haired woman.

Under Dominique's white gaze, the dark-haired man slowly sat back on his heels and rubbed his wrists.

She added as a warning: "A little warning on the side: Don't get any stupid ideas, or you'll never get rid of the ring, and you'll learn what it means to make a witch your enemy."

Since the last parts were meant only for Crowley himself, she hadn't bothered to make her words comprehensible to Adam through gestures.

Crowley simply snorted once, and the hand from his neck disappeared. He would have leaned into the touch, but the witch's words had made it clear where they stood with each other. Dominique trusted the dragon as little as he trusted her.

The dark-haired man had not once taken his gaze off the witch. That's when he noticed that, the moment his hands were able to lift from the ground, a black mark had appeared beneath Dominique's ear. Her magic had to be related to this black mark.

Slowly, Crowley straightened to his full height and looked down at the woman before him.

"I will burn this school to its foundations, and in return, you remove the ring and I can leave. No tricks or loopholes?"

Dominique's grin was friendly, but in her eyes reflected a silent warning as she met the dragon's piercing gaze.

"Believe me, I can't wait to be rid of you," she said, not breaking eye contact as she extended her hand. Crowley held her gaze and hesitated for a brief moment before placing his hand in hers.

"The feeling is mutual, trust me."

Both broke their eye contact to look at Adam.

As though the blonde had done something forbidden, he flinched.

"What do you think of her plan?" Crowley asked him through their telepathic connection.

ADAM

Adam's blue eyes quickly flicked from Dominique's face to Crowley. When he had been sent off, he hadn't known he would drag Crowley into all of this.

Guilt tightened his chest. Had he known that the ring would bind the dragon to him, he would never have accepted the piece of jewelry. It was bad enough that an item in his possession reminded him of his past mistakes.

If he understood the curse correctly, Crowley would follow him if he accompanied Dominique on her mission. But wouldn't they be committing a crime if they just set the magic academy on fire?

"Isn't it a bit drastic to burn down the whole academy? What about the apprentices there who have nothing to do with what happened to you?" Adam asked the witch. Dominique formed her answer this time only with her hands and looked directly at the blonde.

"I can only tell you that during my time there, they kept trying to perform experiments on me. They wanted to know where a witch's magic comes from. Out of jealousy, they kept drugging me again and again."

As she formed her words, tears gathered in her white eyes. Adam was sure they were real tears and she wasn't lying to him.

"The dean just watched in silence. I managed to escape and hide behind the walls of Vitris, but they captured my husband. He is still at the academy. I can feel my powers growing weaker.

If I don't act now, it will be too late. Please, help me save my husband and reduce this academy to rubble."

As she lowered her hands, they trembled with the raw emotions in the room.

Adam's heart would have to be made of stone if he rejected her. "We'll help you."

Crowley simply crossed his arms over his chest but said nothing further.

The blonde man lowered his gaze to his hand and studied the burn scar around his finger.

So Crowley was bound to him by a curse. Did that mean he hadn't done anything willingly since they had left the cave?

A sour feeling started spreading on his tongue. It dripped down his throat and wrapped around his all-too-human heart. So the words and gestures of the dragon, thanks to the curse, were meant to ensure that the dark-haired man would follow him, whether he consciously wanted to or not.

Crowley's voice in his head startled him as it interrupted their conversation.

"Please tell me you have at least a plan, witch? I doubt we can just fly over this academy and set it on fire with just the three of us without someone trying to stop us. And as impressive as a dragon is, we're still just three against a whole wizard school."

Dominique rolled her eyes. "It's an academy for the art of sorcery. Don't call it magic. Anyone can learn parlor tricks with the right guidance."

Adam stopped rubbing at the burn and let his hands fall. He shouldn't think too much about it.

Dominique grabbed a parchment scroll that had been leaning against one of the wooden legs under the kitchen table and unfurled the map that was on it. "The important part is that we make it into the academy undetected. I can handle a few apprentices, but when it comes to raw muscle-" She glanced between Crowley and Adam.

"Wouldn't it be easier if we could also speak with Dominique through our thoughts?" Adam suggested. Crowley's glance from the side was enough to make him discard the idea immediately. Somehow, it was exciting and special that Crowley only let him into his thoughts. The dragon's body language spoke volumes, clearly indicating he would rather turn around and go back to his cave.

And Adam couldn't even blame him.

He had come along to let Dominique remove the golden ring from his chest, and now he had to fulfill another task before she would grant him that wish.

Turning to the witch, he asked: "If Crowley promises to come with you, can't you take the ring off him right away? He doesn't need to be bound to me."

At these words, the blonde man flushed slightly, but before he could get caught up in the ambiguity of his statement, Dominique raised her hands and shook her head.

"I can't do that, unfortunately. I placed the curse on the ring some time ago. Since then, my powers have been weakening. Without my full magic, I cannot remove the ring and break the curse, even if I wanted to."

If that was the case, Adam would do his best to help her regain her powers as quickly as possible. It was his fault Crowley was here. He wasn't selfish and wanted to free the dragon from this ring just as quickly as Crowley wanted to be rid of it.

The blonde's gaze fell back onto the map in front of him. The map was old, with the edges already yellowing.

The two kingdoms, Altos and Oboros, weren't even marked as separate yet.

Dominique waved her fingers in front of the blonde's face, drawing Adam's attention to her hands.

"How much do you know about the geography of the continent and its history?" she asked directly.

Was it that obvious from the way he had stared that he had never seen a map of the continent up close?

His memory was good enough that he could remember directions and key locations when someone described a path.

Adam felt his face warm again. He had never been to school, and his knowledge was based only on what he had learned from knights or other adults when he was a child. His uncle was a strict believer in the old gods. That's why he had never told him much about the All-King Alduin.

"I know that many years ago, a man named Alduin came to the continent and drove out the old gods. After that, his sons fought and divided the land into the two kingdoms that exist today."

Dominique looked as if she were about to argue, but then she seemed to reconsider. Had he made a mistake?

Several centuries ago, the continent had been a united nation under one king: Alduin, a nobleman from the East who had come with his army across the sea. Where exactly, his uncle had either not known or refused to say. That was all Theodore had told him. When asked why the people in the city put up statues of him everywhere and worshipped him, the elder had simply shaken his head.

Dominique looked at Crowley, but he only shrugged. "I know there was once a great king, but that must have been ages ago. My father knew him."

That was the first time Crowley had mentioned his parents. Adam would have liked to know more, but this didn't seem like the right time or place to ask.

The blonde woman sighed and began to unravel the history of the land, smoothing out the curled edges of the old map with her fingers.

"According to legend, King Alduin came from Isla Bula. He managed to unite the fragmented peoples of the continent under one flag and drive out the old gods, who had made the land barren with their hunger."

Adam furrowed his brow.

Something didn't add up. The majority of people he knew from his village and the surrounding clans revered the old gods. They were the ones who distributed elemental magic.

Moreover, Adam had never heard that the old gods had destroyed the land before the All-King had arrived.

Alduin had driven out the gods and apparently crowned himself a god, if one looked at his statues alone in Vitris.

Before he could speak up, Dominique continued: "Under his sons, Brondor and Barnabas, the land split into the two kingdoms that still rule over the two halves of the land today. And among their children, war broke out. What Alduin had united, his bloodline broke apart. After Alduin, no one from the royal family had the power to reunite the continent.

As for the old gods, no one knows exactly what happened to them. They no longer have any influence on the world, but they can still bestow Darshins on the chosen ones."

With that, she finished her brief introduction to the continent's geography and history.

"People who want to learn magic and aren't lucky enough to be blessed by the old gods go to the academy in Oboros. The tricks they learn there aren't real magic. I myself enrolled there because I was curious. But the spells they teach are sleight-of-hand tricks and small rituals. Nothing compared to the elements in the jewelry, my magic, or the magic of the Négul."

At the last word, she looked directly at Crowley. Adam had seen the word before, in one of the old books that Theo or Cain had read to him and Silas.

Négul were beings who rarely, if ever, showed themselves to mortals. Nature spirits so deeply connected to the world that they controlled their own form of magic. In Crowley's case, it was likely his transformation and ability to breathe fire.

Adam didn't want to be the one to interrupt their conversation, but he couldn't help the yawn that was starting to rise.

His gut feeling told him it was already nearing dawn. Their search for Dominique and their conversation had obviously taken more time than expected. Though the blonde tried to hide his yawn behind a hand, Dominique noticed and responded with a small smile.

"You must be really tired. Come, I'll show you where you can sleep tonight. We leave in the morning. Your eyes are about to close. I'll explain everything else to you tomorrow morning, okay?"

With these words, the blonde woman gently ushered the young man into one of the back rooms, almost like a concerned mother.

CROWLEY

The dragon's eyes followed the two until a heavy fabric curtain swallowed them up. He didn't know what to make of the whole situation.

Crowley didn't trust the witch. She seemed to keep information from them and it didn't sit right with the black-haired man to watch her bring Adam away.

But he wouldn't act rashly again.

Dominique had shown that even without her full magic she had ways to keep her defenses up. But if she suddenly jumped from the back and stabbed him, he would bite her head off without regard of their dumb bargain and the even dumber gold ring in his chest.

It started to itch again.

Adam was the least to blame, after all, he was just the ringbearer. Yet, he was now bound to the blonde one. Was that why his body kept reacting so undeniably to the other?

To sort his thoughts, he took another look at the witch's dwelling. Herbs and hand-painted runes and symbols hung from the walls.

He had never met a real witch, but his father had warned him. People born with magic were unnatural and far too powerful for their own good. Crowley hated feeling weak.

"Don't worry, I won't attack you," Dominique said.

Like a startled animal, a deep growl escaped Crowley's throat as he turned in surprise. He hadn't heard her come back. Could she read his thoughts?

Dominique just smiled slightly and began gathering the small teacups. She waved a finger, and the water in the bronze teapot began to boil again, without anyone stoking the fire.

"As a child, I used to play with rainwater. It was my favorite trick. Now, heating water is one of the few things that still works without issue," the pale-haired woman explained before sitting back down at the table.

"Right now, I can only mostly use magic tricks from the Academy because my magic has been weakening more each day. I really need your help."

It was definitely not easy to show such vulnerability to a stranger, and especially to a dragon.

Surprised, Crowley looked at the pale-haired woman. He hadn't expected her to admit so openly how weak her powers were at the moment.

As their gazes met, Crowley believed he saw pity in the witch's dark eyes.

"Did you know the human face has over 20 muscles?" she said before pouring herself more tea. Crowley raised a confused eyebrow and furrowed his brow. Dominique laughed lightly.

"Just now, you used the muscles in your forehead. The human face is much easier to read than one covered in scales, you know?"

Crowley turned his gaze away again; he didn't want this witch reading him so openly.

Dominique sighed softly.

"I know I can't expect you to trust me. After all, I had to deceive you and curse you to get you here. But I'll keep my promise. Once my husband is safe, and the Academy is in ruins, I'll free you from the curse."

Now that they were alone, Crowley could finally ask the burning questions on his mind.

"Why do you need a dragon so badly? You could sneak into the Academy yourself and set it on fire from the inside. I've heard books burn quite well," the black-haired man grinned somewhat smugly.

Dominique stared at him for a moment, speechless, before she had to laugh softly. "I actually imagined a dragon quite differently."

Crowley and the witch weren't going to become close friends, but for now, it was easier to tolerate each other than to fight.

Besides, Crowley appreciated the way Dominique returned his dry humor with her own. The young woman was no stranger to sarcasm. Her pupils looked like black wells in the dim light as she met the dragon's gaze and continued, "But my plan really does need the fire of a real dragon."

"You're not exactly the natural force I was warned about," the black-haired man retorted.

"Just because I can't access my full powers right now," Dominique tilted her head slightly with a grin.

"Besides, I need to know, who is currently in charge of the Academy?" the dragon steered the conversation back to the burning question on his mind.

Surprised by the question, Dominique furrowed her brow.

"The Dean. He's something like a priest of the old gods, but he also answers to the crown. I don't know how that works, but he's kind of an intermediary. He never showed himself the whole time I was at the Academy. And at audiences before the crown, he always wears a robe and a mask. I think he doesn't want to be recognized."

Crowley could already guess why. If he caught Négul, tortured them, and did the most abominable things to them, it would be easier if he stayed unidentified.

"Do you know his last name? Do you know if he's called Nachtgrim?"

The woman thought for a moment but then shook her head.

"I've heard that name before. It belonged to a merchant who was involved in the black market many years ago. But eventually, he disappeared. Maybe he died without leaving any children behind," she said with a shrug.

So, Dominique knew about the man who had captured Crowley all those years ago. Of course, he had died by now.

He had been a simple human, and that cruel time in his long dragon life was now decades in the past.

Dominique might not have even been born back then. It then occurred to him that he had no idea whether witches aged like humans or like other Négul.

His knowledge was limited to the few things his father, his mother, or Orion had taught him, and that was so long ago.

His gaze fell on the plump figure of the small woman in front of him, as she played with one of the teacups she had gathered, twirling it between her fingers.

She seemed like a young woman in her early twenties, not at all how Crowley had imagined a witch.

"How old are you, actually?"

Feigning injury, the pale-haired woman placed a hand over her chest.

"One doesn't ask a lady such a question!" she laughed, shaking her head.

"Not as old as you might think. I left my Coven exactly one hundred years ago, traveled around, met and fell in love with my husband, and then we both went to the Academy."

With a relaxed posture, the witch leaned back in her armchair and snapped her fingers. Immediately, a small black chess piece began to move on the table and stopped on the eastern side of the Latu Mountains in the south.

"Here stands the Dynas, that's the name of the Academy on paper. The Dean has placed a spell on the building. There's only one entrance, and it's carefully controlled who enters and exits. It would be impossible for me to sneak inside. That's why a simple flame won't be enough. I need a dragon to fly with me and set the fire. No one expects an attack from the sky," the pale-haired woman explained matter-of-factly, shrugging her shoulders.

"With the last bit of magic I have, I can put a small invisibility spell on us. Its duration might be limited, but it should be enough for us to approach the Academy."

Surprisingly, her plan made more sense than expected. Of course, people would secure their buildings against ground attacks. The only creatures that flew through the sky were animals and Négul, and none of them would attack a wizarding academy out of nowhere.

"Still, it was a bit of a gamble sending Adam out," the black-haired man commented, lightly pressing the chess piece's head with his fingertip.

"Not really." Dominique seemed to think for a moment about how much she was willing to reveal. But then, the round woman leaned forward, her pale blonde curls spilling over the map.

"I've met Adam before we crossed paths in Vitris. He won't remember it, though, as it was several years ago. Back then, he worked at a barracks near the Latu Mountains. That's why I knew he would know the area. And how did I know you had your lair there?" she smiled.

Crowley felt a chill run down his spine, as if it were so obvious this had been his next question.

"I got the information from one of the unicorns from the forests at the foot of the mountains. Of all the Négul, they're the most cooperative when you have something they can acquire in exchange for their knowledge."

Dominique's eyes sparkled slightly. Crowley snorted and cursed the unicorns inwardly.

For the right price, you could get anything from them. They lived hidden and secluded, and the thought of being betrayed by one of them didn't sit well with the dragon.

"Then why didn't you get a unicorn to help with your plan?" Crowley asked, baring his fangs.

Dominique's voice softened as she answered: "I know you feel betrayed and used. But I promise you, I haven't told anyone else about your lair. I had to ask the Négul for help as a last resort. I needed a real dragon, but finding one of you is harder than finding a needle in a haystack."

Sighing, the pale-haired woman sank back into her armchair.

"And Adam? Is a human life so worthless to you that you send him on a mission where he could have died without explanation? Any other dragon would have attacked him immediately," the black-haired man said, staring at the witch across from him with his unnaturally golden eyes.

"I did consider that possibility," she said slowly, lowering her gaze, and Crowley could actually see a hint of guilt in her eyes.

"But I had to try. What I'm telling you here at this table must remain between us, do you understand, Crowley?" Suddenly, her voice took on a tone that made the black-haired man sit up.

"I don't know how this mind-reading works between you, but you must promise me not to tell Adam anything about this. I want us to trust each other, at least until we part ways again."

Trust was a big word, especially after she had bound him to Adam against his will and now dragged him to Oboros to burn down some academy. She seemed to notice his distrust.

With both hands, she rubbed her eyes.

"I can tell you this much: I chose Adam for two reasons. The first reason might sound dreadful, but I had no ill intentions."

After a brief pause, Dominique quickly continued, "I watched Adam at the barracks back then. He seemed to have no close relatives or friends, so it wouldn't have caused much of a stir if he hadn't returned."

Knowing how her explanation must sound, she raised her hands defensively.

"But I was sure he wasn't an idiot. Then we met again in Vitris and spoke. I didn't want to scare him, but I've never met anyone who lives so fearlessly like Adam, even though he's deaf. I was sure he wouldn't die. Something in my heart tells me that Adam is special."

One of her pale hands pressed against her chest, and Crowley swallowed the initial sour feeling. He tried to put himself in the witch's position. If she sent someone out who no one would search for or miss, should he die, she could easily send someone else.

Still, the thought that Adam could have died didn't sit right. Had the young human become that important to him in such a short time? A brief pulsing of his core under the gold ring seemed to answer that question. A strange feeling crawled through the dragon's veins. His heart. It hurt.

No other human had ever gotten under his skin like this blonde man.

"And what was the second reason?" he asked, before he could focus too much on the growing sensation in his chest.

Dominique sighed, her bright eyes briefly wandering over Crowley's shoulder toward the direction where she had taken Adam for the night.

"Adam doesn't know it, but I think he has royal blood. I can't prove it, but his face seemed so familiar to me when I saw it at the market, after I could finally take a closer look."

Crowley widened his eyes in surprise. What he knew about Adam was that he had been raised by his uncle, Cain, and his wife.

What had happened to his biological parents, the dragon didn't know. The possibility was there, but it was far-fetched to connect the blonde young man in the next room to the royal family.

Dominique leaned back in her chair as if she needed to take a step back before continuing.

"When I came to Vitris, I overheard a rumor that the Queen of Altos had an affair with the King of Oboros. Apparently, this story had been circulating for a few years. I got curious and started digging. But there was no evidence, and everyone knows that people love to gossip when they think a story is valuable enough to spread. Apparently, the rumor had been around long enough that phantom images of a potential heir had been created."

Crowley perked up at this.

Dominique began playing with the chess piece between her fingers as she continued, "A few years ago, I came into possession of one of those drawings."

With a soft creak that echoed too loudly in Crowley's ears, she pushed her chair back and stood. She had to tiptoe to reach the top shelf of her bookshelf.

With a loud rustle, she pulled out a piece of paper and handed it to Crowley.

It was a charcoal drawing of a boy, maybe five years old. Crowley resisted the urge to rub his thumb over the image and smudge the charcoal.

His eyes widened as he studied the boy's features. No doubt about it, the drawing depicted a younger version of the man who was currently sleeping in the next room.

"This can't be a coincidence," Dominique whispered, as if her voice might reveal the secret of the drawing. The charcoal drawing was too accurate, too detailed, to be a coincidence.

It had the same curls, the same curve of full lips, and the same almond-shaped eyes.

"I think so too. And then I met him at the market, as I said. I knew that if anyone could help me with this, it would be him. I don't think he knows about his heritage. Maybe he was adopted as a child. According to the rumors, Adam's supposed father, King Eldor, issued a search warrant and promised a reward to anyone who brought his 'lost son' back. But just like the rumor, the search for the supposed son was eventually abandoned. I found him."

Crowley slowly lowered the piece of paper and raised his gaze to meet the unnaturally light eyes of the witch, which almost seemed white in the weak candlelight.

"What does it change if Adam is a possible descendant of both this kingdom and Oboros? The money reward doesn't interest you, does it?" Dominique fell silent.

She crossed her arms over her chest, as if to shield herself from the answer. Crowley placed the paper on the table, but his gaze remained fixed on the woman beside him.

"You don't need him for his knowledge. Adam is your contingency plan," the black-haired man voiced his suspicion, and the pale-haired woman slowly closed her eyes.

"The Academy is under royal protection. If we can't find another way in, I'll expose who Adam really is. I'm sure the king wants his son back so badly that he'll finally listen to me.

I've tried to talk to the Dean. My letters to the king were intercepted. I'm using everything available to me, Crowley!" she hissed, careful not to raise her voice, though Adam couldn't hear her anyway.

"I need to see the Academy burn. For me and for—" Dominique broke off, turning her gaze away, but both her voice and the rest of her body trembled.

Dominique's arms tensed under the sleeves of her dress as she tightly wrapped her arms around herself. She was scared. The trembling had taken over her entire body, but in her eyes, there was not only fear but also a deep-rooted pain.

Crowley recognized that look, that cold fear that burrowed into the flesh like an icy blade. Whatever had happened to Dominique at this academy, it haunted her to this day.

"Only when this cursed academy burns, with all its books, potions, and secret rooms, only then will I be able to sleep peacefully again," whispered the pale-haired woman in a barely audible voice.

"I feel myself growing weaker from night to night."

She swallowed hard, but it seemed as if she had mostly regained her composure. With one hand, she ran it through her long hair.

"My plan might not succeed, but this is my only chance. If I wait any longer, there won't be enough of my strength left. And who knows what they've done to Lyra in the meantime," the witch buried her face in her hands in despair.

Until now, she had maintained a façade that was now on the verge of crumbling.

Crowley didn't know what to do.

"Is Lyra your husband?" he asked, hoping to prevent her from completely breaking down in tears. He also needed more information.

He wouldn't let Dominique simply hand Adam over.

The academy would burn, he wanted that just as much as the witch. That way, he could destroy the name Nachtgrim. He owed it to himself and Orion.

But he wouldn't trade Adam for that. Just the thought of it burned like acid in Crowley's throat.

He could deny it to himself as much as he wanted, but his damn dragon heart had already made its decision.

Surprised, Dominique looked up, her eyes still sparkling with barely contained tears, but apparently, his question had caught her off guard. Slowly, she nodded.

"After I left my coven, I didn't know where to go for a long time. I took on many different forms and eventually met Lyra. We fell in love and married." Dominique's voice was filled with love.

"Together we went to Oboros and enrolled at the academy. Then, the experiments began little by little. Three years ago, I managed to escape, but he stayed behind to throw them off my trail. Since then, not a day goes by that I don't think of him."

Dominique laughed lightly and wiped her eyes. "Witches live very long lives. It's difficult to find a partner who will bind themselves to one of us. A human life is so short compared to that of a witch or a Négul."

Dragons weren't immortal either; after a few millenia, they could die of old age.

Crowley's gaze subconsciously wandered over his shoulder toward the direction Adam had disappeared.

"Lyra knew that from the start and still married me." The smile on the witch's lips was gentle and loving as she played with the silver ring on her finger.

"If I don't survive, I've made arrangements. I'll make sure you have access to my old coven. There, there's a witch who can lift the curse for you if I ask her to." With these words, Dominique stood up from the table.

"Behind the curtain, you'll find a corridor. On the left, I've placed Adam. You can take the room on the right. Rest. Tomorrow we'll finalize everything and set off. I thought we could join the travelers heading down the main trade road to Oboros. There's a horse station at the gates. I can get us mounts so the journey won't take as long."

Crowley grimaced slightly before standing up as well.

"Animals are afraid of me; they know, even though I look like a human, what I really am. Horses, unfortunately, are out of the question."

Dominique stared at the larger man in disbelief for a moment.

"Can't you fly us then?" the witch asked bluntly. The black-haired man looked at the pale-haired woman as if she were joking, but she was completely serious.

"I'm a dragon, not a pack mule. The ring might have bound me to Adam for now, and we'll help you regain your powers, but I won't allow myself to be seen as a beast of burden just because I'm the only one of us three who can fly."

A journey across the continent was still a long one, even for him in the air.

Besides, the transformations he had gone through up until now had already weakened him far more than he would have liked. Dominique's expression shifted as though Crowley had just destroyed her entire plan.

"The longer our journey takes, the less power I'll have left for the invisibility spell." Crowley shrugged his shoulders.

Dominique's plan had holes all over it; she was obviously no strategist. But if Crowley wanted to get rid of the ring so he could return to his old life, he could help her as much as he could.

However, he wouldn't trade the blonde man for that. The dragon's golden eyes wandered one last time to the curtain behind which Adam must have already fallen asleep.

His core knew it. He knew it himself, even if only since the morning in the barracks.

He wouldn't be able to give Adam up. The young man would have to leave him on his own.

Adam was his.

EPILOG

*What should I say? I'm afraid. My hands are trembling, and everything
inside me is silent, too silent, as if this silence could suffocate me. Sooner
or later, I will lose my heart. In the end, I will be alone again.
I can almost feel it, that emptiness that remains
when someone I love disappears from my life.
It's like a blade slowly digging into me. At first, I barely notice it,
and then… then it tears me apart, piece by piece. Why would it be any
different with Adam? We hardly know each other. He doesn't know how
deep this goes. He has no idea how heavy a dragon's heart can become.
How could he?
I don't let him get too close, afraid that he'll see the monster I was once
thought to be. There's blood on my hands. I know he isn't without regret
either. But still, I'm afraid. I'm responsible for my brother's death. Orion
was the one who pulled me out of the water after I was freed. He himself had*

been injured in his attempt to rescue me. With his last strength, he managed

to drag me to the Isle of the Dead. There, I watched my only family die.

For days, I lay next to my brother's lifeless body until I understood that

he wouldn't leave this island with me. I wish Adam wouldn't go.

That I could protect him, so that he doesn't suffer the same fate.

But he is so fragile, a human whose life can be over in an instant. And

I, who threatens to drown in this single glimmer of hope, the only one

I will ever have. It will tear me apart. Maybe it already has.

He is a human, and I am a dragon.

The mere thought that this could work is foolish and naive. I want to stop

it, make it disappear, just like I could make everything I didn't need vanish.

Suddenly, things like a loud heartbeat or excitement take on a

new meaning. They're not physical signals that I can ignore.

Instead, they pull me in, take me in scales and hair,

dragging me deeper into this whole mess.

And what do I do?

I just want more of this young man.

Am I sick? Or confused? All I want is to wrap myself

around Adam so nothing can happen to him.

He should belong to me, just like my damn heart already belongs to him.

CROWLEY WAS ONLY AFRAID OF LOSING HIS HEART...